PRAISE FOR E[

'Funny, touching and wise'
KIT DE WAAL

'Vivid, funny, sad, thought-provoking,
acutely observed and full of compassion'
HELEN SEDGWICK

'A debut novel to treasure, by turns funny, dark and
heartbreaking and I didn't want it to end!'
LOUISE MUMFORD

'A fascinating and poignant take on friendship
and obsession'
CARON MCKINLAY

'Startling, sly and full of suspense. Not your ordinary
coming-of-age novel'
CATHERINE MAYER

'Full of charm, insight and wit – with the power
to break your heart'
C. E. RILEY

Elissa Soave won the inaugural Primadonna Prize in 2019. She was also a Bloody Scotland Pitch Perfect finalist and has had work published in various journals and anthologies, including *New Writing Scotland*, *Gutter*, and the *Glasgow Review of Books*.

Elissa was a judge on the Primadonna Prize 2022 and the Curae Prize 2023. She currently lives in South Lanarkshire.

Ginger and Me was shortlisted for the Saltire Society Scottish First Book Award 2023

PUBLISHING NOVEMBER 2024
Hardback 9780008673314 £20
eBook 9780008673291 | Audio 9780008673284
For publicity enquiries please contact: HQPressOffice@harpercollins.co.uk

Graffiti Girls

Elissa Soave

ONE PLACE. MANY STORIES

HQ
An imprint of HarperCollins*Publishers* Ltd
1 London Bridge Street
London SE1 9GF

www.harpercollins.co.uk

HarperCollins*Publishers*
Macken House, 39/40 Mayor Street Upper,
Dublin 1, D01 C9W8, Ireland

This edition 2024

1
First published in Great Britain by
HQ, an imprint of HarperCollins*Publishers* Ltd 2024

ISBN: 9780008673314

MIX
Paper | Supporting
responsible forestry
FSC
www.fsc.org
FSC™ C007454

This book contains FSC™ certified paper and other controlled
sources to ensure responsible forest management.

For more information visit: www.harpercollins.co.uk/green

Typeset in Bembo Std by HarperCollins*Publishers* India

Printed and Bound in the UK using 100%
Renewable Electricity at CPI Group (UK) Ltd

For Mum, Amanda, and Carla – the very best
Graffiti Girls I know

Contents

I

The Plan

THE GUY IN THE WHITE Audi TT behind Amy's van honked his horn again. The queue of traffic they were stuck in had been snaking its way from the tree-lined avenues of Ferniegair to the altogether grimier edge of Hamilton town centre for the last half-hour so she wasn't sure where Mr Audi Total Tosser thought his horn-beeping was going to get him. But that was men for you, she thought, all noise and no action.

Amy ignored him and checked ahead to see what the hold-up was. The snow was still falling. It had been inky black outside since five o'clock that afternoon so she couldn't see much beyond the trail of fuzzy car headlights. The gritters had done a poor job and the evening traffic crawled.

Peering out at the identikit bungalows lining one side of the road into town, and the gravelly brown fronts of the ex-council flats on the other, Amy felt smothered by the all-pervading post-Christmas gloom, and not just because of the weather. Like many places, Hamilton had its share of families who had to save up in their credit unions all year to pay for Christmas, only to start saving again for the next one almost as soon as the wrapping was off this year's haul of mechanized plastic and fake Balenciagas. They were currently in the low point of that cycle – one of many reasons she was lucky to have no family of her own to worry about, Amy reminded herself.

A trio of illuminated plastic reindeer in one garden caught her eye, and she glanced towards the house, with its curtains open and all its front windows lit up. She could see the glow of the TV in the far corner, and a couple sitting together on the couch, the light from the screen reflecting on their faces. The woman picked up a large bowl from the coffee table in front of them and turned to offer it to the man. He plucked something out of the bowl but instead of eating it himself, leaned towards the woman and popped it into her mouth. They both laughed and a little girl in pyjamas ran into the room and flopped between them on the couch. They sat close, all three together, the bowl of treats now transferred to the child's lap.

Amy looked away, the warm air in the van suddenly cloying, the Bruce Springsteen she'd been enjoying unbearably loud. She reached down and turned both dials to off and immediately felt better in the silence and cooling air.

But then Mr Audi TT behind her honked again. Amy gave him the finger in her rear-view mirror, enjoying the look of outrage on his face. After her experience at the Miners' Welfare Club last week, she was in no mood to accommodate rude and impatient men. Wait till she told the others about it tonight. She checked the time again and sighed. *They'll be wondering where I am*, she thought. *I'm never late.*

'You'd think since she arranged this night out, and practically sent us all a three-line whip to be here, that for once, just once, Amy could turn up on time,' said Susan, as she stood in the small bar area, which was lit by a fringed red lamp giving off bordello vibes, at the front of the restaurant.

4

She twisted to take off her anorak, removing the blue hairband she wore at work to keep her unruly curls away from her face as she did so. The first thing anybody noticed about Susan was her mass of wiry red – as in ginger not auburn – corkscrew curls. Her naturally pale skin had a tendency to flush when she was annoyed or impatient, and since she was frequently at least one of these things, there was often a contrast between the tones of her face and hair which was not appealing, a fact of which she was well aware. As she'd got older, the colour of her hair had changed and was now slightly more muted so that it was brick-red these days rather than Irn-Bru orange but still, her hair was generally the brightest in the room. There were also threads of grey among the curls now which Susan had done nothing to camouflage despite Lenore's best efforts to persuade her otherwise. Having come straight from the library, she was wearing her pleated navy skirt, sky-blue council blouse and grey cardigan. Her face was clean of make-up, though in a concession to Lenore, she had dabbed at her dry lips with a tinted chapstick.

She checked her phone again and tutted. Although she was generally soft-hearted, she was also easily annoyed if her friends failed to match her own high standards. These included, among other things, punctuality. Giving her curls a couple of ineffectual pats, she said, 'The way she was talking about it being so urgent, couldn't wait for the weekend, you'd think she'd have the grace to be here on time.'

Carole smiled and shook out her own mass of blonde-highlighted hair, the style of which had rarely changed in all the years the women had known each other – she still wore it in thick waves past her shoulders and parted in the centre. If people noticed Susan for her vivid ginger hair, it wouldn't hold their attention for long if Carole was in the room. Her face was as striking as it had always been – a little chubbier perhaps these days than she'd like but her cheekbones were high and prominent under smooth skin that looked healthy and lightly tanned, whatever the weather. She had a dimple in her left cheek which deepened when she smiled, which she did, often, and her eyes were a startling forget-me-not blue. She took her time taking off her own baby pink, pure wool coat. She'd bought it the day before in the House of Fraser as Dennis's Christmas present to her and this was its first outing. But Lenore was too busy looking around for a cocktail menu to see it and Susan never noticed that kind of thing, so she shrugged and arranged it carefully over the bar stool. Beneath the coat she was wearing deep blue jeans and a tight-fitting white blouse, the open neck of which allowed a glimpse of a sparkly quartz necklace. 'Amy's always been like that,' she said, swooshing her hair back from her face. 'Even at school. When she deigned to turn up for school, that is. You remember, Lenore – we used to say Amy's way or—'

'The highway. That's right.' Lenore pulled out the high bar stool next to Carole and sat down, draping the leather strap of her bag over the back of it. 'We might as well get a drink and look at the menu while we wait for her.' She looked around the bar and into the restaurant to find someone to serve them.

The ambience in the Panda Shack was poor. This was partly because no one had any money to go out this soon after Christmas and the place was completely empty. But the general air of neglect and the drooping three-foot Christmas tree in the corner, naked except for a lonely string of red lights that blinked lazily every half a minute or so, didn't help.

The restaurant had been Lenore's choice. One of the

trainee teachers at her school had recommended it when she'd mentioned she was looking for a place to eat. Now they were here, Lenore wondered what the younger teacher thought she and her friends wanted from a night out if she thought the Panda Shack would fit the bill. Although most of her teaching pals were a couple of decades younger than her, Lenore did not consider herself to be old, not at all. She was proud of her gym-fit body and spent most Saturdays in town, browsing the racks of River Island and Zara to keep up to date with the latest trends. She could hold her head high in the company of any of the trainee teachers – or she could if they asked her to join them on one of their nights out.

Still though, this place.

'Personally, I think any restaurant with the word "shack" in its name is to be avoided,' sniffed Susan, looking in at the empty restaurant.

'You book next time then,' said Lenore. 'You always leave the organizing to me then complain about my choices afterwards.'

'Cheer up, girls,' said Carole. 'I didn't leave a house full of gloomy boys to sit with a bunch of gloomy girls.'

She couldn't understand why everyone else was so miserable in January; it was her favourite month of the year. Or perhaps it just seemed relaxing after December, the month where she was run ragged getting everyone exactly what they wanted – with a husband and four sons to cater for, that wasn't easy. In return for her troubles, she would get a dressing-gown from Marks and a selection of bath crystals and coconut-flavoured lotions that she would instantly place on the high shelf in the kitchen cupboard, ready to donate to the school fete in six months' time. Of course Dennis had also told her, as he did every year, to buy herself whatever she wanted from him, 'money no object', which was nice of him. Sometimes though, she missed the days when they'd had no money and he would give her a smooth round pebble he'd picked up on a day out at Croy that he'd painted pink 'to match her lips', or one year, a pair of his old soft Levis that he'd had his mum take in at the waist to fit her perfectly. God, she'd loved those jeans.

A young girl with puffed-up red lips and a fringe that almost hid her eyes came over and said, 'I didn't realize there was anybody waiting. Your table's ready for you.' Lenore treated her to the same look she gave her fifth years when they were messing around at the back of her class but said nothing after Carole shot her a warning glance to be nice. The three women gathered their belongings and followed the waitress to their table in silence.

'Don't think much of the restaurant.' It was Amy, who'd arrived fifteen minutes after the others had sat down.

'Hurray, you made it,' said Carole, indicating the seat next to her.

'Not that you needed to rush,' said Susan, looking round the dingy restaurant for their elusive waitress. 'Honestly, we'd be better jumping on a plane and flying to Beijing for our spicy noodles, it'd be quicker.'

'You can't say that!' Carole laughed.

'Why not? It's true.'

'It's worked out well for me then,' said Amy. 'I thought you'd all be half-finished by the time I got through that traffic.' She hung her anorak on the back of her chair, and looked round the table. 'Where's Lenore?'

'She's in the toilet propping up her hair,' said Susan.

'Does she ever think about anything besides the way she looks— Oh, hi, Lenore,' finished Amy as Lenore sat back at the table, her lipstick reapplied and some fresh blusher across her cheekbones.

'Just because you've given up doesn't mean we all have to,' said Lenore, smacking her lips together so the lipstick was evenly distributed over her top and bottom lips.

'Nice to see you too,' said Amy, smiling broadly at Lenore's assessment of her approach to beauty. They all knew she was right, of course. Amy couldn't care less what she looked like and never had. She possessed what she knew others described, not entirely complimentarily, as a 'strong' face – a deep forehead, only just beginning to reveal her age with some faint vertical lines between her eyebrows, a long Roman nose and a wide mouth, usually open to voice her opinions, of which there were many. Even the V-shaped scar in the middle of her chin suggested that she'd just come back from defending Sparta's honour against the pesky Athenians.

Lenore held the menu out at arm's length so that she could just about make out the letters dancing on the plastic in front of her. 'I should really be good tonight,' she said, more to herself than her three companions. 'I'm already at' – she scrunched up her face as she did some mental calculations – 'Christ, 850 calories for the day, and that's not including all the milk in my tea. Still, we are on a night out. Is anybody else having a starter, or are we just going for mains?' She looked around at the others.

'You can put your glasses on, Lenore, there's no one to impress here,' said Amy from across the table. Even if the place had been full of bright young things, no one would have seen them in any case. Despite the lack of any other customers, they'd

9

still been given the worst table, sandwiched between the ladies' toilets and the kitchen. This was something Amy had noticed since they'd all hit their forties. No new punters were going to walk by and see a group of slightly sozzled, middle-aged women in a restaurant and feel the urge to be just like them, hence no more prime tables in the window – unless they sent Carole on ahead to charm whoever was allocating the seats.

That clearly hadn't happened tonight, so the worst table in the place it was. An hour later, it bore two empty bottles of house red and plates smeared with hot sauce and the remains of the mountain of sticky ribs and hot wings they'd manage to get through between them.

Lenore was looking at the menu again. 'Is anyone else having a dessert?' she said hopefully, straining to see the items on the dessert section at the bottom of the menu.

'Please put your glasses on, Lenore,' said Amy, 'and for God's sake, have a dessert if you want one, you don't need our permission.'

Lenore dropped the menu. 'But it's January.'

The others looked at her blankly.

'You know,' she explained. 'New year, new start, new diet and all that.' She looked longingly at the dessert section again. 'And I've been so good up till now.' She pushed the menu away resolutely. 'I've lost three pounds, did I tell you? Partly due to the diet and partly down to a line dancing class I've started at my new gym.'

'Line dancing!' said Amy. 'How can you be bothered? It was bad enough we were forced to do it at school.'

Carole looked up from her phone. 'I wouldn't mind going line dancing, actually,' she said. 'It'd be a break from the kids.'

'Is Dennis still refusing to do his share?'

'Don't start on Dennis again, Amy,' said Lenore quickly.

'Exactly, thank you, Lenore.'

'Why do you stick up for that loser, Lenore? You always have done. Ever since school,' said Amy. 'And I don't know why because he's managed to sire four children, yet not do a hand's turn to look after any of them.'

'It's not like that, Amy.' Carole jumped in to defend her husband. 'I keep telling you. He works very hard, you know. You don't earn the kind of money he does without putting in the hours, so he's tired when he comes home. And it's not like I've got anything else to do apart from the kids and the house – I've never had to work, Dennis provides for us all.'

'How very 1950s,' said Amy, wiping the last of the hot sauce from her fingers and deliberately not looking at her friend so she wouldn't be tempted to say more about what she thought of her domestic life. She couldn't understand why Carole had never tried to put her years of dance training to good use, or gone back to study something else, or . . . done something, anyway.

'Let's change the subject,' said Susan, sensing the mood was beginning to turn.

Amy swirled the last of the one glass of wine she'd allowed herself and added quietly, 'As long as you're happy, Carole. It's just, you were going to go to London and be a dancer. Till Dirty Den got his hands on you. I never understood how you could let all that training go to waste. You could have taught dancing after you had the kids, or done anything you wanted, you were so talented.'

Carole waited till their waitress had picked up some of the debris from their table and headed back through to the kitchen with it before she answered.

'You know perfectly well why, Amy. I was going to, I would have when Dan went to nursery, except then I got pregnant with Thomas, didn't I? Dennis always said I was the lucky one getting to spend all that time with them, that we'd never get these years back again. And he was right, the older two hardly want to know me these days.'

'Maybe you'll be allowed off the leash a bit more then,' said Amy, lifting up the bottle nearest her and draining the dregs left there into Carole's glass.

'I'm out as often as Susan is, sure I am, Susan? Susan!'

Susan looked up from her phone, startled back into the company. 'Sorry,' she said. 'I was checking in on Fraser. I left him his dinner in front of the microwave but he wouldn't have known how long to put it in for.'

'God's sake, Susan, what is he now – fifteen?'

'Sixteen.' Susan had the grace to redden a little.

'Sixteen. We've got kids at my school who've been looking after themselves for years by that age. In fact most of them have already left school by sixteen.' Lenore stacked some of the dirty plates still on the table as she took Susan to task.

'Well, anyway,' Carole continued addressing Amy. 'I'm out tonight, aren't I? And what's this big plan that couldn't wait for the weekend for you to tell us about?'

'Yes,' said Susan. 'What did you want to tell us? I need to get home soon.'

'It's only half nine,' said Lenore. 'How am I supposed to meet someone if I've no wingmen? Women? Wingwomen? People to come out with me, you know what I mean.'

Amy turned to Susan. 'Why do you need to be home early?'

'For wee Fraser. I need to—'

'Wee Fraser? Wee— Are you kidding me? He's shaving already!' Lenore balanced one more plate on top of the pile and wondered why she was doing their waitress's job for her.

Susan smiled. 'Only occasionally, it's just cute little fuzz, right here.' She turned to face Amy and ran a finger across her own upper lip, which, truth to tell, could have benefited from some attention from a razor itself but Amy didn't say so. Susan carried on. 'It's so cute. But I still need to put his school uniform out for tomorrow, check he's done his homework, and he won't have had any supper with me out gallivanting. They don't stop needing you at sixteen, you know.'

'More like she needs him,' whispered Carole to Lenore.

'I can hear you, you know,' called Susan across the table. 'But that's not true. It's different for Fraser than for your boys, Carole. They've got two parents looking out for them, Fraser's only ever had me.'

'Sorry,' said Carole. 'You're right.'

Susan waved away Carole's apology with a smile. 'It's Amy's fault really, just because she's not responsible for anyone, she thinks we're all footloose and fancy-free.'

'Speak for yourself, Susan,' said Lenore. 'I *am* footloose and fancy-free. And actually Amy's not her own boss these days, what about Tess? I'm sure she'd have plenty to say about Amy staying out late – if we ever got to meet her, that is?'

Amy was fiddling with her unused dessert spoon and making a big show of looking round for the waitress to order coffees.

'Well, are we ever going to meet her?' Lenore asked again. 'I'm starting to think you've made her up. Either that, or she doesn't want to know us.'

'Listen, guys, I love you but not every lesbian wants to spend all their time hanging out with a bunch of straight women, you know, however lovely you are.' Amy was spared the faux outrage of her friends as the waitress came back and asked in a bored voice, looking at none of them as she did so, 'Desserts? Coffee for anyone?' in a tone that made it clear she couldn't have cared less about the answer.

'Just a black coffee for me,' said Lenore quickly, pushing the menu towards the waitress before she could change her mind. The others ordered a variety of hot drinks, no one went for the dessert.

'Anyway,' said Carole, 'we're happy to see you go out with someone for longer than a month at a time, Amy. And yes, we would love to meet her, since we can tell from the way you talk about her that you've found someone special at last.' Susan and Lenore backed her up, saying, 'Definitely' and 'Of course we would'.

Amy folded and refolded her napkin and shuffled in her seat. 'I don't know what you're talking about, you make it sound like Tess and me . . . She only moved in to help me pay my mortgage, you know. Having your own business is all very well in theory but it's not the same as someone else paying you a sum of money every month, no matter how well or badly you perform. But business is picking up a bit now – lots of leaky taps and frozen pipes, thank God – so I don't need that kind of help at the moment. You might as well know, Tess . . . moved out . . . a few weeks ago now. Look, it's not that important.'

'Oh Amy, I'm sorry to hear that, you seemed so—'

Amy dismissed her friend's sympathy. 'It's absolutely fine.'

'Less work and a few good nights out will cheer you up then,' said Carole.

'I'm not *un*happy,' snapped Amy. 'And this conversation started with me saying you could do with a few more nights out, if you remember,' she added, deftly changing the subject.

'I'm out tonight, aren't I? So, what's this big plan that couldn't wait for the weekend for you to tell us about it?'

Amy huffed a bit more and said, 'If you'd let me get a few words in edgeways, I'd tell you.'

'The floor is yours, madame,' said Lenore, looking with longing at Susan's large cappuccino, doused in chocolate. She sighed as she picked up her own strong black coffee and wished she'd remembered her sweeteners.

'Thank you,' said Amy. 'Finally.'

Satisfied that she had their full attention, she started to speak. 'Something happened to me last week. And it's happened before but this time, it really got my goat . . .'

The previous Tuesday, Amy had parked her van on the main road opposite the Miners' Welfare Club in Viewpark. She looked across the road at the building which seemed so quiet and shuttered she wondered if it was still closed after Christmas. She checked her phone again. 'Nope, this is definitely the right place and time.' She grabbed the large canvas bag from the passenger seat next to her and made her way across the road.

There was no bell that she could see so she rapped hard on the door then stepped back, waiting. There was no reply so she rapped again, harder this time, looking up at the front of the building as though the straight red bricks could give her access.

She heard heavy footsteps behind the door and bent down to pick up her tool bag.

The door was opened by a big man with a scraggy neck and

a nose you couldn't miss. He looked Amy up and down, taking in her hair shorn to her scalp, her grease-stained, green canvas overalls and the large bag of tools weighing her down. He came slightly forward and looked along the street, as though expecting someone to come rushing from behind the building and shout, 'Surprise.' Finally, he addressed Amy. 'Yes? Can I help you?'

'Are you the caretaker?'

The man nodded his head just vigorously enough to shake the loose skin of his neck.

'Then I think it's more likely I can help you,' said Amy. 'You called Double X Plumbers? About your leak?'

'About my . . .?'

'Your leaky whatsit,' said Amy impatiently. 'Tap on the men's urinals?'

The man flinched.

'Running all the time, won't stop leaking?'

The man appeared to suddenly cotton on. 'That's right. I told the wife to call a plumber.' He looked Amy up and down again then stepped back into the clubhouse and shouted, 'Sarah? Sarah!'

A small blonde woman appeared, wearing an apron with 'Tuesday' on the front and pearly pink lipstick smeared across her lower lip.

'Yes, dear?' she said, wiping her hands on the apron.

'Who the hell's this?' He indicated Amy with a swish of his hand.

'I don't know, Robert,' said the woman. She turned to Amy, 'Can we help you at all?'

Amy was beginning to lose her patience. 'Look, I'm the plumber. You called Double X Plumbers? That's me, so do you want me to stand out here all day or do you want me to come in and fix your leaky tap?'

'I think come in and—'

'Over my dead body,' said Robert, moving in between his wife and Amy so that the woman was completely obscured from Amy's view. 'If you think a wee lassie like you is coming in to fiddle with my tap you've got another think coming. This is the Viewpark Miners' Welfare Club. For men. Mostly. So, no, you can't come in and fix my tap.'

'But, dear—' began Sarah from behind her husband.

'Look,' he said, turning so that he faced his wife and his back was to Amy. 'You stick to cleaning the bar. I'm the caretaker here so I'll get us a plumber. Don't know why I left it to you in the first place, might have known you'd get it all wrong.' He looked round at Amy again and laughed. 'This wee dame? A plumber? You wouldn't ask a man to watch the kids or clean a toilet, would you?'

'Chance'd be a fine thing,' muttered Sarah, twisting her apron in her fingers.

'What's that?'

'No, nothing, dear,' said Sarah quickly.

The man gave Amy one last look and said, 'Thanks for coming, doll, but you're wasting your time. I can attend to my own stopcock, thanks very much.' He shut the door in Amy's face.

'That's good,' said Amy to herself as she picked up her tool bag, 'because I'm pretty sure no one else would want to.' She marched back to her van, flung the tool bag in the back and roared away from the pavement without a backward glance.

★

Amy sat back, throwing the napkin she'd been twisting in her hands across the table so that it landed in the stack of dirty dishes the world's worst waitress still hadn't managed to clear. She looked at the others, awaiting their reaction.

Uncharacteristically, Susan spoke first. 'I don't like to say I told you so but when you first told us about starting this plumbing business, did I not tell you so?'

Amy sat up, her face reddening with sudden anger. 'What do you mean? Do you not think that's outrageous? In this day and age? I wasn't even allowed in to fix a poxy leaky tap. How am I supposed to make a go of this business if folk like him won't even let me through the door? A leaky tap? I could've fixed that with my eyes shut.'

'I believe you,' said Lenore. 'Remember that time you sneaked over to mine to fix the mess Tommy had made at the weekend? I told him he wasn't capable of fixing a toilet himself but he wouldn't have it.'

'Though why I had to do it on the sly, I don't know,' said Amy, looking accusingly at Lenore.

'Because that's what he was like – couldn't bear to admit he couldn't do something, or ask for help, or directions, or anything really. I remember once I insisted on stopping this woman to ask the best way to Barshaw Park and because she told us to go right, he took nothing but left turns for the next hour to prove her wrong – took us the best part of two hours to get from here to Paisley, honest to God. He'd have been absolutely raging if I'd told him you were coming to fix his DIY.'

'One of the very many reasons you're well shot of him, in my opinion,' said Susan. 'But look, Amy, I agree with you, the west of Scotland male is definitely closer to his Neanderthal ancestors than we would like, but what's that got to do with this big plan of yours? You said we were going to take back control? Control of what, exactly?'

'That sounds like something you would say right enough, Amy,' said Carole. 'You've been talking like that since school.'

Amy smiled at Carole. 'I know, it's true. But' – she looked round at her friends, lowering her voice and leaning forward as she spoke – 'that happening to me the other day got me thinking. I mean really thinking about all the crap we're agreeing to in our lives.'

'Speak for yourself, I'm not agreeing to any crap.' Carole threw her own napkin at Amy and it narrowly missed her, landing on Susan's half-empty coffee cup. 'Watch it,' she said.

Now it was Lenore's turn to sit forward impatiently. 'Seconded. I am most certainly not accepting crap from anyone. Never have. Look at me, what man could say no to this?' She swept a hand down her sparkling top, from which her pushed-up breasts were overflowing, and the skintight jeans which sheathed her gym-slim thighs.

'My life's also going perfectly fine, thanks very much,' chimed in Susan. 'No crap last time I looked.'

Amy looked at each of them for a few seconds in turn, incredulous at their denials. She took a deep breath then said, 'Really? You really think so? You, Lenore, were unceremoniously dumped by that arsehole husband of yours practically the minute you turned forty and your boobs went from 32 perky to 38 double long, which just happened to coincide with him getting his redundancy money and being able to swan off into the sunset with a younger version whose boobs still bounce.'

Leaving Lenore looking at her breasts in dismay, Amy turned

to Susan. 'I'm hard pushed to say there's any crap in your life, Susan, but that's because there's nothing very much in it at all. That son of yours is almost a grown man and you're still running after him like a five-year-old and what thanks do you get? None. He'll be off to university before you know it and that'll be the last you see of him till he skulks home with enough washing to turn your house into a Chinese laundry, doubling up as a Chinese takeaway at night while you cook his favourite sweet 'n' sour.'

Ignoring Susan's attempts to come in and stop her in her tracks, Amy turned finally to Carole. 'You, on the other hand, Carole, live in a house full of sweaty boys – I include your husband in that, by the way – who make you wait on them hand and foot. Meanwhile, Dirty Den is swanning around in his plush office in the West End, wheeling and dealing and bringing home the bacon, looking forward to getting back to his nest – cleaned by you – to eat his meat and three veg – cooked by you – and ignore his offspring – looked after entirely by you.'

Amy ignored Carole's attempts to explain she'd been misrepresented and her life was nothing like that, and sat back in her chair, her blood pressure raised at the injustice of it all.

'Does that sound like the lives we dreamed of when we were at school? I mean, you tell me, does it? We're *better* than this, we *deserve* better than this crap.'

There was silence round the table as Lenore, Susan and Carole stared at Amy then back at each other, breathless from Amy's blistering attack. They'd known each other for over thirty years, been through playground scuffles and skinned knees together, through the transition to big school, they'd talked each other round from break-ups, dissuaded each other from makeups, started out in the world of work together, gone to this one's wedding, cried at that one's divorce, admired newborns, comforted miscarriages. They'd done it all but never had they criticized each other's choices in this way. It was a punch to the gut and it was hard to know whether to be offended or grateful to be seen.

Lenore soon decided she was in the latter camp. 'I suppose when you put it like that . . .'

'I mean, maybe . . .' agreed Carole.

The three of them turned to Susan, waiting for her verdict. Slowly, she wiped the cappuccino froth from her top lip and pushed away her empty cup. 'I suppose Fraser can wait a bit longer for his cheese and pickle. Right then, Amy, what's this big plan of yours to remedy our dull and dutiful lives? We're all ears.'

The following evening, Carole was ignoring the pleas of her two younger sons while she cleared the table after dinner. Archie was moaning about someone having taken his iPad charger and could she please help him find it, whilst Glover was treating her to myriad facts about reptiles and why corn snakes in particular made excellent pets. Her oldest son, Daniel, floated into the room, asking his mother about his clean T-shirt.

'You know the one I mean? With a picture of Grimes on the back? White? Was white anyway before you got your hands on it.'

Carole carried on filling the dishwasher with plates and said if he didn't like the way she did the washing he could always do it himself. He stopped in front of her and she stood up, wiping her hands on the tea towel. 'Mind you, I suppose I could always throw in one of those Vanish tabs with the whites.'

'That sounds more like it,' said Daniel.

Carole glanced across the room at Dennis, waiting for him to tell his son not to treat her like his own personal laundry mistress. But Dennis was oblivious to his family as he peered at his laptop, his lips moving slightly as his eyes moved along the screen. Carole turned back to Daniel but he was already halfway out of the room, his retrieved white T-shirt over his head, so there seemed little point in saying anything. She bit her tongue and pushed the door of the dishwasher shut.

'Right, you two,' she said to her younger sons. 'Finish whatever it is you're doing and get yourselves ready for the bath. Mummy's going out tonight.'

That got Dennis's attention, and he pulled himself up from the sofa to swivel round and face Carole.

'You're going out again? You were out last night.' He pointed to the rows of figures streaming across his screen. 'I was half-thinking of going back to the office later to get a head start on all this before tomorrow's stock meeting.' His voice had a whining tone to it that Carole remembered finding so childlike and endearing when they'd first met all those years ago. Now, it reminded her of Archie or Glover bleating about more juice or complaining about having to brush their teeth when they'd already done it the night before.

'It's not really out out. I'm only going to an exercise class with some of the girls. I told you about it last week,' she fibbed. 'Remember?'

'No,' Dennis sulked.

'I did. Anyway, you've been working all the hours God sends recently, I'm sure they can manage without you putting in the night shift. And you're going out tomorrow night.' She didn't add that Dennis went out almost every Friday and Saturday and had done for years while she stayed at home with the boys.

'Knock knock,' called Amy from the hall. She walked into the huge, white kitchen, smiling at Carole and throwing her hand up in a wave at Dennis, who closed his laptop and walked over to the kitchen counter.

'I did knock,' she said, 'but no answer. Are you ready?'

Dennis's eyes travelled slowly up and down Amy's figure, taking in her buzz cut and head-to-toe black outfit. 'If it isn't Morticia for the gender-fluid generation. Or did someone's cat die?'

Carole threw the tea towel she was still holding at her husband. 'Ignore Dennis, Amy. He thinks women should be swishing about in Laura Ashley and stilettos. His ideal woman's Mrs Hinch.'

'Who?' Amy pointedly kept her back to Dennis and addressed only Carole.

'Mrs Hinch. That woman that's all over social media trying to persuade women cleaning is the new rock 'n' roll.'

'Don't knock Mrs Hinch,' said Dennis, slouching against the counter so that Amy had to move further along to keep ignoring him. 'There's a reason Mr Hinch is happy with what he's got, you know.'

'Yeah, his wife's making enough to keep both of them in style, no doubt,' said Amy. She watched Carole drying the surface she'd just washed. 'You ready, Mrs Hinch?'

'Almost.' She turned to Dennis. 'Right, that's everything cleared away, the packed lunches are all in the fridge for tomorrow, their pyjamas are on the beds and their supper's plated for after their bath.'

23

Amy looked from Carole to Dennis in disbelief. 'Your hands, is it?'

'Eh?'

'I thought there must be something wrong with your hands, you can't do any of that stuff yourself? Or have you had a hard day buying low and selling high?'

Carole stepped in before her husband could answer. 'Never mind her. I've run the bath, you can put the two of them in together.'

Archie looked up and whined, 'Muuum, don't make me share a bath with him again, he keeps farting.'

Amy shoved Carole in front of her, pushing her along the hall to the front door. 'Call it a Jacuzzi then,' she called over her shoulder to Archie. 'Just make sure none of it goes up your nose. Come on, Carole, we've to meet the others at half past.'

'Where are you going anyway, dressed up like Catwoman and her not-so-glamorous assistant?' Dennis followed them into the hall as Daniel came sauntering back down the stairs.

'More like Itchy and Scratchy,' he said, giving his dad a high five.

Amy waved her hand in front of Dennis to let him know exactly what she thought of his regulation Hugo Boss office trousers and shirt. 'Coming from the world's greatest fashion icon, we'll take that as a compliment,' she said.

'I didn't realize I was internationally recognized, Amy, thank you.'

'Honestly, you two,' said Carole. 'Give it a rest.' Addressing her husband, she said, 'I told you, we're going to give aerobics bootcamp a try.'

'Sounds like a good idea,' said Dennis. 'Get rid of some of that post-Christmas flab.'

Amy watched as Carole's face fell.

'No, wait, I didn't mean—' began Dennis, but Amy butted in.

'Congratulations,' she said.

'On what?'

'Your new personal best.'

'I'm not with you,' said Dennis, narrowing his eyes in dislike at his wife's best friend.

Undeterred, Amy continued. 'On the absolute twatometer. Tonight's personal best of 98 beats your previous best of 97.5.'

'Out of?'

'A hundred, obviously.'

Before Dennis could respond, Carole pushed Amy out of the door, closing it tightly behind them.

'For God's sake,' muttered Amy as they slipped and slid their way across Carole's lawn. She watched Carole raise her face to the red velvet sky and breathe in the bitter late-evening air like a prisoner released from confinement. 'Why do you put up with that? He might not be as hot-headed as he used to be but it's like going back in time spending any more than ten minutes with him. And it's beginning to rub off on your boys too.'

'Dennis isn't as bad as you make out. They're only joking, him and Dan, they don't mean anything by it. You need to be able to take a joke in a house full of men.' She stopped slightly ahead of Amy and swivelled round to look at her backside in her tight black leggings. 'I'm not sure if I'm comfortable in this outfit. Dennis is right, I have put on weight. These leggings are too tight. Do they make my bum look big?'

Amy glanced down at Carole's backside and looked away quickly, saying, 'No, it's . . . perfect.'

'What?'

'I mean, it's fine. You look fine in what you're wearing. Whatever.' She got into the van.

Carole swithered outside then got in. 'Are you annoyed about something?' she asked her friend as she looped her seat belt round her.

'No. I suppose I'm a bit apprehensive about tonight. What about you?' Amy started the engine and rolled out of Carole's massive driveway, managing to avoid the sandpit at the edge of the lawn which was currently filled with sludgy grey snow rather than the sand it was meant for, and two small, frost-covered bikes which were propped up against the fence. 'Are you ready to do something radical?'

'To be honest, I'm quite nervous too. It sounded great last night after a few vino rossos but now I'm a bit . . . We won't get caught, will we?'

'Arsehole.' Amy swerved as the driver of a white van gave her the finger as he sped past her. 'You need more braking time in the frost, you eejit,' she shouted to the disappearing tail lights. 'Sorry? What? No, we won't get caught, don't worry. Look how dark it is, and if we go round the back of the club, it's hardly lit at all. They'll all be too busy spending the housekeeping money on flat ale to notice us outside. Folk won't see what we've done till the morning.' She put the van into fourth gear and they gathered some speed.

Carole watched the snow-tipped trees whizz by and thought how much prettier everywhere looked with a light dusting of snow, even Ferniegair which was a lovely part of town whatever the weather. They'd moved here about five years ago, following Dennis's most successful trading year to date and a pay rise that more than covered the extra mortgage payments. She knew she was lucky to live the life she did, whatever Amy said. She turned to her friend suddenly. 'We don't want to do anything silly though, do we? Maybe . . . I mean, maybe we could just shout in through the windows or something? You know, disrupt their night out without actually doing anything . . . illegal?'

'Ppff. How's that radical? We need to put the message out there, Carole, get change on the agenda.'

Carole started laughing, a high-pitched nervous sort of laugh, but she was amused by her oldest friend. 'Why are you like this, Amy? You've always been . . . I don't know, raging against someone, or something, looking for the unfairness, the prejudice. Even at school. Whenever you came to school, that is.'

'Yeah, and you never have to look very far to find it, do you?' She shot a quick look at Carole out of the corner of her eye. 'Anyway, it's better than dying a slow death living with a man I met at school and sticking it out for the kids and the huge house, do you not think?'

Carole looked down at her lap then out of the window before she said in a quieter voice, 'Don't talk about what you don't understand, Amy.'

'Sorry,' said Amy immediately, reaching over to squeeze her friend's shoulder. 'You're right, it's none of my business. We'd better get a move on, the others are probably there already.'

Susan and Lenore were in the car park at the side of the Miners' Welfare Club, leaning against the bonnet of Lenore's car. Both were dressed from head to toe in black, as Amy had instructed, Susan covering her tight exercise kit with a bulky old black cardigan.

She pulled it closer to herself, shivering as a bitter January wind blew her ginger curls across her face. 'I don't know why we had to wear these stupid outfits,' she said. 'Even Fraser commented on it when I left tonight and he never notices what I'm wearing. Never notices me at all these days, to be honest, unless I'm fetching him a pizza while he's at his pc, or he wants me to iron his shirt. He's so well-turned out, my Fraser, always has been.'

Lenore stopped examining her long red nails and said, 'He's always had you to do everything for him, that's why. You're not doing him any favours, you know – who's going to do all that stuff for him when he's away at uni?'

'Don't talk about that. Maybe he'll go to Glasgow, eh, and stay at home? Don't most students stay at home with their parents these days? It's a while off yet anyway, I can't deal with that right now.' She checked her watch then around the deserted lane where they were parked. 'Where are those two? Amy definitely said half eight, didn't she? It's already quarter to nine and I'm freezing in this stupid outfit.'

'You know Amy,' said Lenore. 'Works on a completely different time zone to everyone else.' She watched as Susan wrapped her shapeless cardigan round herself again. As if to accentuate the differences between their figures, she stood up and stretched, looking down at her own slim thighs in their skintight leggings as she did so. 'I don't mind the outfits, actually. I know I've said it before but it's true – Tommy leaving was the best thing that ever happened to me. I'm at the gym every night now I've got the time to take care of myself. I can get away with lycra.' She did a few star jumps on the spot to illustrate the point. 'Not like most women our age – boobs like baked potatoes and underarms you could attach a string to and take for a spin round the park.'

'Thanks very much,' said Susan, lifting her arm and dropping it again to see if it wobbled.

'I didn't mean you,' said Lenore, and Susan smiled, until her friend added, 'You don't care what you look like.'

'I'm like Kim Kardashian in this outfit,' she said, swivelling round to check out her own backside, in the manner of women everywhere.

'Who?' said Susan.

'Kim Kardashian.' Lenore stopped as she noticed Susan's puzzled face. 'Come on, even you must have heard of Kim Kardashian? From *Keeping Up With the Kardashians*?'

'No, what does she do?'

Lenore thought for a moment. 'She's . . . she does . . . I mean, she's always on the TV. In every magazine, showing off her booty, as they call it these days.' She gave her own a little shake.

Susan was none the wiser. 'Why is she on TV? Is she talented?'

'Well, no, she . . . I mean, her whole family . . .'

'Her whole family's talented?'

'They're all part of it, what we're interested in.'

Susan was not convinced. 'But why are we interested in them? I've never heard of them.'

'Are you serious? You're not, are you? She's . . . everywhere.'

'But why?' Susan persisted. 'Is she a singer?'

Lenore shook her head.

'An actress then? A beautiful actress?'

Lenore sighed. 'She *is* beautiful. She's . . .' She indicated large breasts and bottom, awkwardly. 'You know?'

'Not really, no,' said Susan, her forehead wrinkling.

'Oh, for God's sake, Susan— Ah, here's Amy and Carole, thank God! At last,' she said, raising her eyebrows at Carole.

'Aye-aye,' said Carole, pointing to Lenore's outfit. 'Who invited Kim Kardashian?'

'How does everyone—' began Susan before Lenore cut across her and said to Carole, 'Don't even start that conversation, trust me.'

She turned to Amy. 'Thanks for showing up, Captain.'

'Not Amy's fault tonight,' said Carole, before Amy could reply. 'It was me that held us up, sorry.'

'Never mind, we're all here now. Are we ready for this? Where's the stuff?' Lenore checked behind Amy to see if she had left anything in front of the van.

'It's in the back,' said Amy. 'I wanted to make sure there's no one about first.'

'Not a soul,' said Susan, stamping her trainers on the hard ground to try and heat up her feet which were so cold she could no longer feel them.

'Right, let's get everything from the van then, come on.'

Ten minutes later, the women gathered together, close to the back of the club house. Each woman held a slim canister of white spray paint in her hand, and there were a couple of small tins of green paint and a pile of soft brushes at their feet. They were all looking round them nervously, except Amy who was bouncing back and forward on the balls of her feet, raring to go.

'Okay then, who wants to go first? Who's bursting with something they want to say to the world?'

Susan pulled her cardigan closer to her chest and fiddled with her hair, Lenore kicked some dirty snow across the car park, and Carole looked into the middle distance as though she was waiting for inspiration to strike.

Amy put her hands on her hips and looked directly at Lenore who was standing closest to her. 'Lenore, come on, what about you? Is there nothing you'd like to shout from the rooftops to Tommy, and men like him everywhere that marry young women in their prime then suck the life out of them and leave them dried-up husks of used-up ovaries and menopausal flushes?'

Lenore kicked some iced dirt in Amy's direction and said indignantly, 'Eh, excuse me, I hope you're not including me in that category. I'm still very much menstrual, thank you, and just about to reach my prime. Some may say. What?'

She looked around as she heard the others sniggering.

'Two hours a day at the gym, lifting weights and living off pineapple chunks to keep yourself looking like that. Bloody boxing the other day! And for whose benefit? Do you really want another man that only wants you for the firmness of your flesh and the distance between your thighs?'

'The distance between my . . .? Boxing's about empowerment, Susan, not about the shape of your thighs. Although . . .' She looked down at her own thighs with approval.

Amy tutted and turned her attention to Carole. 'What about you then? Is there a message you'd like to send to that lump of lard you call your husband, or those equally domestically challenged boys of yours?'

'Don't insult my boys. That's just the way they are.'

'Just the way they are. Exactly.' Amy pounced on the phrase. 'And we are just the way we are, and do you know what way that is?'

'Feeling stupid in black lycra?' said Susan, pulling the clingy material away from her stomach.

'No, it's *better* than them.'

Lenore, Carole and Susan all said at the same time, 'What?'

Amy laughed at their incredulous faces. 'Women are better than men. End of. And it's time we started saying it, loud and proud. In fact,' she said, pulling the cap off the can of spray paint in her hand, 'that's the perfect place to start.'

The others watched as Amy shook the can and raised it high into the air. She stood back, choosing the best place on the wall to start.

'She won't,' whispered Susan to Carole.

'Watch me,' said Amy. She pressed hard on the nozzle, and the can hissed before unleashing an arc of paint, spraying little flecks of white back on to Amy's cheeks as she reached up high as she could and scrawled halfway up the wall, **WOMEN ARE BETTER THAN MEN. END OF**.

She stood back to admire what she'd written.

'Oh my God, Amy. What have you—' began Lenore, as Carole stepped forward, rolled up her sleeve and threw the lid of her paint can on to the ground.

'Right,' she murmured under her breath. 'Here goes.'

'Yes! Come on, Susan, you too, make a name for yourself. Lenore, get going, we haven't got all night.'

Susan caught Lenore's eye. She raised her shoulders slightly and grinned, and they both shook their paint cans and joined their friends.

Lenore chose a section of the wall to the left of Amy's slogan and, in the swirly white capitals her pupils used to graffiti the front of their jotters, quickly sprayed **BRAINS ARE BETTER THAN BOOBS** before she could change her mind. She stepped back for a moment to consider what she'd painted, then put down the can, dipped a brush into one of the paint pots and used the green paint to dab a smiley face on the Os for good measure. Satisfied, she walked along to see what the others were writing and watched as Susan finished painting a slightly shoogly but still legible, **MEN DRINK THE HOUSEKEEPING MONEY, WOMEN STRETCH IT**.

'Love it, Susan!' cried Lenore. 'That's exactly right – these men are out here every night, some of them, drinking away the family's money while women have to make do with what's left. There's kids in my school can't even go on school trips while these men think nothing of spending twenty, thirty quid a night on booze.'

Carole was the only one still painting as Amy pointed to her watch and said they'd better hurry. 'Just this last bit,' she said, kneeling close to the wall and using one of the small brushes to add the final touches.

Amy moved closer to check her friend's handiwork. 'You've been keeping your artistic urges well hidden, I see, Carole. That's brilliant.'

'Why thank you, kind friend.' Carole's eyes were shining, Amy couldn't remember when she'd last seen her look so happy.

She bent down to read the last couple of words. 'What does that mean at the end—'

'Sssshhh,' hissed Lenore suddenly, from behind them. 'Sssshhh, wait, what's that?'

All four women stood still, paint dripping from their brushes, as they looked towards the lane at the side of the building, where they could hear shuffling noises, followed by a loud bang and a male voice saying, 'Shit, my knee.'

'Oh God,' said Susan. 'There's someone coming. Why did I ever let you talk me into this, Amy?' She looked all round then threw her spray can into the shrubbery. 'I can't go to prison, wee Fraser couldn't manage on his own—'

'Sssshhh, Susan, if anyone's going to get us caught it's you.'

The women stood, gripping their spray cans and trying not to make a sound, as the voice behind the wall started singing.

'Will I go and see who it is?' whispered Carole.

'No, wait,' said Lenore. 'It's some drunk taking a pee against a wall, that's all.'

'What is it with these men, the way they feel they can whip out their willies at any opportunity?' said Carole.

'They've no option when their bloody urinal's still broken, have they?' said Amy. 'If they'd just let me mend it—'

'Are you really going on about that now, Amy? We're all going to get caught and—'

'What's that smell? Like . . . turps or something,' came the man's voice, closer now than before.

The women all looked at each other, Susan mouthing 'Oh God,' her hands in her hair.

'Paddy!' It was a different voice. 'What're you lurking about out here for, we've been looking for you? It's your round, mate.'

'Give me a minute, Rab, I'm just taking a leak. It's up to the ankles in pish in there.'

'Told you,' said Amy smugly to the rest of the women, who ignored her.

They remained in a jittery semicircle, as they heard the sounds of a door slamming, followed by some more swearing from Paddy and scuffling noises as he finished what he was doing, then a second set of footsteps, getting fainter as he headed back into the club. Finally, the side door slammed again.

'Right,' said Amy, raising her hand and pointing towards the van, like a general leading her army back to safety. 'That's our cue. Everyone – get going! *Now.*'

The women grabbed the paint and brushes and ran from the club towards their vehicles. Stashing everything in Amy's boot, they drove off into the night, leaving the paint to dry on the wall behind them.

Back home, Susan thanked Lenore for the lift and locked the front door behind her. All the downstairs lights were off and the house was silent. She saw a light on in Fraser's room but decided to make a cup of tea before going up to check on him. As she waited for the kettle to boil, she noticed her paint-splattered leggings and smiled to herself. If only her loyal customers at the library could see her now, she thought. She drummed her fingers on the worktop then flicked the switch on the kettle and walked to the fridge instead. She took out the bottle of white wine that had been sitting there unopened since her birthday and poured herself a large glass.

I deserve this, she thought, as she flopped on to the couch and put her feet up on the coffee table in front of her.

She heard heavy footsteps coming down the stairs and her son poked his head round the living-room door.

'Mum, where have you been? Are you . . . drinking wine?' He made a face. 'I've had nothing to eat since dinner.'

'I was out with friends, Fraser. I told you. Maybe you weren't listening.' She took another sip of wine and crossed her legs.

'Well?' said Fraser, still hovering round the doorway.

Susan smiled. 'Yes, I had a good time, thanks. An interesting time anyway, maybe I'll tell you about it one day—'

'I wasn't asking about your night, Mum. What do I care what a bunch of wee wifies from school talk about while they're out getting gassed. I meant, well, can you make me my supper now? It's way after the usual time.' He sniffed, to let her know what an inconvenience it all was.

Susan put her glass down on the table but kept her eyes on the stem before saying hesitantly, 'Could you not have made yourself a sandwich if you were hungry, Fraser? There's everything in, I bought that crusty loaf you like and the ham with the smelly herb round it.'

Fraser's head snapped back in astonishment. 'Make it myself? But . . . you always make my supper for me.'

It was true, most evenings she took her son up a sandwich, or a bowl of black grapes maybe, something he liked anyway. She looked forward to that small moment, in fact, a quick ruffle of his strawberry blond hair as she set the offering on his desk, or a high five as his eyes remained glued to his screen.

'Could you bring it up to my room like you usually do?' said Fraser. 'A battle's about to start and I'm strategy boss, the whole team's looking to me to keep it all together.' He disappeared then stuck his head back in the room again. 'Mum?'

Susan looked up hopefully.

'You put too much butter on it last night, watch how much you're putting on tonight, will you? Thanks, Mum,' he added, 'you're the best cook I know.'

Susan heard his footsteps retreating to his room and the door slam behind him. She took a last sip of her wine, then, sighing, got up and went into the kitchen to make her son his sandwich. The words Carole had written – **WE ARE NOT HERE TO SERVE** – had never seemed more apt.

★

Lenore parked the car in her driveway and looked up into the gloom for a few minutes to steel herself to go into the empty house. She knew she was lucky to own such a lovely home, which had become entirely hers as part of the divorce settlement. Her friends could say what they liked about Tommy, but she knew how guilty he'd felt at leaving her, so much so that he'd insisted on taking nothing but his clothes and the massive record and CD collection he'd been amassing since he was a teenager. Her solicitor had had her sign that offer document before the ink was dry in case he changed his mind. Lenore was still wishing he would as she signed all the papers that were put in front of her.

She headed straight to the kitchen and opened the fridge, humming to herself to alleviate the silence that was still new to her. She saw the shelves full of lettuce and plum tomatoes, half-fat yoghurts and the dreaded pineapple chunks, and cursed under her breath. She slammed the fridge door and walked over to the cupboard to take out the Ryvita. Slouched against the counter, she nibbled the edge of the dusty crispbread before making a face. 'What sick mind invented these and called them food? Enough!'

She reached into the back of the freezer, where she'd hidden the ice cream behind the frozen peas and ice cubes, and pulled out a full carton of raspberry ripple. She yanked the top off impatiently and grabbed a spoon from the drawer, digging in immediately. 'As befits the arch criminal Amy has turned me into. Now, where's my laptop?'

Settling herself on to the sofa, ice cream in hand, she logged in to an online dating site and started to scroll.

Time to see what else is out there, she thought.

★

Amy drew the van up to Carole's driveway and turned off the engine. They both sat on in silence after the vehicle had come to a halt.

'Here we are then,' said Amy finally.

Carole looked up to her house, the bottom half of which was in darkness, but didn't get out. 'Yup, here we are. Thanks for tonight. It was a lot more fun being a criminal than I thought.' She turned to face Amy. 'Mind you, we could've done without Paddy the piss artist almost catching us in the act. You don't think he saw anything, do you? Or heard us?'

'No, it'll be fine, I promise. He was too drunk to have any idea what was going on behind the club.'

'Why do men get like that?'

'Drunk?'

'Yeah, but out of it drunk, not having a good laugh with mates drunk. Why are men like that?'

'Don't ask me,' said Amy. 'I'm the last person to know anything about men.'

Carole smiled. 'We don't get like that, do we?'

'Mostly, no. Though it has been known. Do you remember that time we got out of our faces on cider and blackcurrant on that trip to Irvine and they wouldn't let us back in the hostel?'

'I haven't thought about that for years. With that posh girl from Bothwell – remember her, Pamela or Camilla, something like that, wasn't it? Hair the wrong side of auburn and smelled like mature cheese?'

'That's right. She kept saying, "My father will have this place shut down, let us in this instant."'

'They wouldn't though, and we ended up spending the night

huddled together under the picnic table in the backyard. What happened to Pamela, I wonder?'

'I don't know, I just remember cuddling up with you under your hoodie.' Amy avoided Carole's eye. 'To keep warm, I mean, it was freezing, remember?'

'Yeah, I remember.'

They were both silent for a few seconds then Amy cleared her throat and said, 'Anyway, should you not be getting in? There's no lights on in that mansion of yours, looks like they're all in bed already.'

Carole looked towards the house and said, 'I hope so.' She turned back to Amy. 'It's been a good night. I've felt . . . like myself again. Reminded me of old times. Before . . . you know, the kids and everything, reminded me of being young, I suppose.'

'We're not past it yet,' said Amy.

'No, I suppose we're not.' Carole smiled. 'Okay, I'd better be getting in.'

'Yeah. Night, Carole.' Amy started the engine and Carole reluctantly got out of the van and stumbled across the expanse of frozen lawn in the darkness, sliding a little as her trainer caught the ice, and turned back to wave to Amy from her front door.

As the tail lights disappeared into the distance, Carole closed over the storm doors then the front door behind her. She didn't bother putting on the hall light and held tight to the bannister on her way up the stairs. She stopped at the first door off the upstairs hall and peeked in on her two youngest sons who were both sleeping soundly under their Power Rangers duvets. Archie's leg was poking out the bed, his little foot almost on the floor. Carole smiled and gently lifted his foot back on the bed and placed his duvet over him. His warm hand brushed against her cheek and she caught it and kissed it, wishing all her children could stay this age for ever. 'Night night,' she whispered into the darkness and closed the door.

She padded soundlessly across the thickly carpeted hall to Thomas's bedroom and chapped the door before poking her head round. Thomas was in bed but still awake, his face lit up by the light reflecting from his phone screen. 'I'm snapping Jaxx,' he mouthed at her, frowning and pointing to his phone. Carole motioned to her watch to indicate that it was too late for him to still be awake but she didn't push it as he'd been so much happier recently since he'd made friends with Jack and she didn't want to spoil it for him.

Her last stop before her own bedroom was Daniel's room. After a quick chap on the door, she put her head round and was met with the strong smell of sweaty feet and the lingering aroma of bacon sandwiches, the remains of which she could see curling up at the edges on Daniel's desk. She knew the plate and its congealed contents would still be there waiting for her to remove them in the morning. Daniel himself was sprawled on his unmade bed, his eyes twitching as he scrolled Reddit. He didn't even look up as he waved her away. She clicked his door behind her and made her way to her own bedroom at the far end of the hall.

The light was off, and the sleeping bulk of Dennis was under their soft white duvet, spreadeagled in the middle of the bed. She perched on the edge and bent to untie her trainers.

'Good night, was it?'

Carole jumped. 'Christ, Dennis, you gave me the fright of my life, I thought you were sleeping.'

Dennis sat up in the bed, his silhouette looming against the velvet wallpaper on the back wall. 'Kind of late for an aerobics class, isn't it?'

'Amy and I stayed chatting in her van for ages afterwards. You know, Daniel and Thomas are both up. You shouldn't go to bed and leave them to their own devices. They'll probably be awake all night and it's school tomorrow.'

'They're big boys now, Carole, they can choose their own bedtimes. Anyway, I'm tired, I've done all your jobs for you tonight, no wonder I need my sleep.'

Carole swung round. 'What do you mean – you've done all *my* jobs?'

'What do you think I mean? Putting the kids in the bath, feeding them their supper, putting them to bed. It's a lot to do after you've been working all day.'

'I know it is, Dennis,' said Carole. 'I do it every night when you're working late or off out at some work do or other.'

Dennis laughed. 'I know and you're so good at it.' He flashed Carole one of his special smiles and reached for her. Carole softened immediately and said, 'Okay, let me go to the bathroom and freshen up first. You put the candle on.'.

'Why all the fuss, every time?' He lay back, his arms behind his head.

'I won't be long, I promise.' She reached over and kissed him deeply before pulling away from him, saying, 'Five minutes, wait for me. I'll be worth it.' She grabbed a silk teddy from her drawer and nipped through to their en suite.

She smiled and hummed to herself as she moisturized her neck and shoulders before changing into the pretty pink bodysuit, trying to ignore how much tighter it felt round her waist than the last time she'd worn it. Actually, she couldn't remember the last time she'd had occasion to wear such a thing. Dennis was always so busy these days and it was hard to be enthusiastic about sex after you'd spent a day descaling the downstairs toilet or reorganizing the pantry. But tonight, she felt alive, buzzing after her adventures with Amy and the girls, and ready for anything. After she'd flossed her teeth, she perched on the edge of the bath and sent a short text to the group, 'We've started something. C x' then put out the bathroom light and hurried back to the bedroom, minty fresh, to show Dennis how good she looked in silk.

When she opened the door, the thick church candle was flickering romantically and casting shadows on the long velvet curtains. She smiled and crept into bed. Dennis was facing away from her so she stroked his back and whispered, 'Dennis. Dennis?' There was no movement from her husband's side of the bed. Carole sat back a little, wondering if she should try again, when suddenly Dennis grunted, turned on to his back and simultaneously farted and started snoring. Carole sighed, knowing she'd taken too long and he hadn't bothered to wait for her. As he continued to snore heavily by her side, she lay back, lips tight and eyes staring into the gloom as she wondered how they'd got to this point. Finally, she got up and snuffed out the candle.

Amy parked the van in the space reserved for her second-floor flat and thought about dumping the spray paint canisters and paint pots in the bin, before changing her mind. *That can wait till morning*, she thought as she grabbed her jacket and locked up the van. She crossed the car park, meeting no one at that time of night. One of the things she'd liked about these flats they'd built beside the racecourse was that they were mainly for single people like her, no young families running around to remind her what she didn't have, and was never likely to have. But sometimes, she did wonder what all the other residents did with their lives. She was usually away too early in the morning to see any of the office workers heading out to town, and often out at callouts in the evenings or weekends so that she sometimes had the impression she was living in a ghost town. It had been fine when Tess was living with her, but now she could go days without seeing anyone at all, beyond the people whose taps and toilets she fixed. There had even been a couple of occasions recently when she'd considered getting in touch with her father and trying to re-establish some sort of relationship with him, but then Carole would call her, or Susan or Lenore would text to arrange something and she'd be reminded that she didn't need a family after all. Thank God for her friends, she thought, as she unlocked her front door.

She was met with the usual deep silence of an unoccupied home and quickly turned on the main light so that the living room was flooded with warmth. 'Mrs Cooper?' she called. 'Mrs Cooper, are you there?' She waited for a few seconds and smiled broadly as her little striped rescue cat came padding out of her bedroom, yawning and stretching.

Amy bent to stroke her. 'Were you on my bed again, naughty girl?' she said, in a voice that showed she wasn't angry at all. 'Did you miss me? Hmm, did you miss Amy? Come on, let's get you a little treat.' Mrs Cooper followed Amy through to the kitchen obediently.

At first, Amy had been annoyed when Tess hadn't come back for her cat like she'd said she would. 'I can't be responsible for a cat,' she'd told her. But she'd surprised herself by how much she could care for another creature, and how she looked forward to seeing her when she got home. If Tess came back for the cat now, Amy didn't know what she'd do. Mrs Cooper had become part of the furniture.

She checked her phone as she waited for the kettle to boil, then again as she flopped on to the couch, coffee in hand. There were no messages or missed calls. She had her shower and set out her jeans and T-shirt for the morning. She had an early callout in Rutherglen so she set her alarm for six. Before she got into bed, she checked her phone again and pursed her lips at the blank screen. Mrs Cooper was already curled up on the other pillow so she put out the light and lay down in the dark. A few minutes later, her phone buzzed and she reached out for it beside her bed. She smiled as she read the message from Carole. 'Yes, Carole, we have started something,' she said, and lay back down to sleep.

The following Sunday, the women agreed to meet at Café Nisi for breakfast. Susan had left Fraser's sausages and bacon warming in the oven, with instructions to make two slices of toast and heat the beans in the microwave, which she felt sure he could manage to do himself. Dennis had had to go into the office to discuss some deal or other with a new client so Carole had paid Daniel a tenner to keep an eye on his younger brothers while she was out. He'd wanted more but since Carole knew he would spend the whole time on his Xbox, only intervening in the event of blood being drawn, and then only to call her, she'd stuck to her guns. Lenore had been to the gym earlier than usual and done an extra fifteen minutes on the cross-trainer so she could treat herself to a small cappuccino and still be within the day's calorie intake. Amy had fed Mrs Cooper and marched into town so that she was only ten minutes later than everyone else. They were all there.

Susan pushed away her breakfast plate and got up to order more coffee. Carole helped Amy stack the dirty plates so they'd have room on the table to put out the papers. When Susan came back with her fresh latte, she said, 'It's all they're talking about at the library, you know. One of the guys in my book club said this is what happens when you let women vote. Can you believe that? I said, Mr Heggarty, did you actually read what was written on the wall? Maybe these women feel they're being unfairly treated by society, and do you know what he said? They weren't complaining when it was men that had to go off and fight in the trenches, were they? I mean, how can you even argue with someone like that?'

Lenore shook her head. 'Tommy always used to say when it comes to women, it only takes one bad apple to infect the rest.'

'Like we're a crate of rotten fruit. Charming,' said Amy.

A young mum with a double buggy passed by close to their table. The buggy contained a screaming boy, red in the face with his determination to grab a toy car from his sister, who was equally determined not to let him have it.

'Please, Leah, let your brother have the car,' said the exhausted woman. She grabbed it from the girl and gave it to the boy and immediately their roles were reversed, with the boy smiling and the girl squealing fit to raise the roof. 'You've got your dolly, Leah, there, give it a cuddle, that's better. Good girl, it's good to be kind.' The girl's sobbing subsided and she buried her face in her doll's stringy hair. The boy grinned and drew circles in the air with his car in front of his sister's face.

Amy tilted her head towards the woman as she left the

café. 'That's exactly the kind of woman who needs to read the messages we're putting out there.'

'Sssshhh,' said Carole. 'We don't want everyone to know it was us, do we? Although the local papers are doing a good job of letting people know about it.' She picked up the *Hamilton Advertiser* from the small pile in front of them, and read aloud, '"Local miners' welfare club defaced by Graffiti Girls".'

Susan picked up the *Bellshill Speaker*. 'Or what about this one – "Graffiti Girls tell the darts team to get back to their kids". I don't think we said that, did we?' She looked around at the others.

'Listen to the *Motherwell Times*,' said Lenore. '"Graffiti Girls – who do they think they are?"'

'Please,' said Amy. 'Don't keep repeating it, it's bad enough it's in all the papers.'

Susan looked at Amy in surprise. 'What do you mean?'

'That . . . that abomination of a name you signed on the wall, Carole, and now they've saddled us with it.'

'Graffiti Girls? I think that was brilliant, Carole. I wish I'd thought of it, don't you, Lenore?'

'Yeah,' said Lenore. 'I've never been in a proper group, with a name and a mission and everything. Not for years, anyway. What's wrong with it?'

Amy treated them all to one of her glares then snapped her hand against the table. 'Graffiti Girls? Graffiti *Girls*? Come on, we're not exactly girls, are we?'

Lenore frowned. 'I don't know about you, Amy, but last time I looked I was *definitely* a girl.'

'No, I mean we're women. *Women*. We're in our forties, for God's sake. Lenore, you're the oldest, you're already forty-two, aren't you?'

'Only just, and I'd prefer you didn't tell the whole world if you don't mind—'

'We're all in our forties anyway, what does it matter? The point is, we are grown women. We're as adult as we're ever going to be and calling us girls dismisses us, surely you can see that?'

'But how are they dismissing us when they're writing about us? We're all over the local papers,' said Susan.

'Exactly,' agreed Carole.

'Look,' said Amy. 'Imagine this. Let's say Tommy and Dennis decided they'd had enough and wanted to do something radical . . .'

Lenore spluttered over the remains of her coffee. 'Tommy? Are you joking? He'd be more likely to go down the pub and play darts than do what we've done.'

'I know that, Lenore, he's a man, isn't he?' Amy paused while the others laughed and nudged each other. 'But let's say, just for a moment, they got their act together long enough to devise a plan to do something really radical, like, well, like . . .' The others waited as Amy tried hard to think of something Tommy and Dennis would be capable of carrying out. 'Look, doesn't matter what they do but let's say they carry out this plan that affects the whole town, maybe the next town too as other men get involved, they start a movement say, and social media joins in, other groups meet up and do this same radical thing . . .'

'Whatever that is,' said Carole, checking her phone in case Dan had texted.

'Yes, whatever that is,' said Amy. 'And before they know it, they're in the papers, not the local rags but the big ones, the *Guardian*, say. Do you really think, in your wildest dreams, the best tag line they'd come up with would be "the Doodle Dudes"? Or that they'd say "Who's annoyed the Graffiti Boys?"

47

Can you imagine picking up a paper that screams, "Who do the Letter-Writing Lads think they are?"'

'You're good at this,' said Lenore.

Amy ignored the compliment. 'But you get my point? Calling us girls, focusing on that stupid nickname takes the sting out of what we've done, makes it, I don't know, domestic or something. Keeps the girls in their place.'

There was a silence round the table as Carole, Lenore and Susan all thought about what Amy was saying.

Slowly, Susan sat up and said, 'Do you know, I think Amy's right. I think if men had done what we did, people would stop and ask why.'

'Yes,' said Lenore. 'They'd wonder what had gone wrong, how the men had been failed that they felt bad enough to go and deface public property.'

Carole stopped worrying about what might be happening at home and joined in. 'And if they kept it up, there'd be initiatives, ten-point plans, the men would be invited to speak with the First Minister.'

'And not to talk about their feelings either, but to talk about how things could be made better.'

'For the men who did this radical thing, and for all men,' added Lenore.

At last Amy was smiling. 'Now you're getting it. We are *not* girls' – she banged her fist on the table as she said this and the old couple at the table on the back wall jumped – 'and we will *not* be dismissed.' She picked up the papers and laid them on the floor. Then she sat forward with her elbows on the table and said, 'Right, here's the plan . . .'

II

Lenore

'BUT MR BURNS, JANEY STARTED it. She said my hair extensions looked like the ends of a dirty mop so I—'

'I couldn't care less what Janey McLeod said about your hair, Chloe Baxter, you cannot disrupt the whole of S2 Special Maths by flinging pencils and rubbers across the room to avenge your stringy hair extensions.'

But, sir, what— Wait, what do you mean stringy?'

'Excuse me,' said Lenore, turning sideways and squeezing past the aggrieved second year to make her way into the staffroom. Mr Burns raised his unkempt eyebrows at her and shrugged his shoulders in a 'here we go again' gesture so Lenore gave him a small smile of solidarity. It soon changed to a frown as he said, 'Mine's a white coffee if you're making one, I'll be finished here in two minutes.'

That'll be right, thought Lenore. She hadn't been released from years of domestic servitude for Tommy to be put back in the harness by the likes of bushy-browed George Burns when she got to work. She indicated her bottle of Diet Pepsi apologetically and looked round the busy staffroom to see if Nadia had made it over from the Modern Languages' block yet.

Like their pupils, the teachers tended to stick together in

their own well-defined tribes. In the far corner sat the Maths and Science teachers, dismayingly male, middle-aged and tweed, every last one. Considering all the talk of equality and STEM opportunities being made available to girls, it was a mystery why the demographic of the teaching staff remained the same as it had been in Lenore's own schooldays. The comfiest chairs closest to the kettle and microwave were the preserve of the Home Economics crowd. Smaller, and perhaps consequently, closer knit, this group consisted of two elderly sisters, Kate and Prue Elliott, and a new arrival this year, a sturdy-looking girl who couldn't be more than twenty, and certainly seemed too young for her daily preoccupation of knitting the world's largest purple scarf. Lenore's own tribe, the dozen or so teachers from English and Social Subjects, usually occupied the big oval table in the middle of the room, which was permanently strewn with greasy-rimmed cups, half-finished Pot Noodle cartons, and days' old copies of the *Guardian*. Lenore got on well with her colleagues but preferred to sit with Nadia and have a laugh at breaktimes rather than make small talk with the others. She waved and smiled broadly though, making sure they didn't take it personally.

Standing beside the kettle, drumming his fingers on the worktop as he waited for it to boil, was a teacher Lenore hadn't seen before. The navy Nike tracksuit indicated he was in the PE department and Lenore was admiring the tightness and fit of his white T-shirt as he turned round and gave her a quick smile, pushing his hair back from his face as he did so. She felt her colour rising and looked away.

She spotted Nadia in one of the two hard seats beside the window and gave her a wave as she made her way towards her.

'Still sticking to the diet, I see?' said Nadia, as Lenore twisted open the lid of her fizzy drink and placed her Ryvita snacks on the window ledge.

'Definitely,' said Lenore enthusiastically. 'I feel great for it. Soon be as thin as you,' she added.

Nadia smiled though they both knew Lenore would never look like Nadia. Lenore was at least ten years older, for one thing, but she also lacked her friend's naturally slim frame and the delicate bone structure of her face, not to mention the younger woman's Mediterranean glow, glossy black hair and eyes framed by perfect Sophia Loren-style eyeliner with an uptick on each eyelid. There was a reason Higher Italian was so popular with the fifth-year boys and it wasn't entirely to do with the annual field trip to Lucca.

Lenore tried not to feel jealous as her friend took another bite of her Twix and a delicate sip of full-sugar cola.

'I had a meeting with Mr McLoughlin yesterday about some ideas I had for the new Italian assessment. Complete waste of time, of course, he never listens to a word anyone says. And that laugh, God, it grates on you. You never told me how your last meeting with him went? Your proposal to introduce new writers?'

'Oh that, yes, fine. Well, no, he was never going to agree to my proposal but he did say he'd think about it so that's something, I suppose.'

In fact, Lenore had forgotten all about the meeting with the head, after all the shenanigans with Amy and the others a couple of weeks ago. This was the thing with Amy, she got a bee in her bonnet about something and they all had to join in, no matter what other stuff they had going on in their lives. Yet she'd been working on her proposal for Mr McLoughlin for weeks and when she'd practised what she was going to say in front of the mirror it had gone a lot better than the reality.

She'd knocked on his door with the same trepidation she used to feel on being called to the office when she was a pupil here herself. Usually, the misdemeanour would have been some stunt or other organized by Amy and gone along with by the rest of them for an easy life. Then it would have been up to Lenore, or sometimes Carole, to talk their own headteacher, Mrs McHugh, into letting them off with no detention and a promise to do better in the future.

Mr McLoughlin was an altogether different beast from the grey-bunned and traditional Mrs McHugh. He'd been the deputy head when Lenore was at school, young enough to have enthusiasm and hair, but the intervening years had seen him develop his real passion – for targets and efficiency, and three-point initiatives. His overriding obsession was staying on top of the league tables, and certainly ahead of their nearest rival, Hamilton Grammar.

He was tapping away on his keyboard and didn't look up for a full two minutes after Lenore had entered his office. She stood in front of his desk, her nose twitching at his Brut aftershave and watching his eyes slide across the screen as he typed.

Finally, he was done. He tapped the return key with a flourish and swung his chair round to face Lenore.

'Mrs Radcliffe – to what do I owe the pleasure? Please, sit.' Mr McLoughlin indicated the soft armchairs opposite his desk and Lenore had no option but to flop down into one, suddenly at a disadvantage as she looked up into his pink-rimmed chipmunk eyes.

'It's Ms,' she said reflexively. 'And we have an appointment?'

Mr McLoughlin shuffled some papers on his desk as though they would provide him with the subject of the meeting.

'To discuss the S1 introduction to literature programme?' supplied Lenore, shifting herself on the armchair to try to raise herself up a little.

'Of course. You wanted to change some of the required reading texts, am I right?' His nose wrinkled as he spoke and he eyed the door as though he was already mentally ushering her out of it.

'That's right. As you'll have read in my proposal' – Mr McLoughlin's gaze fell to his desk again as though he was searching for it – 'I really feel very strongly that we should include more contemporary women writers on the list. After all, this is the children's first real introduction to literature so it's important to choose the right texts.'

Mr McLoughlin swung back on his chair and looked at Lenore appraisingly. She tried again to pull herself up to her full height but it was impossible.

'And you don't think Wilfred Owen and Shakespeare' – he said this last name so there was a pause between Shake and Speare – 'Shake . . . ah . . . speare and even our homegrown Grassic Gibbon quite cut the mustard, is that it?'

'No, of course they're perfectly good examples of excellent literature but what about Jackie Kay or Janice Galloway or Liz Lochhead, or even Diane Weston? She still lives in Uddingston, you know, although I believe she's a bit of a recluse now, but she might be persuaded to come and talk to our pupils since it's only along the road. I mean, honestly, I could list Scottish women writers as long as your arm, Mr McLoughlin, all of whom would inspire our first years.'

'I appreciate your enthusiasm, Mrs Radcliffe, but I don't think there's any need for us to go all radical, or what's that term they use now – "woke".' The inverted commas were palpable and Lenore winced but Mr McLoughlin continued. 'Messrs Owen and Shake . . . ah . . . speare have served our pupils well for all the years I've been head, and I daresay before that as well.' He turned and brought up a spreadsheet on his screen, pointing to the last column of figures with a nicotine-stained finger. 'Look, there, you see. We are currently meeting, no, *exceeding* our target in terms of Higher passes in English and that's what we are here for, isn't it?'

Lenore wanted to say that no, the purpose of English, the way she wanted to teach it at any rate, was not to tick the boxes and pass exams – that would flow naturally from what she was proposing – it was to open young minds, especially female minds, to the possibility of wonderful, inspiring, mind-blowing literature written by women, women like them from small towns in Scotland with no privilege or old boys' network to propel them to success. She opened her mouth to say as much but Mr McLoughlin had already moved on to the next topic so there seemed little point.

'And will you be attending our fundraiser next month for the trip to London to see *Macbeth*? I take it you have nothing against *Macbeth*, Mrs Radcliffe?' He treated Lenore to his impossible laugh which sounded like 'Boyoyoyo'.

Lenore fought the dual urge to vomit and to remind him again that it was Ms, and instead said of course she would be there.

'Boyoyoyo, excellent. And is there anything else I can help you with at the moment?'

Lenore struggled out of the armchair and said no, that was everything. As she reached the door, she turned and said, 'If you could read the proposal I emailed you, there might be a book or two we could at least get for the library?'

'Indeed,' said Mr McLoughlin non-committally, his back already facing her, and his mind returned to the spreadsheet of coloured columns and figures on his screen. 'See you at the fundraiser, keep up the good work.'

She was halfway out of the office when he flung at her over his shoulder, 'Good job on taking the notes of our last training day, by the way. I think we'll need to promote you to official minute taker at meetings, what do you say?'

Nothing that can be repeated out loud, thought Lenore, resisting the urge to slam the door behind her.

Nadia tipped her head to one side sympathetically. 'What a shame. After all that work you put in, too.'

'I didn't really expect any different,' she said, scrunching up her Ryvita wrapper. 'With the pace of change round here, we can probably expect to see a few more women authors on the curriculum by the time we retire.'

Nadia laughed and generously ignored Lenore's implication that they would both reach retirement age at the same time.

'Anyway, in other news . . .' Nadia raised her left hand and waved it close to Lenore's face.

Lenore looked over in the direction Nadia's hand was waving towards. She noticed the new PE teacher hadn't received the memo on where to sit as he'd perched himself on the edge of the table and was swinging his legs enthusiastically so that his giant blue and orange training shoe came perilously close to

Prue Elliott's shoulder. Lenore stifled a laugh as she watched Miss Elliott swing her upper body away from the new teacher in an exaggerated motion to indicate her displeasure. Her eye caught that of the PE teacher and he smirked back at her, raising an eyebrow and swinging his leg again for the sheer hell of it. Lenore shifted her gaze and made a show of fixing her hair as she scanned the rest of the room to see what Nadia was pointing at. She could see nothing unusual.

'What?' she said. 'What is it?'

'No, Lenore, look.' Nadia raised her hand again and wiggled the ring finger lower than the rest.

Lenore caught the glint of a diamond solitaire sitting proudly on Nadia's hand.

'Nadia? Tony proposed? When— Wow, congratulations!'

Her friend's face was pink with delight. 'Thank you!' She beamed. 'It was last night at Andiamo. He took me there for a pre-theatre and just before they brought out the profiteroles, Tony got down on one knee in front of me, this music – Pavarotti I think – started playing and he said, "Nadia, will you marry me?" It was perfect.'

Lenore swallowed the urge to voice her first thoughts which were: profiteroles on a Wednesday, you lucky cow; and: down on one knee at the local pizzeria, hardly original; and: Pavarotti, pulease; and: judging by the size of the diamond it must be nice to know you're not marrying a spendthrift; and said instead: 'How romantic, let me see that gorgeous ring. Congratulations, Nadia!'

The other teachers heard the commotion and the younger Miss Elliott came over and said, 'Ooh, you've got a keeper there' and Mrs Knowles from Modern Studies said, 'It'll be babies next, just you wait' while Nadia's face turned even pinker, and Mr Burns and Mr Connolly, Maths and Physics respectively, shouted 'Aye-aye' and 'Congrats' without bothering to get up off their seats.

The bell rang for the next period and Lenore gathered up her empty Diet Pepsi bottle and Ryvita wrappers and made her way slowly back to the English block to enlighten her third years on the benefits of the first-person narrative.

She stopped by Tesco on her way home for more tuna in brine and some fat-free yoghurts. The rest of the day had left her flat and listless. It wasn't that she wasn't happy for Nadia, of course not, it was just that it seemed a long time since she herself had been so excited about life and looking forward to the next stage. At forty-two, she found herself wondering if this was it for her – teaching the words of antiquated male writers all day and buying calorie-counted foods on her way home to a dozen cats. Not that she had any cats yet, she was thinking about it, but didn't that practically shout defeat? To hell with it, maybe she should buy a family-sized tub of Caramel Chew-Chew and be done with it.

'You're away in your own world there, Lenore,' came a familiar voice behind her. She started and dropped the treacherous tub of Ben and Jerry's back into the deep freezer.

'Amy, you startled me.'

Amy smiled. 'Yes, I have that effect on people, apparently. Might be the hair. Lack of.' She rubbed her palm over her stubbly head.

'I was about to say. When did you do that? It's a bit extreme, even for you.'

'It was annoying me. Even short, I still had to faff with hair gel and flicking bits this way and that. This is much easier.'

'Very aerodynamic. You'll be under those sinks before some old guy can say, "Wait, you're a woman." They probably still won't let you into the Miners' Welfare though. Leaky urinal or not.'

'Ha!' said Amy. 'As if I care. Anyway, what's up with you? You've got a face like a deflated balloon.'

Lenore tutted. 'Thanks very much. Time for a coffee?'

'As long as you can bear to be seen with me? Come on, too late for Nisi's, need to be Costa now. I'll treat you.'

Amy told Lenore to find a seat while she queued for their coffees. She took the couch at the back of the café and was immediately annoyed by the way her thighs squished against the well-worn sofa as she sat down. It didn't seem to matter how little she ate or how much exercise she did, she was never going to have thighs like that woman Tommy had run off with.

'Here we are,' said Amy, setting down the laden tray.

'I don't know who those chocolate muffins are for, Amy, but I certainly won't be eating one. Look at this!' She grabbed a handful of flesh at the top of her thigh and clicked her tongue. 'At this rate, I'll be back to how I was at school – fat and ugly. Big, fat Lenore, always wants more.' Her nose reddened and she could feel her eyes sting and threaten to overflow.

'Aw, come on, Lenore,' said Amy. 'Enough of that. What on earth's brought all this on?' She passed Lenore one of the napkins from under the muffins and told her to use it as a hanky.

'Thanks,' sniffed Lenore. 'Sorry, I don't know what came over me there, I'm fine, honest I am.' She dabbed the napkin at her eyes, leaving chocolate smears across her face which Amy decided not to mention.

'You're clearly not fine so what's been happening in the last couple of weeks? You were okay last time we saw you at Café Nisi. Here, take your coffee.'

'Is it skimmed milk?' said Lenore before she put it to her lips.

'Yes,' lied Amy, waving her hand impatiently. 'You know, I think you're taking this dieting lark too far. You've got nothing to prove. Tommy's the one in the wrong, he left you, you don't need to redeem yourself or anything stupid like that.'

'It's not about that. It's . . . oh I don't know, maybe it is. All I know is that when we were all at school, I was the fat girl who never had a boyfriend while everyone else was out enjoying themselves. You never had a boyfriend either, of course, but you never seemed to want to go out with anyone, whereas I really did. Just . . . no one was interested in going out with someone like me. I spent the whole of my last year at school up in my bedroom, reading and eating Tunnock's teacakes. No wonder no one fancied me. As soon as I lost the weight at uni, that's when life started for me. Boys and dates and having someone to do stuff with.'

Amy was incredulous. 'I don't know what you're talking about, Lenore. You were always popular at school. What about' – she thought for a moment – 'well, there was Big Alfie for one. You went out with him in fifth year, and he was really popular. And didn't he even get into a fight with Dennis over you at one of the Christmas discos, before he started going out with Carole?'

Lenore almost choked on her coffee. 'Big Alfie, so you remember him?' She put down her coffee cup on the low table. 'Yes, you're right, I suppose, there was Alfie.' She'd almost managed to wipe him from her memory but of course, Amy and the others had no idea what had really happened with Alfie, she'd been so careful at the time to manage what she'd told them.

She'd been waiting on Susan coming out of the library. As fifth years they had several free periods a week and when they weren't spinning out a Coke and a couple of portions of chips between them at the Safeway café, they were usually to be found in the school library. Even then Susan had been a bookworm and always wanted to spend far longer among the books than the rest of them could stand. Lenore loved books too, but even she found it tedious to hang about while Susan trawled each shelf meticulously, checking desperately to see whether any new titles had been added.

'I'll see you outside, Susan, I need to get some air.'

Susan had her nose in a Margaret Atwood and hardly noticed her leave.

Lenore leaned against the wall and thought about taking out her Walkman to listen to some music. As she was reaching into her bag, she became aware of a looming presence behind her. She turned and saw Alfie Haynes, lolling against the office block opposite, and staring at her. Avoiding his eye, she pushed back her hair and put on the large black headphones she'd got for Christmas. Her fingers fumbled with the buttons on her Walkman and she wished Susan would hurry up and come out of the library.

'All right?' said Alfie coming over and standing directly in front of her. He was close enough for her to smell the leather of his jacket and something else, sweet and perfumed, maybe hair gel or Lynx.

Lenore looked all round to check it was definitely her he was talking to. 'Me?' she said, poking herself in the chest, and pushing the headphones off her ears.

Alfie laughed, showing his large white teeth, hyena-style. He was handsome though, taller than her dad and eyelashes to rival Carole's.

'What are you listening to?'

'Em, The Verve. It's not mine, it's . . . my friend's,' she added, in case he didn't like her favourite group.

'I love The Verve, did you see them on *Top of the Pops* on Thursday?'

Damn, thought Lenore, wishing she could take it back and admit the CD was hers. 'Yeah, they were brilliant.'

There was a silence. Lenore wracked her brains for something to say but couldn't concentrate for wondering why this hulking great sixth-year boy would spend any time talking to her, a nobody from the year below.

Alfie was looking at her through narrowed eyes. 'Do you want to go for a walk through the Palace Gardens?'

'I . . . what, now? There's still two periods left.'

'So? What are you missing that you can't catch up?'

'I . . . I suppose . . .' Lenore glanced back at the library but there was still no sign of Susan and Lenore suddenly thought why shouldn't she go? This was the first time in her sixteen years that a boy had shown any interest in her and he wasn't a slimy fifth year either, he was Alfie from sixth year.

She smiled and said okay and they walked out of the school gate and down the hill towards the park behind the sports centre. They didn't speak much as they walked past the museum, then the ice-skating rink where she and Carole went skating. Lenore was trying so hard to think of something to say that would impress Alfie her head hurt. All her friends would have known exactly what to say to a boy, she thought, and kicked herself for being so immature. As they entered the park, she turned to ask him what his hobbies were when he lunged at her and pulled her behind the statue of Davie Cooper, kissing her roughly on the mouth. It wasn't unpleasant and she was quite keen for him to do it again but he stepped back, smiled at her and suggested they walk a bit further into the park.

'Okay,' she said. 'I hope it doesn't start raining though, I haven't got a hood on this—'

Alfie lunged again, this time grabbing her by the lapels of her jacket and sticking his tongue into her mouth. That didn't feel so pleasant and Lenore pulled away, wiping her mouth with the back of her hand. 'Wait a minute,' she began, her bag falling off her shoulder and landing on the ground between them.

Alfie laughed loudly. 'What's the matter? No one can see us.'

That wasn't the comfort he seemed to think it was, and Lenore stood for a moment, shifting her weight from one leg to the other, unsure of her next move. But when Alfie came towards her again, she grabbed her bag and marched back the way they'd come, without looking back. She felt Alfie's eyes on her the whole way up the hill to school but she didn't stop till she got to French class and had to apologize to Miss McCrae for being so late.

Later, at Carole's house, the other three wanted to know what had happened to her.

'You're never late, Miss Perfect,' said Carole. 'Where were you?'

'Yeah,' said Susan. 'One minute you were waiting for me outside the library, the next you'd disappeared.'

'You were taking for ever,' said Lenore, pretending to look through Carole's CDs.

'I saw Big Alfie lounging about at the office and almost thought you'd gone off with him,' added Susan.

Carole and Amy laughed. 'As if,' said Carole, then seeing Lenore's face, she added, 'I meant because he's a sixth year, he wouldn't be seen dead with the likes of us, not because you're, you know . . .'

'No, what?' said Lenore. But, like a meteor, it hit her, something that had been at the back of her mind as they'd all got older, but that she hadn't acknowledged even to herself. At sixteen, Lenore was a size 14 in clothes. She'd never weighed herself so had no idea what she weighed. She was hardly fat but she certainly wasn't the skinny little size 8 of Carole and Susan, and nowhere near the lithe, athletic build of Amy. It had never bothered her though. So she couldn't wear the tiny skirts and midriff tops from Primark and Etam like the others, hers were all from the ladies' range at Marks and Spencer or her mum's catalogue, but she always altered them so that they looked pretty much the same, or added her own touches here and there. It didn't mean she couldn't go ice skating with Carole every Saturday, or stop her doing anything else she wanted. But now she wondered if the others saw her as the fat girl, Carole had almost said as much.

Chin jutted forward, she said, 'For your information, I *was* with Alfie. He asked me to go to the park with him and I . . . went. That's why I was late.'

Amy started laughing then stopped as she saw Lenore's face. 'Oh, you're serious. But, why? Do you like him?'

'It's not a question of whether *I* like *him*,' said Lenore, uncertainly. 'He liked me. Enough to kiss me, in fact.' Her face burned and she plucked at the *Friends* duvet on Carole's bed.

'What? Tell us more,' cried Carole.

So she did. She told them it had been wonderful, kissing behind the statue of Davie Cooper, how gentle Alfie had been, how romantic. She described the scene as it should have been and enjoyed her friends' envy.

'Don't chase him too much, that would be my advice,' said Carole. 'Remember wee Angie Green with Spud at that party last year? She fancied him for months before they got together and he only said yes because she agreed to go upstairs with him. None of the boys would touch her with a bargepole after that.'

'Carole's right. The eggs don't swim to the sperm, you know.'

'Listen to you two. And that's disgusting, Amy,' said Lenore, and grabbed Carole's prized Matt Le Blanc cushion and threw it directly at Amy's head.

Later that evening, she lay on her own bed and prayed that she'd be able to avoid Alfie for the rest of her time at school. She thought it wouldn't be that hard since she generally managed to be invisible to the boys most of the time. At half nine, her brother Craig shouted up there was someone on the phone for her. She couldn't be bothered chatting any more to her friends, she was fed up already of trying to make her time with Alfie sound better than it had been, but then Craig added, 'It's some boy' and she hurtled down the stairs three at a time to get to the phone in the downstairs hall.

'Hello?' she said breathlessly, twirling the phone cord as far as it would go round her waist, whilst simultaneously shooing away Craig who was standing with his back to her, his arms wrapped around his body and making disgusting sucking noises.

'Hi, it's Alfie.'

And apparently that was all it took for them to be officially going out.

Lenore loved the feeling of being someone important, part of a couple, as she hopped off the school bus in the morning and Alfie was waiting for her at the gate. She was the envy of the girls when she was invited to a sixth-year house party which Carole did her make-up for, and Susan gave her advice on not drinking anything unless she'd actually seen it being poured, while Amy looked on disinterestedly. And after the party, they didn't need to know that some of the sixth-year girls had actually sniggered as she'd passed by them and she was sure she'd heard one of them whisper 'chunky monkey', or that she'd spent half the night in the kitchen pretending to like Whitesnake's new CD, and the other half in one of the back bedrooms fighting off Alfie who was a lot more pushy after downing two large tumblers of cider. The point was, she'd started living, she was going out with a boy and her friends were envious. As to whether she actually liked Alfie or not, she didn't stop to consider. And then he'd done what he'd done to her, and thank God for Dennis because otherwise . . .

'Oh come on, Lenore, don't start crying again, you know I can't do this touchy-feely stuff.' Amy plucked one of the napkins off the tray and threw it across the table to Lenore.

'Sorry,' said Lenore. 'Honestly, I don't know what's wrong with me. It's just . . .' She patted the napkin against her nose. 'Today, one of the other teachers, you know Nadia, I'm sure I've mentioned her, glamorous Italian teacher?'

'Not really,' said Amy, 'but go on.'

'She announced today that she was getting married and it made me think about all the exciting stuff she has in front of her whereas my life, it's so . . . boring at times. There doesn't seem to be anything to look forward to.'

Amy put down her empty coffee cup and sat forward in a way that let Lenore know she was in for one of her lectures. 'Lenore, do you still not get it? This is the great lie that's been perpetrated by the world at women's expense for centuries. This idea that the only thing women have to look forward to, to work towards, is snaffling a man and getting married. It's *married* life that's boring. Day after day with the same person, and most of them don't have the energy to power a hairdryer so you're tending to their every whim, cooking the meat and three veg *he* likes rather than sitting in front of the telly with a pile of hot toast, cleaning the toilet that smells because *he* can't pee straight, spending your weekends at B&Q looking at power tools because *he* wants them rather than having a few wines and a laugh with your pals. *That's* what's boring, not a life without men.'

Lenore sniffed. 'Do you think so?'

'I know it. I am not the "we" of anyone and that's exactly how I like it,' said Amy, her voice loud enough that the young man sitting behind his laptop at the next table glanced over.

'Sorry,' mouthed Lenore.

'Do not apologize to him,' said Amy, and the man returned his attention to whatever was on his screen, hunkering down slightly so his face couldn't be seen.

'Seriously, Lenore, I'm fed up telling you that you don't need a man to support you. Half of them can't support a full moustache, never mind a full-blooded woman.'

Lenore smiled at last and said, 'Maybe you're right.' She wiped her nose with her hand.

Amy passed her the last napkin and said, 'Of course I'm right! Our lives without a significant other are not boring. What about the other night? Didn't we do something special, making sure those men at the Miners' Welfare took notice? And not just them, everyone in Hamilton is talking about it, probably Bothwell and Uddingston too.'

'It was a laugh, I suppose,' said Lenore doubtfully.

'More than a laugh, it was about us striking back, making our voices heard. And you need to do more of that. Stop waiting for Tommy to notice how slim you are—'

'I'm not waiting—'

'You are, and it needs to stop. You've been on this treadmill for years now. Literally. When are you going to learn that there's more to life than how many calories there are in a tomato? You need to start living your life for yourself again, having fun. In fact, come on, this caffeine's not hitting the mark at all, let's go to Jilts for something stronger.'

'What, on a school night? I can't—'

Amy got up and put on her anorak. 'Yes, you can. You're always telling me you could teach those whiny old male writers in your sleep. Get your jacket on, we're going.'

When Amy was in bossy mode like this, it was useless to resist. Lenore twisted round in her seat, picked up her green suede jacket and swung it over her shoulder as she followed Amy out of the café. She could hear the low tut of the man at the next table as they left but this time, she ignored him.

★

The women had been going to Jilts regularly since they'd been in their teens. Although the décor had changed several times, the place had always remained in the same hands, owned by an ex-professional footballer and now run by his grown-up daughter. This gave it a familiar, even nostalgic feel as they took their usual booth in one of the bay windows of the bar, overlooking Brandon Street.

'Cheers, Big Ears,' said Amy, clinking her pint of Guinness against Lenore's small dry white.

'Cheers,' said Lenore, taking a sip of wine. 'Although actually alcohol's not allowed on—' she began but Amy shushed her and for once, Lenore agreed with her that the diet could go to hell.

'Should we call the others?' she said, suddenly in the mood for a night out.

'Nah, what's the point? Carole wouldn't be allowed out at such short notice and Susan wouldn't leave Fraser.'

'You're probably right,' said Lenore, sitting back and taking in the Thursday night clientele. 'The pleasures of the single life right enough.'

Over in their usual corner were the domino players. Two of them had taught Amy and Lenore when they'd first started school but they never acknowledged them. They seemed impossibly old now, with their bulbous noses and squabbles over dominoes, and primary school was a lifetime ago. Propping up the bar were local celebrity, Justin – he'd played for Hamilton Accies a few years back but a hamstring injury ended his playing days and he'd been determined to drink himself into oblivion ever since – and a duo who looked like father and son, looking straight ahead and saying nothing as they slowly emptied their pint glasses. At the next booth sat a group of three younger women, over-made-up and under-dressed, their eyes alternating between their screens and the door, which they looked up at hopefully every time it opened.

It seemed unusually quiet for a Thursday. Lenore was beginning to wonder whether they should drink up and head somewhere more lively but when Amy came back from the bar with fresh drinks she told her to pick up her jacket, they were going through to the lounge.

'Why?' said Lenore, but doing as Amy instructed as usual. 'Will it not be even quieter in there now they've stopped serving food?'

'No, it's tribute night. The lounge is the place to be.'

They walked through the half-empty bar and headed past the ladies' toilets to the lounge. They both tried not to stare at the teenage girl with panda eyes, crying on her friend's shoulder about her two-timing boyfriend and how she'd have done anything for him, *anything*. Amy raised her eyebrows at Lenore to say, see? See what happens when you get involved with men? Lenore didn't respond and pushed her friend through the double swing doors ahead of them.

The lounge was packed. In the far corner, next to the bar, they'd set up a makeshift stage. It was occupied by a young woman dressed in sports gear, her bare midriff gleaming at them as she sang 'Word Up' in a high-pitched voice. 'Now this is more like it,' shouted Amy to Lenore over the music. 'You go and grab that table, I'll see if they've got any bar snacks.'

'Not for . . .' Lenore began then shrugged her shoulders, knowing it would make no difference what she said.

The chatter and the laughter died down gradually as the main act stepped up. Lenore read on the drum 'The Jamm' and nudged Amy as the second-rate Paul Weller strutted across the stage. His hair was mousy brown and parted in the centre, a little curl in front of each ear. His pot belly and narrow shoulders were not reminiscent of the Eighties Jam front man but his shiny suit, slim black tie and long-toed Chelsea boots could just about persuade you you were about to hear something special.

'Bit before our time,' said Amy to Lenore, but the atmosphere in the place was catching. Lenore estimated there were about sixty people crammed into the lounge but it felt more like hundreds. There was a tingling in the air, a low murmuring from the crowd, some of whom were dressed up for the occasion in their Lonsdale tops or mid-length trench coats, appropriate for early February in Scotland but sweltering in the bar. Lenore found that she was almost willing the band to be good, and to give them a night to remember. The drummer in the foppish orange shirt and spray-on white Levis raised his drumsticks into the air, held them there for a second or two, then banged them down on the drums, beating out the quick-fire introduction to 'Going Underground'. Lenore and Amy watched a group of young guys push their way to the front, as the band blasted their way through the best-known Jam tracks, rightly reading the crowd's desire for well-loved tunes, taking some of them back to school, others to university nights. 'Paul' was playing his guitar like he was cracking a whip and spinning crazily close to the edge of the stage. Suddenly his pot belly and crazy hair didn't matter. He was Paul Weller, playing for the fans.

'This is brilliant,' shouted Lenore to Amy, as they got up and stood at the edge of crowd, watching the others dance and point, and shout out the lyrics to their friends.

'Phew,' said Amy sliding back into her seat as the tribute act took their well-deserved bows. 'Wasn't expecting that tonight, were you?'

Lenore laughed and pointed to Amy's empty glass. 'I'll go and get us another, shall I? The night's young.'

'Check you out, enjoying being single at last,' teased Amy, rubbing her hand over her buzz cut. 'But actually, I should probably be getting home. I've got an eight thirty callout tomorrow.'

'Just one more.' Lenore ignored her friend's reservations and made her way through the crowd to the bar.

'Excuse me.' 'Sorry, can I—' 'Thank you.' 'Coming through.'

Finally she reached the front and stood waving her card in the direction of the harassed young students serving behind the bar. She rested her elbow on the counter and surveyed the room as she waited to be served. A group of lads on a night out caught her eye. They were younger than her – who wasn't when she went out these days, she thought ruefully – and enjoying chatting up two women to their left, who were trying and failing to look uninterested. The girl nearest the boys was particularly pretty – blonde hair straightened to a shimmering waterfall, glittery pink lips and the kind of figure Lenore would have killed for at eighteen. The girl was talking to her friend but really her eye was on the boy next to her, the most handsome of the group with a hundred-watt smile that would have earned him a place in a boy band. The boy tapped the girl on her bare shoulder and pointed to his mobile phone. Lenore watched in fascination as the girl's mouth went into an automatic pout and she slid her hand on her hip, one shoulder pushed forward, accentuating her delicate collarbones. How at ease she was with her photo being taken, how happy she was to pose.

★

Not like Lenore. Surely Alfie had noticed how uncomfortable she'd been. And of course, it wasn't like now, with everybody taking selfies, and photographing every little event as it happened on a daily basis. They hadn't had phones when they were teenagers but Alfie had been given a Minolta Maxxum 7000 for his seventeenth birthday and he was keen to show it off. He spent ages telling Lenore about the superb autofocus and the shutterspeed and the gadgets it had that prevented overexposure. It was the first time Lenore had been in his bedroom and she was hardly listening as her eyes darted round the messy little room, taking in the posters – she remembered one of a sleek white Porsche, another of the very camera he held in his hand, but with all the parts of it labelled and described – and the pile of dirty clothes, including navy blue boxer shorts(!) sitting unashamedly on top of the pile. She remembered the unfamiliar smell of boy's sweat, and something else, something unwashed and exciting, and of course, in the middle of it all, his unmade bed, small and single, yet dominating the room.

He was behind her and stopped talking about his camera and started talking about art shots and how beautiful the human form was, especially the female nude, what did she think? Lenore snapped round at the mention of the word 'nude' and kept her eye on the door.

'I . . . I suppose it can be beautiful. If the model's slim and gorgeous obviously.' She waved a hand at her own body, so unlike the stick-thin ones with the jutting bones and angles she and her friends admired in magazines, and she felt sure Alfie admired too. 'Not . . . not like me, I mean.'

Alfie was looking at her body appraisingly now. 'Don't be daft, plenty of men like fat women.'

'Is that how you think of me then – fat?' Lenore could feel sudden tears and wondered if she should leave.

Alfie concentrated on the lens of his camera. 'You're not thin, are you? But I like that. I think that can be beautiful too. Here, let me show you.' He turned the camera round so that its lens was eyeing Lenore.

'What do you mean? What are you doing? Don't photograph me.'

Lenore tried to shield her face behind her hand as Alfie snapped away with his camera, very close to her face.

'Sorry,' he said, dropping the camera on the bed suddenly and placing his hands on Lenore's shoulders. 'I didn't mean to make you uncomfortable.' Lenore relaxed against him, and laid her head against his chest as he carried on talking. 'But you know, what I'd really love is if you would let me photograph you properly, you know, pose for me?'

He lifted her chin up and held her gaze. 'I mean, I thought we were going out together, you should trust me to take some photos of you.'

'We are, I do, it's just . . . what do you mean, proper photographs? Do you want me to smile or stand in a particular way? What do you want me to do?'

Alfie smiled and told her a good start would be if she took off her long cardigan so he could photograph her in her T-shirt. Lenore was uncomfortable showing her arms which she knew were beefier than they should be but after a bit more cajoling, and some kissing, she agreed. Alfie sat her on the bed and told her to sit side on so he could take a few profile shots.

'You've got a really pretty face, you know that, Lenore, try pushing your hair back so I can see your shoulder, that's it. These shots are going to be gorgeous, I can already tell. Maybe if you, could you pull the sleeve off your shoulder a bit so we can see it better, that's it, and now maybe turn to face me and bend forward a bit so I can see . . .'

'Like this?' Lenore's bra straps had slid down to the middle of her arms so that when she kneeled on the bed and leaned forward, Alfie could see the deep valley of her breasts and almost all the flesh of each breast.

'That's gorgeous,' he said in a soft voice, 'really beautiful.'

Lenore felt more attractive than she'd ever done in her life. She could tell by the way Alfie was complimenting her and moving closer towards her that he really meant what he was saying. She wasn't slightly overweight, sixteen-year-old Lenore that nobody noticed, she was a model, being photographed by her talented boyfriend. So when he reached into her T-shirt and took her breasts in his hands, she didn't pull away, she leaned into him, enjoying the feeling of his chest pressing against hers. And then suddenly her loose top was round her waist and Alfie was fumbling at her back, trying to undo the clasp of her bra. She pulled away and said, 'No, I need to keep—'

'Come on, Lenore, you can't let me get this far and then not let me take your bra off. Please.' His voice was soft and wheedling. His hands were kneading her shoulders now and it felt so good that she didn't want it to stop. 'Please, come on, we've been going out together for ages now, there's nothing wrong with it, just what's natural.'

His breath was at her ear, his hands moving slowly up and down her back as he talked.

'It's just—' she tried again, but he kissed her mouth gently, whilst at the same time undoing the clasp of her bra. They both gasped as her heavy breasts fell and Lenore automatically reached round to cover herself. 'What if someone comes in?' she whispered.

'Don't worry about that.' Alfie was all business now. He picked up his camera and started taking shots. Lenore looked away as the camera kept flashing, she was aware of him pulling her hands away from her breasts and placing them at her waist.

'Like that,' he said. 'That's perfect.'

Lenore watched as the perfect young girl next to her stuck out her tongue at the boy taking the picture. 'You owe me a drink now,' she said, and pointed to her empty bottle of Wkd. Lenore wanted to reach across the boy and speak directly to the girl. She wanted to say, 'Don't let him take your picture, don't give him the power, he could send that image viral in less time than it takes you to finish that drink he's bought you.'

'Being served?' The barman drummed his fingers on the counter impatiently.

Lenore turned back to the bar, trying not to notice the boy winking at his friends or the way they sniggered in response. 'A Guinness and a white wine please,' she said. 'Make it a large. And . . . and crisps please, two packets of cheese and onion crisps.'

'You took your time,' said Amy, taking her drink from Lenore. 'Crisps?'

'Why not? We deserve them,' said Lenore. 'Cheers.'

Amy wiped the froth of her Guinness from her top lip. She tapped her feet to Beyoncé and watched a group of girls egg each other on to the dance floor. The boys at the bar stopped talking to watch them move in a tight circle, giggling and dancing like there was no one else in the place.

'To be confident like that, eh?' said Amy, putting down her drink. 'I'm nipping to the toilet then we'd better head.' She glanced over at Lenore, who appeared to be mesmerized by the girls making the dance floor their own. 'I'll be back in a minute.'

Confidence. Lenore knew for a brief period what that felt like. After Alfie had taken the photographs of her, Lenore suddenly felt able to take on the world. She was beautiful. She was loved. She could pose with her top off and reduce the boy in front of her to begging for more. She hadn't actually seen the photos when they were developed but Alfie had told her how artistic and beautiful they were. She started to walk with her head held that little bit higher; she hadn't lost any weight but she felt lighter, taller, more confident. And it showed. Suddenly people noticed her when she walked into the library, her friends asked her if she'd been on a diet, her mum worried she would attract the wrong sort of attention. Lenore felt reborn. She started to be invited to all the sixth-year parties, not just those that Alfie decided she should accompany him to. The other guys asked her whether she preferred Blur or Oasis, what her opinion was on Tony Blair, and one of Alfie's friends, Paul, asked her if she wanted to go and see *Titanic* at the Odeon in town with him the first Saturday it opened.

But it turned out Alfie didn't like having a popular girlfriend.

'Why do you always have to show off so much, everywhere we go?'

Lenore was stung. 'What do you mean?'

'At Eilis's party, did you have to dance with every single guy there? What was the point of that?'

'I was only dancing with people who asked me. Everyone was dancing.'

'But you're going out with me,' he sulked.

'But you didn't want to dance.' Lenore was beginning to think going out with someone wasn't all it was cracked up to be and she wondered whether maybe the time had come for her to finish things with Alfie and start really enjoying herself. 'Maybe . . . we shouldn't go out with each other any more then? If you're not happy with the way I dance at parties, I mean.' They were in Alfie's bedroom and she was sitting on his still unmade bed, which suddenly struck her as sloppy and unhygienic rather than romantic.

Alfie snapped his head up. 'What do you mean? *You're* breaking up with *me*?' He couldn't believe it.

'Well, yeah, I don't think you really like me, do you? You seem so . . . angry with me all the time.'

'Fuck off then,' said Alfie. 'Like I give a shit. I was about to break up with you anyway.'

Lenore stayed where she was.

'Didn't you hear me? Get lost, get out and shut the door behind you.'

Lenore scuttled off the bed and made her way out of the house, stunned that he'd been so sharp with her, but relieved to be out of it.

That Monday morning, she walked into the Maths block and saw Alfie and his gang immediately, huddled in a corner, passing round the photographs. Of course she knew instantly what they were. Topless photographs of her, being passed round the sixth years. The boys were all sniggering and laughing, one drawing fake breasts on himself in the air while another pretended to

79

pant with desire. Alfie spotted her first and nudged his pals who all turned to stare.

Dennis appeared suddenly behind the group, in his black leather jacket and jeans, the silver sleeper glinting in his ear. Lenore's heart plunged deeper. Dennis and Alfie were mates, of course Alfie would pass the photos to him. She braced herself for his reaction. But, she discovered later, the pair had fallen out after Alfie had drunk Dennis's share of the carryout at Eilis's last party, and Dennis was not a boy to take such things lightly. He slouched in the corner and watched for a few moments, his eyes narrowing as it became clear to him what was going on. Strutting into the centre of the group, he snatched the photos from Alfie and, quick as a cat, slid them into Lenore's hands.

'What the hell—' started Alfie, rolling his shoulders and squaring up for a fight.

'You really want to do that?' said Dennis, drawing himself up to his full height and balling his massive hands into fists.

'Leave it, Alfie,' said one of his pals. 'Just walk away.'

A look passed between Alfie and Dennis, neither boy prepared to back down in front of the crowd, each calculating his own chance of success if they did fight.

'What's it going to be, Alfie?' said Dennis, jerking his black Nike bag off his shoulder and on to the ground in readiness. 'Are you going to put your money where your mouth is, or are you going to bottle it?'

That was all it took.

Alfie swung his first punch so fast he completely missed his aim and his fist flew by the side of Dennis's head, allowing Dennis to whack Alfie on the chin before following up with a kick to his stomach. Alfie's pals wavered as they saw him writhing on the ground but Dennis's eyes were flashing and he was on the balls of his feet, nimble, ready for them. 'Come on,' said one boy, nodding his head to the others. They scarpered, leaving their friend to it.

'That's enough,' cried Lenore, panicking, 'I've got the photos,' but Dennis was not ready to stop yet. Before Lenore could pull him back, he socked Alfie a punch under his left eye, which they heard later had fractured his cheekbone.

'Humiliating girls, that the best you've got?' Dennis spat at Alfie's flailing form before he stalked off, leaving Lenore to stuff the offending photos into her own pink Nike bag and rush upstairs to her Maths class.

Lenore tried a couple of times to thank Dennis for intervening and even started to fantasize that they might get together after that. He could be her knight in shining armour, making sure the likes of Alfie and his pals stayed well away. But he ignored her completely and as soon as Carole had shown up in her flared jeans moulded round her slinky hips and wearing gold hoops the size of cooker rings in her ears, Lenore stood no chance.

Later, when she examined the photos in the privacy of her bedroom, she realized she was not beautiful at all. The girl in the photos looked uncomfortable and embarrassed, and in a couple of them her arm was wrapped in front of her as though she was trying to shield herself from the person taking the pictures. And the more she looked, the more she could see the soft, white flab of her upper arms – was the skin puckering even? – and breasts that were low-slung and heavy – was the right one bigger than the left? – and you couldn't see her belly button because of the roll of fat curling over her lower tummy. Crying, Lenore flung the photographs across the room. She felt betrayed. Ashamed.

Embarrassed. Most of all, she felt utterly powerless and knew she couldn't face anyone at school again.

She'd faked a tummy bug for the rest of the week but her mum finally had enough and insisted she went back to school. She dreaded running into Alfie but he passed her in the corridor at the end of the week and didn't acknowledge her presence, not even when one of his pals squeezed himself tight into the wall when she passed, muttering that the corridor wasn't big enough for both of them. Lenore pretended she hadn't heard him and dashed to class. That evening, she took a second then a third helping of custard, ignoring her mum's raised eyebrows and the teasing from Craig about being the size of a house.

'Ready to go? Lenore. Anybody home?'

Lenore looked up to see Amy slinging her jacket across her shoulders. 'Sorry, I was miles away. Yes, let's get out of here.'

They left Jilts at midnight and when she got home, Lenore unearthed an ancient bottle of whisky – the only alcohol she had in the house – and settled herself on the sofa. She drank till her insides felt velvety and crawled into bed at three.

The alarm went off at seven the next morning and Lenore opened her eyes. She closed them again swiftly as there was something very wrong with her head. She raised her hand to meet her face and pulled the damp hair away from her forehead. She tried opening her eyes again. The mint wallpaper, which she'd changed after Tommy left, and chosen for its calming effect, had become electric overnight. She turned on her back and looked up at the ceiling, trying to keep hold of the grey spot next to the art deco shade hanging directly above her. Success. The room was now static, though her head was still busy thumping and pulsing. She cursed Amy for talking her into a night out on a Thursday, like they were still teenagers. Thank God it was Friday, and her first class wasn't till after break.

An hour later, she wiped the steam off the mirror and took in the face that greeted her. Puffy, black-circled eyes and dry patches round her mouth. She could still taste the whisky even though she'd brushed her teeth hard. As the hot water streamed into the bath, she scanned her shelf full of bath salts, fizzing bombs and luxurious scented crystals that were one of her greatest indulgences since Tommy left. He'd hated clutter, detested the lotions and potions that Lenore loved. She smiled to herself as she selected one of the dimpled glass bottles, poured out a generous handful of blue crystals and watched as the water turned into an Icelandic hot spring. She eased herself in, relishing the soothing heat and clouds of steam, telling herself she was running late anyway, what difference did a reviving bath make.

She closed her aching eyes and felt the heaviness recede. Her hands ran their daily checks of her body, sliding across her stomach – still reassuringly flat, down into the bowl of her hips – concave, the reclaimed hipbones still visible, and along her thighs – they remained smooth and slim. Relieved that what she still thought of as her 'new' body had not betrayed her, she couldn't yet banish the memories of what her body had become, after Alfie and the photographs. She'd known instinctively that if she'd told her mum or a teacher what had happened, how violated she'd felt, how diminished, they'd have told her to chalk it up to experience, not to tell anyone or talk about it, and be thankful Alfie had at least had the decency to hand over the negatives in the end. So she'd built a fortress of fat instead, safely tucked away in her bedroom, stuffing down Mars bars and coffee cake. She deferred her place at Leeds, took a gap year and hardly saw the girls at all, she was so ashamed of how she looked. The ground was quicksand beneath her feet, everything had started to slope and slither, and she ate more to steady herself, till she was a pufferfish whose gills had expanded to fill any space she was in. But when the letter came in to ask whether she was ready to take her place at university the following year, she decided that yes, she was ready, finally, to move on and make a new start away from everyone who knew Big Fat Lenore. She would go to uni, lose all the weight and became a new person, a disciplined person, in control of her appetites.

She couldn't let it all slip away now, could never go back to being that person she'd been in her teens. No one, and certainly not Tommy, was going to do that to her, hence the gym, the diets, the rigour, the scented baths and creams. She was determined to keep her body – and her life – under her own control.

She got to school five minutes after break had ended.

To hell with it, she thought. *I'm late anyway, I might as well get my coffee first.*

Waiting for the kettle to boil, she stood at the window and looked out of the staffroom towards the empty, grey playground. The huge bin was overflowing with crisp packets and Coke cans, a couple of straggly bushes waved dispiritedly in the breeze, and a latecomer, head down and grimacing at the cold in his school blazer, made his way to the main entrance. It was nearly March already so spring was definitely round the corner, thought Lenore. Some people loved spring, viewed it as a new beginning, paving the way to summer, such as it was in Scotland. Not Lenore though, she always thought the spring months were so dull. No longer beautiful and sparkly like the winter months, and not yet warm and hazy like the best of the Scottish summer. Just dishwater grey February days like this one.

'Penny for them?'

'Oh,' said Lenore, startled. 'I thought everyone else had gone to class.'

It was the new PE teacher, standing straight like a soldier in front of the kettle and Lenore's waiting mug. He was tall and rangy, more like a cross-country runner than a rugby player. His hooked nose and thin lips prevented him from being classically handsome, but still, there was something in his weather-roughened face and slightly too long blond hair which Lenore did find appealing.

'You were miles away there,' he said. 'Something interesting?'

'No, not really, I'm . . . running a bit late.'

'I won't tell. I just came in for a quick coffee before the S3 fitness assessments.'

'Who'd be that age again?' said Lenore, pouring her own coffee, and indicating a second mug to ask whether he'd like her to pour one for him.

'Yes please,' he said, with a smile. 'Black, no sugar. I'm Dave, by the way. PE.'

'Pleased to meet you,' said Lenore, shaking his outreached hand. 'Lenore.'

'That's a pretty name. Unusual.'

'It's definitely unusual,' she agreed, smiling and looking up at him from beneath her eyelashes. The clock on the back wall struck half past and snapped her out of it. 'I'll need to go, class started ten minutes ago.'

Dave stepped aside to let her past, putting his hand on her waist as she walked by. She stopped, unsure of herself suddenly.

'You look as though you'd pass anyway,' he said, raising his cup to his mouth.

'Pass?'

'A fitness assessment.' He grinned and sat on the couch next to the door. He crossed one long, tracksuited leg over the other. 'See you at lunchtime maybe?'

'Yes, ah, yes, maybe,' said Lenore, blushing like her sixteen-year-old self, as she dashed down the corridor to face the second years, her hangover suddenly lifting.

By lunchtime, she felt back to normal, her intention never to drink again already wavering. She was heading into town to buy something healthy for lunch when she ran into Dave again in the car park. He was getting into a white Audi TT but stopped when he saw her, and shouted over, 'Are you going into town? Want a lift?' He patted the bonnet of his car proudly.

'If you don't mind, yeah, that'd be great.'

He smiled and held the door open for her.

Over the Guns N' Roses that he had on at high volume, she asked him how he was enjoying working at the school.

'Oh, it's not too bad. You get some kids who are really into their sport and then there's the rest of them. You know what I mean?' He puffed out his cheeks and lifted both elbows.

'Sorry, I don't know what you—'

'The fatties. The ones whose only exercise is going to the fridge and back.' He sniffed. 'There's no need for it. It's the parents I blame.'

Lenore reddened and thanked God there were no treacherous Facebook pictures from her schooldays to give her away.

'Anyway,' he carried on. 'I'm only here on a short-term contract. I spend most of my time at the gym.'

Lenore looked at him.

'I mean, I own a gym. It's the Dave Bates Gym down the bottom of the arcade.'

'That's yours? I've just joined!'

'I thought you looked like a woman who takes care of herself,' said Dave approvingly. 'Fitness is so important, especially as we get— Well, at all ages, in fact. Healthy body, healthy mind, am I right?'

Lenore laughed encouragingly, thinking that if one of her friends had said that she'd have told them to stop spouting such inane rubbish. Somehow, when an attractive man said it, however . . .

'Here we are – outside Marks and Spencer okay for you?'

'Yes, great, thanks for the lift.' Lenore turned round in her seat to face him. 'I'll . . . see you in school, I guess.' She got out of the car.

'Lenore,' he called after her. 'Do you want . . . would you maybe fancy meeting up some time? Outside school I mean?'

'I . . . yes,' said Lenore. 'That would be lovely.'

Things were looking up.

'Sounds like a complete tosser,' said Amy, holding up her half-finished pint of Guinness to the light to admire its deep ruby tones.

'No, he isn't, not at all. Why would you say that? This is the first time a man's been interested in me since Tommy left, and he's a nice man, not someone who sends me emails from Ohio, or swipes right on some dating site but will never want to meet me. This is a real-live, flesh and blood man.'

'No one could ever accuse you of having unrealistic standards, Lenore, if flesh and blood are the only prerequisites,' said Susan, looking up from her phone once she'd seen that Fraser hadn't replied to her text.

'You two are impossible. At least let me tell you how the date went before you start carping.'

'Yeah, come on, girls, give her a chance,' said Carole. 'Start at the beginning, Lenore, and tell us every detail.'

'Oh Lord,' said Amy. 'I'd better get another pint then before you start.'

Dave had picked her up at half seven precisely, as he'd promised. Lenore was glad to see she was not the only who'd made an effort. Dave scrubbed up well in his black jeans and checked shirt, and the air in his car smelled of Eau Sauvage which he'd clearly applied in generous measures.

'I booked us a table at Andiamo, thought we should go somewhere special for our first date,' he said, as he reached across her to take the seat belt from her and buckle her in.

'Lovely,' she said, deciding that it might be twee for a wedding proposal but it would do very nicely for a first date.

They had burgers, rare with extra salad, and without the buns or cheese. Dave ordered for them both, which was a bit annoying but after all, quite romantic. He'd be happy for her to have alcohol, he said, though he himself rarely drank and certainly never on a week night.

'Have you ever tried cranberry juice?'

'No, I don't think I have,' said Lenore, trying not to eye the carafe of icy white wine sitting on the table of the couple next to them. 'But I believe it's very good for you.'

'Yes,' said Dave. 'Great for preventing urinary infections! I drink it a lot.' He smiled like he deserved some praise.

'That's, erm, good,' said Lenore.

'Excellent, I'll order us both a cranberry juice then. With ice.'

The drinks arrived and Lenore said 'Cheers' and clinked her glass against Dave's before surveying the restaurant, which was full of couples who all seemed to be talking a lot more than they were. Dave was more reserved than he'd been at school, and the conversation was ebbing more than it was flowing. As she crunched her cucumbers, Lenore fell back on asking him about his fitness routine, and then had to listen politely to his answers – very comprehensive answers on the number and depth of press-ups he did morning and night (excellent for the core, apparently), the perils of too much fat in one's diet (cheese being the devil's work), and his strategy for scoring a PB of under three hours twenty in the next marathon he ran.

'And do you run?' he'd asked over black coffee, no dessert.

'Yes, well, actually no, but I have read *Running Like A Girl*. It was . . . a very good book,' she finished lamely, seeing Dave's disappointed look. 'I do go to the gym a lot though,' she said with a big smile. 'It's just . . . running has never been for me.'

'We must remedy that right away,' said Dave. 'Running is for everyone, the mental boost, not to mention the carb-busting propensities of running, make it the gold standard of exercise.'

Lenore felt she'd let him down somehow and found herself simpering, 'I'd love to take up running, if I had someone to train me and tell me all about distances and speeds and things.' She waved her hand in the air and screwed up her eyes as though it was all rocket science to her.

Dave gave her a broad grin. 'Of course I'll help you,' he said. 'We can start tomorrow morning. Before school.'

Lenore choked on her coffee and murmured that she couldn't wait.

'So, do you mean to tell us that in addition to the usual schedule of boxercise, weight-lifting, bums and tums, and God knows what else, you are now pounding the pavements with Dashing Dave before school every morning?' Amy eyed Lenore accusingly, though exactly what she was guilty of wasn't quite clear.

'Not every morning. But yeah, twice this week already, and we were out at half six this morning.' She yawned. 'I can't lie, it is tiring but look at this, I mean the weight is falling off me.'

'Never mind that,' said Carole. 'What's he like then, apart from being an exercise fanatic? Are we going to meet him any time soon?'

'Give me a chance, Carole, I've only just met him myself. But yeah, he's . . . nice, I like him.' She covered her cheek with her hand to hide her embarrassment. The others noticed and Carole and Susan elbowed each other while Amy blew a low wolf whistle under her breath.

'Honestly,' said Lenore. 'It's like being back at school with you lot.' But she laughed it off, thinking how much she would have loved this sort of attention when they'd all been at school and no one had noticed her.

'When are you seeing him again?'

'Tomorrow night, we're going to the gym then back to his for a smoothie.'

'Is that what they're calling it these days?' Amy winked at Carole. 'Cheers to the smoothie then, may it be long and thick.'

'You lot are impossible!'

'Come on, Lenore, come on.' Dave was breathing heavily and urging her on. The sweat was dripping from their bodies, they'd never done it this long before.

'I can't . . . last much longer . . .' panted Lenore. 'It's too much.'

'Don't let me down now, we're nearly there, come on.' Dave's blond fringe was sticking to his forehead, his cheeks red and his lips parted as he breathed heavily.

'We're there,' he shouted finally, jumping off the running machine next to Lenore's and slowing hers down to a halt.

They both stood at the ends of their machines, hearts racing, staring at each other.

'See you after your shower,' said Dave, winking at Lenore. Her cheeks coloured furiously but she was already so red from the exercise you couldn't tell. She tried not to think about what her friends would say if they'd been there.

She and Dave had been seeing each other for almost three weeks, and Dave was becoming increasingly keen for Lenore to stay over, or to allow him to spend the night at hers. Lenore couldn't explain her reluctance, she liked him well enough, he obviously had a great body and had told her enough times about his heart rate and slow pulse that she could imagine he'd be good in bed. And yet.

This time, Lenore was determined to take things slowly. She was no longer the stupid young woman she'd been when she'd run into Susan unexpectedly after she came back to take up her first teaching post at a school in Tollcross. Twenty-three years old by then, and the slimmest and fittest she'd ever been, there couldn't have been a better time to bump into an old school friend who hadn't seen you since you were in your teens and the bathroom scales had quivered when you approached them.

She almost hadn't gone to the book festival but the thought of seeing James Kelman, ten years post-Booker Prize but still angry, and many of her other favourite authors, made it impossible to miss. She took the midday train through to Edinburgh, ignoring the appreciative stares of a group of Hibs fans at the next table along, but pleased they'd noticed her all the same.

As the Castle and the jagged rooftops of the Old Town came into view, she had a strong sense of being home and belonging here. She'd loved her time in Yorkshire but she remained true to her Scottish roots, and the piper on the Royal Mile and the biting Scottish wind masquerading as a summer breeze made her nostalgic for the times she'd spent with her pals and the fun they'd had. When she got to Charlotte Square, she browsed through the arty postcards at the entrance to the book tent, and a black postcard with a red hood illustrating *The Handmaid's Tale* made her think of Susan. She wondered if she was still as big an Atwood fan as she'd been at school—

'Sorry—'

'Excuse me—'

They both apologized at the same time in true Scots fashion though neither was guilty of anything.

'Lenore? It is you, isn't it?' The small woman with the big hair and a face full of freckles was staring at Lenore.

'Susan? How are you? I can't believe it, I was literally just thinking about you! It's been, what, three, four years?'

'Longer than that, I think. We haven't seen sight nor sound of you since you went to Leeds, when was that now? Must be about five years anyway. You look amazing!' Susan stepped back to look at Lenore properly. 'No, honestly, you really do.'

'Thank-you. You too, you haven't changed at all.'

It was true. She looked exactly as Lenore remembered from school, her distinctive hair in particular, still falling to her shoulders in fiery red corkscrew curls. Susan tugged at the ends of it apologetically. 'Not much I can do about this, I'm afraid.'

'No, you look great too. And how are you? Do you still see Carole and Amy?'

'Of course, I was out with them last night, in fact. Dennis too – if you remember him? He and Carole are still together.' Susan had to move out of the way of a crowd of students excited to see their literary heroes. 'Listen, we should catch up properly. Shall we swap numbers?'

'Definitely,' said Lenore, proudly taking out her new Nokia. 'Give me your number and I'll call you and set something up.'

And that was it. The following Saturday, she'd met up with the girls at the Bay Horse and it was like they'd never been apart. Her old friends weren't the only ones who thought she looked amazing. That was the night she'd met Tommy, who'd spilled half his pint on her then insisted on buying them all a drink in recompense. The others thought he was arrogant for assuming that a group of girls on a night out would rather listen to him take over the conversation than talk among themselves. But as she got to know him, she realized the opposite was true – he was trying too hard to be liked because he was insecure, particularly around women with the attitude and lip of Amy on cider and black – and that vulnerability was one of the reasons she'd fallen for him.

'Tosser,' said Amy, when he finally left, having written down his number for Lenore on a receipt from Marks and Spencer. 'Probably goes shopping with his mother in there to buy his white Y-fronts.'

The rest of the girls laughed but Lenore liked him even then, thought he had something, spirit maybe, or a little spark in his eye. She didn't say anything to the girls, this was their night to reconnect, but she pocketed the receipt with Tommy's scrawl and every so often for the rest of the night, reached into her pocket and tapped the paper reassuringly to make sure it was still there.

She and Tommy were only going out for three months when she had the pregnancy scare. They weren't upset about it; they took it as confirmation of their grand love affair and promptly got married at Hamilton town hall, a small ceremony with their families and close friends. If the girls disapproved of her choice of husband, they didn't say so, well, maybe Amy did say something about not needing to get married to the first person who came along, but she ignored her. She was deliriously happy as she threw her bouquet into the waiting group of four or five women – Amy refused to join in – on Cadzow Bridge. She couldn't remember who'd caught it because she was too busy snogging her new husband and wondering if the world would always be this bright. A month later she lost the baby but Tommy had been brilliant, saying he didn't blame her at all, and they'd proved any doubters wrong by staying married for the next sixteen years, happy together, or at least Lenore had been. Perhaps Tommy had been unhappy all along and she hadn't realized. After he left, she wondered whether she was not the best judge of men.

★

Dave told Lenore to wait for him in reception while he went downstairs to check all the lights were off. She wandered round looking at posters advertising body conditioning classes and protein shakes, aware of the receptionist's envious eye upon her as she did so. The girl finished packing her bag, but stood for a few moments at the door with her coat on, as though she wanted to say something before she left.

Lenore waited, raising an eyebrow in the way she did to her surly fifth years.

The girl shrugged. 'Night then,' she said finally, zipping up her coat and leaving.

The place suddenly felt eerily quiet and Lenore looked across at the empty pool behind the reception area, the water still and shadows playing on the back wall. There was a row of lockers to the right of the reception desk and the locks were blank eyes, staring back at Lenore as though telling her to watch out. She started as Dave popped up from behind the reception desk.

'You look like you've seen a ghost,' he said, grinning. Lenore had never noticed before how wide his mouth was, how many pointed, dazzling white teeth.

'That's everything,' he said. 'Close the door behind you and I'll set the alarm.'

The lane outside the gym was empty apart from a line of black bins which were starting to smell. There was a full moon high in the sky – a bomber's moon, her granny used to say. Lenore shivered as she remembered. She pulled her jacket closer, wishing she'd worn her coat against the still-bitter March wind. Her hair was damp from the shower and she wondered suddenly what on earth she was doing there, waiting about in the cold for a man she hardly knew when all she really wanted was to go home and put her feet up in front of *Montalbano*.

Dave came out of the gym, his wet hair sleeked back from his forehead, and his tight blue jeans fitting where they touched. He saw Lenore looking at him and she averted her eyes and started unzipping her gym bag as though she was searching for something in it.

Dave smiled and came a bit closer. 'Back to mine then? I did promise you a smoothie.' He looked her up and down appraisingly, liking what he saw.

Lenore was tired after a day's teaching, not to mention that forty-minute stretch on the cross trainer. The thought of having to be her best for one minute longer made her feel exhausted and she wanted to be back in her own house, sitting on her couch in a fluffy blanket and sipping Canderel-sweetened tea.

'Actually, Dave,' she said, backing away slightly so that she was almost flat against the white wall. 'Can we leave it tonight? I'm too tired after all that exercise. I think I'll call it a night.'

'Don't be silly, what have I told you about the invigorating effects of exercise? All those endorphins, remember?' He moved towards her and planted his legs apart so that he was directly in front of her, a leg on each side of her body.

The wall felt cold and hard on her back and she wasn't entirely comfortable with Dave being that close. She tried to squirm out to the side of him but he moved his leg again so that he was blocking her way.

'Dave?'

'Come on, just one kiss and I guarantee you'll want to come back to mine.'

He pulled her close to him again so that her unzipped bag

fell to the ground, her sweaty leggings and wet towel flopping out of it. Dave kicked it a little further away and pinned Lenore's arms to her sides.

'You're so beautiful, Lenore, I thought that the first time I saw you.' He bent his head to her face and started to kiss her. Lenore tried to relax into the kiss – she did like Dave after all, and maybe she wasn't as tired as she'd thought.

Dave drew back and smiled. 'That's more like it,' he murmured. 'Don't worry, no one can see us here.'

Lenore snapped out of it and pulled her head back. 'What did you say?' But he didn't respond because he was too busy moving his hands from her arms and reaching round under her jacket to grab her buttocks.

'Ow, Dave, that hurts. Right, that's it, I've had enough, I'm going home now.'

They struggled, Lenore trying to get out from Dave's grip, but he was much stronger than she was and determined to keep her pinned against the wall. His lips were loose and wet and she could see the saliva gleaming on his bottom lip. He dipped his head to her breasts and Lenore looked up at the empty lane, and started to scream.

'What the hell's the matter with you?' Dave's voice was low and thin, almost a hiss. 'You're not going to get a man's blood up like that then refuse to see it through, are you?'

'What's going on here? Is everything okay?' A man emerged from the shadows at the opening of the lane.

Dave backed off immediately and peered into the darkness. 'We're fine, mate, just keep walking.'

Lenore seized her opportunity, grabbed her bag, and with a furious backwards glare at Dave, ran up to where the man was standing. 'Thank you,' she mouthed to the stranger and raced up a silent Quarry Street towards her car.

When she was safely inside, she threw her bag on to the back seat, and tried to calm down before starting the engine. What was she thinking, that she could start again after Tommy as though she was still sixteen years old. And she still hadn't learned how to give off the right signals so that men knew what she wanted and what she didn't want. The tears started to fall and she put her head down against the steering wheel, letting them flow.

There was a tap against her passenger window and she jumped. It was the man from the lane. Once he had her attention, he backed off with his hands in the air.

Lenore wiped her wet cheeks with the back of her hand, opened the window across from her and called over. 'Yes? What is it?'

'Don't be alarmed,' said the man. 'I'm a police officer, I wanted to check you were okay?'

Lenore relaxed back into her seat. 'Yes, yes, I'm fine thanks. Thanks for coming along when you did, and for . . . coming to see if I was okay.'

'Like I said, I'm a policeman so that's my job – even when I'm off duty.' He gestured down towards his low-slung jeans and soft plaid shirt. Unlike Dave, this man wore his hair very short, and his green eyes were open and trustworthy, his mouth shaped into a tentative smile of concern. 'You know, you could press charges if you're unhappy about the way that guy was treating you?'

'Oh no,' said Lenore. 'It was nothing, honestly. Probably my fault for leading him on.' She gave a little laugh, uncertainly.

'No, it wasn't your fault. There's no such thing as leading a man on so that he can't stop whatever he's doing if you want him to stop.' The man smiled again; really a very nice smile – like one your best friend would give you if she were giving similar advice.

'You're right, of course. I'll be more careful who I go out with in future.'

'Okay then, drive safely, won't you?' The man backed away from the car.

'I will, and thanks, um . . .?'

'Mark,' said the man. 'PC Mark Lown if you decide later you do want to make a complaint.'

'Okay, thanks, Mark. And goodnight.'

He stood and waved as she pulled away slowly from the kerb.

'I feel so stupid but if that policeman hadn't been there, who knows what would have happened.' Lenore held out her empty glass to Carole who was standing over her with a fresh bottle of white wine.

It was the following evening, Friday, and the women were at Carole's house. Lenore already felt better for telling her friends what had happened.

'Don't feel stupid at all, that's what these men want, that's what they count on. They expect us to keep quiet and take it. God, it makes me angry.' Susan gripped the stem of her wine glass so tightly her knuckles were white against the glass.

Carole glanced at Susan, surprised at the ferocity of her reaction. 'It's not all men, of course,' she felt bound to add, as the mother of four boys.

'No one said it was all men, but for fuck's sake—'

'Susan!' Carole stared at her friend. 'That's so unlike you, to . . . swear like that.'

'What? You're going to tell me off for bad language while that bastard—'

'At least keep your voice down,' said Carole, nodding her head through to the other room where her boys were still up.

'Sorry.' Susan put down her drink and balled her hands into tight fists in her lap.

'No need to be sorry, Susan,' said Amy. 'We're all angry about it. But listen, Lenore, did you not meet him at the school? Will you have to see him again?'

'No, thank God, he was only there for three weeks, as part of the Sporty Kids Scotland programme. As long as I don't go back to the gym – yes, before you ask, of course I've cancelled my membership – I won't see Dave Bates again.'

'Wait a minute, his name's Dave Bates?' A smile spread across Amy's face. 'That means he was Master Bates all through school. Are you kidding me?'

'I hadn't thought of that, but it explains a lot,' said Lenore drily, and the others laughed, Carole so much so that she almost fell off her chair, causing more hilarity all round. Susan said, 'What? I don't get it,' which made the others laugh all the harder.

Amy sliced the air with her hand and shouted, 'Order, order. Remember the point of this meeting was supposed to be to discuss the Graffiti Girls' next move. The plan was to let our first message sink in then keep the pressure on and get our message out there. It's been two months since our first outing so it's time to remind the powers that be we're still here and we're not going anywhere any time soon.' She looked round at her friends. 'And it seems to me we've got exactly the message we need.'

The others stared at her.

'No means no. Obviously,' she said.

'Now you're talking, Amy,' said Carole. 'Where and when?' She took a notepad out of the kitchen drawer and found an old green crayon to write notes with. 'Hang on, didn't you say he owns that gym, Lenore?'

'I see where you're going, Carole. Perfect,' said Amy.

'Wait a minute though — won't he know right away I had something to do with it, if he suddenly gets graffiti scrawled up his wall?'

'Listen, Lenore, I hate to break it to you but if Dashing Dave's tried this on with you after three weeks' seduction on the cross trainer, I think you'll find there are plenty more women out there like you who fell for his charms.'

'How could I have been so stupid?' Lenore put her head in her hands, and then raised it again as Carole's youngest son came into the kitchen looking for food.

'No more sweets tonight, Glover, you already had a big bag of Maltesers after dinner,' said Carole, pushing her son back out of the room.

'Can I have a corn snake then?' He recognized his mum had had some wine and thought he might as well try his luck.

'This isn't the time to talk about that. It's almost time for bed, but I tell you what, if you disappear back into the living room, I'll forget you're still up, okay?'

The boy grinned and grabbed his chance, disappearing out of the room.

'It is getting late, Fraser will be wondering where I am,' said Susan. 'I'd better be getting back.'

'Wait a minute, what's the plan?' Amy was not letting anyone leave till they had their next move pinned down.

'I say we make our feelings known via the walls of Dave's gym, if you know what I mean? Let's show him he can't mess with women without consequences.' Carole was standing up, her arm outstretched with her glass of wine in hand. 'Who's with me?'

Amy stared at Carole admiringly. She loved the way her old friend was reappearing, revived and excited by this new adventure they'd started. She stood up immediately and clinked her glass against Carole's. 'I'm in.'

'I don't like it,' said Susan. 'What if we get caught?'

'We didn't get caught last time, did we?'

'True, but . . .' Susan still wasn't convinced.

'A minute ago you were ready to hang, draw and quarter him,' said Amy impatiently. 'Come on, we can do this. Or do we let these men get away with this shit for ever?'

Susan lips tightened. 'Definitely not.' She sighed, but stood up and said, 'Okay then.'

'Lenore?'

Lenore didn't disappoint them. She picked up her glass, clinked it against the others, and said, 'Yup, let's show him.'

Bates's Gym was located in a lane off the main shopping drag in the centre of Hamilton. The shops and nearby cafés were all closed at eleven at night, the time Amy had instructed them all to be there. They were standing at the bottom of Quarry Street in a huddle beside Susan's car.

'Okay, Carole, you go and check the coast is clear, you two come with me back to the van to get the stuff. Carole, here's your whistle, signal to us when it's clear for us to come round.' Amy was all business.

'Bossy as ever, Captain,' said Lenore, but ready to do what she was told.

'Someone needs to take charge. Come on, let's do this as fast as we can and get out of here.'

'At least you didn't insist on those ridiculous outfits this time,' said Susan, feeling more comfortable in her usual jeans and jumper.

'No need. Lenore told me it was up this back lane so there'll be no one about.'

'Although that policeman did come up the other night, didn't he?'

'That's true,' Amy conceded. 'But I think we'd be very unlucky for anyone to see us here at this time of night.'

'I'm glad it was no black gym kit required,' said Carole. 'I don't think Dennis would have bought the boot camp excuse again tonight.'

'Where does he think you are then?'

'Actually, he doesn't know I'm out. He's working late again, Daniel's babysitting. Charging me a fortune for the privilege as usual.'

Amy screwed her eyes up. 'Dennis is putting in a lot of hours, isn't he, even for the king of finance?'

'The markets are crazy, even an investment manager with Dennis's years of experience needs to keep trawling to find new stock.' Carole was repeating almost word for word the reply Dennis had given to her own similar query earlier that evening. 'It's nearly bonus time again too so they're all putting in the hours.'

'Mmhhmm.' Amy sounded sceptical.

Carole was about to say more in Dennis's defence but Susan said impatiently, 'Come on, we can't stand round chatting all night. I've left Fraser in on his own, for one thing.'

'You're right, action stations,' said Amy and sprinted back to the van.

Five minutes later, they were standing in front of the wall, which looked as though it had been freshly whitewashed.

'Right, Lenore, this is your show. What do you want to say?' Amy stood with her hands on her hips, facing Lenore.

Lenore chewed on the end of her hair, pondering. 'I don't know, I'm wondering now if Dave did have a point. I mean, we had been seeing each other for a few weeks and I hadn't exactly been holding him back. Maybe I was leading him on . . .?'

Amy scowled. 'That's what he wants you to think. That's what they all want us to think.'

'Wait a minute, Amy, Dennis has never been like that.'

'Oh really? So you've never had sex with him when you didn't really want to, when you'd told him you were too tired, didn't fancy it, just couldn't be bothered?'

'I . . . no, you're right, there have been times, especially when the boys were little, when I really wasn't up for it but it seemed like, well, it seemed like he would be in a mood if I didn't. But . . . I mean, we're married, aren't we?'

'So that gives him the right to access your body whenever he feels like it? Even if you don't feel like it?'

'No, of course not.'

'What do you think all these actresses and singers are complaining about at last? The systematic abuse of women by men. They're the men we've come to get back at tonight. The question is, what do we want to say to them?'

When none of the women answered, Amy turned to Susan and tried a different tack.

'Guess who I saw in Asda the other day?'

'Who?'

'Mr Mould. Remember him? Our old art teacher?'

'Don't remind me,' said Susan. 'Remember he asked me and Carole to model for him when we were in second year and when we went up to his room, he asked us to put on leotards. We didn't know how to say no so we stood there half-dressed while he drew us in charcoal. Remember, Carole? You were in the chair with your knees up and I had to stand behind it, bending over slightly so that my curls would be in your face. I can't believe we agreed to that. I was mortified.'

'I haven't thought about that for years,' said Carole. 'The way old Mouldy put it, it felt like we had no choice. He didn't have the right to do that to us, but he did it anyway. And what about all the other guys we met while we were growing up – with their cajoling and wheedling to get what they wanted, and the way they made us feel like there was something wrong with us if we didn't want to do all the things they wanted to do?'

Lenore stood with her mouth open. That had happened to other people too? She hadn't told anyone about posing for Alfie and how she'd felt when he'd begged her to take her clothes off, how it seemed churlish to say no, babyish even, when they were going out together and he kept telling her how gorgeous she was. But now it seemed like she could have told her friends, they could have helped her, shown her that she hadn't been wrong not to want to, Alfie had been wrong to keep asking. And now look what had happened with Dave. Had she learned nothing in her forty-odd years, that she almost fell for the same trick again?

'Do you know, this is exactly where it happened?' she said. 'Dave and his refusing to take no for an answer, he pushed me right up against this wall. I don't know what would have happened if that guy hadn't come along at the right time.'

Susan stepped over the cans of spray paint and put her arm round Lenore. 'Don't let him upset you.'

Lenore patted Susan's arm. 'No, you're right, I won't. Because I'm going to get even instead.' She picked up the can closest to her – Green Satin, bought especially for the occasion by Amy. The others watched as she reached up as high as she could and sprayed in clear round capitals, **NO MEANS NO**.

'That's what I should have said to Dave the other night,' she said. 'Exactly that.' She stood back and wiped her hand across her face, her eyes shining. 'That felt good. Go on, Carole, you next.'

Carole dithered for a moment then picked up a can and walked a little further on from the spot on the wall that Lenore had graffitied. She sprayed in smaller but thicker letters, which gave it a menacing feel, **MY BODY, MY CHOICE, NOT YOURS TO TAKE**.

After a quick look up and down the lane, Susan sprayed in neat blocky letters beside Lenore's message, **#METOO. SOLIDARITY**.

'Well done, girls, and one more from me,' said Amy. She bent down and along the bottom of the wall running all the way to the front door of the gym she wrote, **DAVE BATES DOES NOT RESPECT WOMEN**.

'There, that should do it.'

The women stood back and admired their handiwork.

'Wait a minute,' said Carole. 'We forgot our signature.' She bent down and added in flowery letters, **Graffiti Girls** and added two entwined G's beside it.

'Now we've even got a motif,' she said.

Amy tutted but laughed along with the others. 'Perfect, Carole. Now let's get out of here.'

It was a week later and Susan was almost finished helping Lenore to put up the pupils' posters depicting scenes from *Macbeth* around the school hall.

'Thanks for helping, Susan. We're down to the wire with our preparations as usual. The event actually started ten minutes ago.'

Susan made a face as she pinned up a large image of a skeletal hand, covered in splodges, splatters and drips of viscous red paint, with the tag line in bubble lettering along the bottom reading, 'All the perfumes of Arabia'. She turned back to Lenore. 'Don't mention it. I'm actually glad to have something to take my mind off' – she looked all round before whispering – 'you know, the other night. *At the gym,*' she added, with all the melodrama of Lady Macbeth herself.

'You worry too much. Dave Bates got what was coming to him, I don't feel the slightest guilt about it.'

Dave had been calling Lenore daily since she'd cancelled her gym membership, his messages ranging in tone between incomprehension, disbelief and irritation at her refusal to speak to him. But Lenore had stuck to her guns, he wasn't worth her attention, Amy was right.

'Where is Amy anyway? And Carole said she'd be here too.' Lenore looked round at the crowds spilling into the hall. 'Looks like it's going to be packed.'

Outside, Amy was drawing up to the school car park in her van.

'We'll be lucky to get a space,' she said to Carole, who was checking her hair in the mirror.

'Carole. Are you listening? I said we'll be lucky— Oh wait, there's one there.'

Amy parked up and turned to look at Carole. 'What's wrong with you tonight? I told you, no one saw us at the gym, there's no way the graffiti will be linked to us.'

'It's not that.'

'What is it then? You've hardly said a word since I picked you up, and you could've cut the atmosphere in your house with a knife.'

'I know, sorry. That was Dennis being Dennis.'

'He didn't want to babysit?'

'You don't babysit your own kids, Amy, as you're always telling me,' said Carole sharply. 'Sorry.' She quickly relented. 'Nothing's wrong, honestly, just life, isn't it?'

She lifted her arm to push back the mirror and as her sleeve fell, Amy saw the chunky gold band, studded with diamonds the size of pills, slide down her wrist.

'New bracelet?'

Carole dropped her arm immediately. 'Yeah, Dennis bought me it.'

'What for? Your birthday's not for a couple of months yet.'

'He's allowed to buy me a piece of jewellery when it's not my birthday, you know. He gave me it yesterday. As a surprise.' Her cheeks were splotchy red and she suddenly felt on the verge of tears.

'Okay, sorry, I didn't mean to upset you. Of course he can buy you whatever he likes. He must be doing well, right enough, that's not from H. Samuel, is it?' Amy reached across Carole's knees to take out a pack of tissues from the glove compartment.

'Here,' she said, turning round at the same time as Carole

bent forward so their noses almost touched. Amy could see the deep V between Carole's breasts as her top gaped and smell the expensive, spicy aroma of her perfume rising up from her body.

'Sorry,' she said again, snapping back to her own seat, and looking straight ahead.

Carole was wiping her nose with the hanky. 'Don't worry about it, it's not you that's upsetting me. It's things at home . . . Anyway, I don't want to talk about it, we're on a night out.'

Amy snorted. 'If a school fundraiser is what passes for a night out these days, things are worse than I thought. Come on, cheer up, are we meeting the other two in there?'

'Yeah, Lenore said she'd see us by the tombola.'

The event was crammed with bored-looking men, spruced up in tweed jackets with their jeans, and many more women, overdressed and overexcited to be out of the house for the evening, even if it was only at the local school fundraiser. The hall remained cold and echoey despite the attempts to jazz it up with balloon arches and paper tablecloths. The sweet aroma from the chocolate fountain in the far corner almost, but not quite, covered the feral smell of sweaty sixth-year boys, mixed with the scent of teenage embarrassment that permeated the very walls of the place.

'Weird to be back in our old school, eh? I wonder if Lenore feels like this every day,' said Amy, as she admired the pupils' handiwork in the giant posters pinned up round the hall.

'Lots of blood and witches in the artwork, I see – Lenore's influence, I bet. And speaking of witches—'

'Hi, Lenore,' they both said at once and laughed, Carole looping one hand through Amy's arm, and waving their friend over with the other.

'You made it,' said Lenore. 'And not even that late either, Amy, you must have come with Carole.'

'Yup, she kept me on time.'

'For once,' laughed Carole. 'Good turnout,' she said to Lenore.

'Yes, just as well since we need to raise quite a bit to put all the kids up in a hotel in London for the night. And you know this catchment area, very few of the parents have cash to spare for theatre trips.'

'You should get Dennis to throw in a few quid. He's got plenty to spare at the moment.'

Carole pulled away from Amy and said, 'Give it a rest. There's Susan at the bingo, I'm going to join her. See you later.'

Lenore watched Amy watching Carole make her way across the hall to join Susan.

'Did something happen between you two?'

Amy turned back to Lenore. 'No, what do you mean? We're fine. More importantly, are you fine? After the other night, and Dave and everything?'

Lenore brushed Amy's concerns aside. 'Absolutely. Something and nothing, and anyway we made sure he got what was coming to him.'

'Definitely. Plenty more fish in the sea. Speaking of which, what about him?'

Lenore looked over to where Amy was pointing and saw a skinny guy sporting a lime jacket and a newborn goatee.

'Are you kidding me? That's the new trainee History guy, twenty-two if he's a day. What am I – Madonna now?'

Amy laughed and they made their way through the crowd to the home-baking stand.

Over at the bingo, Carole called 'House' and was surprised to hear she'd won a lamp.

'A lamp? Who gives out lamps as prizes in the bingo?' she said to Susan as they headed towards the coffees, Carole carrying a table lamp with a fringed blue shade awkwardly in her right hand.

'At least you won, don't knock it.'

There was a long queue at the coffee urn and the two women took their place behind a small group of mothers who were chatting animatedly.

'I mean, normally I wouldn't condone vandalism obviously—'

'Is it vandalism though? You know Lesley? You do, Lesley, whose sister works with Sarah, the receptionist at the council? She told me that her friend Margaret told her that that Dave Bates has gone through four receptionists in the last six months, all of them complained about him being an octopus.'

'An octopus?'

'You know, hands everywhere. He had to pay the last one off, she was threatening to take him to court. If you ask me, the Graffiti Girls did the right thing letting everyone know what he's like.' She folded her arms. 'These men, they think they can get away with whatever they like and women will be too embarrassed to say anything. Dave Bates isn't thinking that now, is he?'

Carole stole a look at Susan out of the corner of her eye, but neither said a word.

Two much younger girls joined the queue behind them.

'I'd love to know who they are,' the smaller brunette was saying to her friend.

'You wouldn't report them, would you? As far as I'm

concerned, they're doing a public service. You should hear some of the stories my mum's told me about the way men used to behave towards them. Teachers even, I'm not kidding!'

The first girl cried, 'No, not to report them, are you crazy? To join them.'

Susan bit her lip to stop her smile from spreading across her face, and Carole whispered, 'Wait till we tell the others.'

As the evening wore on, and the plastic tumblers of warm white wine and cheap rosé started to take effect, the noise in the hall grew thunderous. Most of the home-made millionaire's shortbread and banana loaves had been sold and devoured, the floor was littered with discarded raffle tickets and plastic stirrers, and people were wandering round the hall carrying Body Shop sets, bottles of Lidl's vodka, and the already-drooping plants they'd won at the various stands.

'Trust me to get landed with a bloody lamp,' moaned Carole to her friends, making a face as she took another sip of wine, her lipstick staining the rim of the plastic cup she'd been clutching most of the evening.

'Could be worse,' said Lenore. 'You could've won cheap shower gel.' She held up the three miniature bottles in a box she'd won for correctly guessing the weight of a giant SpongeBob.

'Dewberry, urgh,' said Amy.

'Excuse me.' A woman Carole vaguely recognized from the school gate approached their group. 'I like your lamp,' she said.

'Um, thanks,' said Carole.

Amy noticed her tumbler was empty and wandered off to see if there was any more wine. Susan took out her phone to text Fraser and Lenore went to tell the sixth-year volunteers they could start the clear-up any time now.

The woman turned to Carole. 'I'm glad to see you here, actually, because I wanted to introduce myself properly, although we've said hi at the school. I'm Jaxx's mum.'

Carole looked at the woman blankly for a moment.

'Jaxx? Thomas's friend.'

'Right, yes, Jack. We've suddenly started hearing quite a bit about Jack, always good when the kids make new friends.'

'Isn't it? Especially our two, since they're both, you know . . .' The woman made a fey gesture with her hand.

Carole raised her chin. 'They're both . . .?'

'You know, they're . . . they're a bit different to some of the others. You know what I mean.'

'No,' said Carole. 'No, what do you mean?'

Amy came back with three fresh tumblers of wine.

'None for me thanks,' said Jaxx's mum. 'I need to get back. Nice to speak to you,' she said to Carole, before making her way out of the hall.

Amy said goodbye to the woman then turned to Carole. 'What's up with your face? Here, drink your cat's pee and pretend it's Pinot.'

Carole gave a deep sigh. 'I don't know what's wrong with me tonight, everything seems a bit . . .'

Amy waited.

Carole leaned in a bit closer. 'Between you and me, I'm not sure what Dennis is up to a lot of the time.'

'He's not still picking fights with everyone that looks at him sideways, is he?'

Carole shook her head.

'What then? Women?'

'No!' she said. 'Why would you say that? Do you think he's

seeing someone else? Do you think that's what the bracelet was for – because he feels guilty?'

'How would I know?' said Amy. 'But if you don't know what he's up to, did it never occur to you that he might be seeing someone?'

'Oh God,' said Carole. 'I hope not. But . . . maybe. He says he's working harder than ever and he is making all this money, he says that's the only reason he does it but . . . I mean, what's the point of working so hard you never get to see your own family? And even when he is home, he's a million miles away, I can't reach him any more.'

'You've been married for years, you can't expect it to be like your honeymoon for ever, and him hanging on your every word.'

'I know that, I'm not stupid.'

Amy touched her friend's arm. 'Why do you stay, Carole? He clearly doesn't make you happy.'

'What are you talking about? I love him! Anyway, you've got no idea, Amy, you don't have kids. I could never leave, not when there's so many people depending on me, needing me for stuff.' She took another sip of wine and made a face.

'But your kids are all fine, aren't they? Children are resilient, that's what everyone says. They'd all cope if you decided to leave Dennis.'

'Would they? Glover maybe, he's young enough, but Archie's permanently anxious about something or other, I couldn't bear to give him more to worry about. Daniel's anger, well, it reminds me of Dennis when he was that age, I'm so worried he's going to get into a fight and do someone serious damage one of these days, and as for Thomas . . .' She hesitated. 'Have you ever noticed anything . . . odd about Thomas?'

Amy stared into her wine. 'Depends what you mean by odd.'

'So you have noticed something?'

Amy looked round the hall before answering. 'Look, Carole, everyone's different, just let kids be who they are.' She paused.

'Go on,' said Carole.

'No, nothing, just – you've always accepted me without judgement, haven't you?'

'Of course. What do you mean?'

'Do the same for Thomas and he'll be fine, Carole, I promise. I'm more worried about you—'

Carole smiled suddenly and said out of nowhere, 'Yes, it's been a great night, hasn't it?' as Lenore and Susan came to join them. Amy pursed her lips but said no more.

'It's been brilliant,' said Lenore. 'Apparently they've raised over four hundred quid from the entry tickets alone, so the kids' trip to London is on.' She raised her plastic tumbler and twirled round the leftovers of her lukewarm rosé, knocking Carole's lamp off the table.

'Mind my lamp,' said Carole. 'That's having pride of place. In my utility room anyway.'

Lenore laughed as she picked it up and put it back on the table at Carole's elbow. Susan placed a giant lemon cupcake, tied up in cellophane and a yellow bow, carefully beside it. 'That's for Fraser,' she said. 'Don't want to get it crushed.'

'God forbid,' said Amy. 'But let's not forget the real triumph of the week – a shoutout from Michelle McManus, no less, praising the Graffiti Girls for, and I quote, "raising awareness of issues affecting many women in Lanarkshire".'

'No! Really?' said Lenore.

'Really,' said Amy. 'So in summary – Master Bates's hand has been stopped in its tracks—'

'Amy!' cried Susan and Lenore together, as Carole laughed.

'—Lenore's honour—'

'Such as it was,' joked Carole, and Lenore jostled her.

'—has been avenged, and judging by the comments we've heard here tonight, it seems very much like the good people of Hamilton are beginning to wake up to the fact that women have rights too. So, girls, please raise your glasses to' – she leaned in to the group and whispered – 'the Graffiti Girls.'

'Seconded,' shouted Lenore.

'Thirded,' agreed Susan in a quieter voice, and looking all round to check no one was listening.

'And fourthed,' finished Carole, and they all raised their plastic cups in the air, laughing as Carole's lamp toppled from the table once more and rolled across the wooden floor.

Later that evening, Lenore was in her bedroom hanging up her denim skirt and thinking about the fundraiser. Everyone said it had been a huge success and Mr McLoughlin had congratulated his staff on their efforts. They could probably have done without Chloe Baxter tippexing the tiles in the girls' toilets (though as Amy pointed out, who was Lenore to talk), and it would have been nice if a few more sixth years had stayed on to help so she didn't have to clean the entire chocolate fountain herself but still, they'd raised plenty of money for the trip so she was satisfied. She was contemplating a late-night bubble bath with one more glass of wine – after all, she thought, smiling, there was no one to tell her she couldn't – when Dave's number flashed up on her screen. Lenore stood in front of her wardrobe for a moment, swithering about whether or not to take his call. If any of her friends had been there they'd tell her to ignore it then wipe his number from her contacts immediately. But the other women weren't there and all the rosé she'd knocked back to get her through the evening was swirling treacherously round her bloodstream. The phone rang out insistently and Lenore clicked the wardrobe doors shut and answered it.

'Thanks for picking up, Lenore. It's me, Dave. From the gym?'

'I know who you are, Dave,' said Lenore, pushing a pile of towels off her bed and sitting down.

'Sorry, I know, sorry. I wanted to tell you that I was thinking about what happened the other week, you know, outside the gym, and I realize now it was wrong of me to keep kissing you.'

Lenore said nothing.

'Lenore?'

'Yes, I'm listening.'

'It's not as though my intentions were bad, I just, maybe, misinterpreted the signals you were giving me.'

'Wait, are you saying it was my fault?'

'No, no at all.' There was a pause. 'Maybe a little. I mean, not that it matters . . .'

I think it does, thought Lenore, but she didn't interrupt him.

'It's just . . . I've had a terrible week. Some bitches vandalized my property, painted all over the walls of the gym, spreading all sorts of lies about me as well!'

Lenore tightened her grip on her phone. 'Bitches, did you say?'

'Yeah, they even signed it. "Graffiti Girls". One of my girls, the receptionist, told me it's some group of crazy wimmin's libbers that are going about vandalizing property. They were in the papers for doing the same thing to the Miners' Welfare Club a few weeks back. No idea what they're trying to prove but I'd just had those walls painted. It's been a complete nightmare for me.'

'Poor you,' said Lenore. 'Listen, Dave, don't call me again, okay?'

'What? Wait, Lenore—'

But Lenore had hung up the phone.

III

Susan

SUSAN LOOKED OVER AT THE clock, wondering why the hands were going so slowly today. She bit her lower lip and winced as she felt the chapped skin break and bleed. She vowed again to stop biting her lips and smoothed her fingers over her scabbed mouth.

She started as her colleague Marion reached behind her to place two large atlases on the returned shelf.

'Sorry,' said Marion. 'So jumpy,' then stood there quietly until Susan, as usual, felt compelled to break the silence.

'I'm not jumpy,' she lied. 'Just got a lot going on. And you keep appearing behind me.'

'That's where the returned books go.'

Susan knew she was right. She was skittish as a box of frogs and had been since Amy and the others had persuaded her to graffiti the gym. Amy had made it sound so reasonable at the time – yes of course Dave Bates deserved to be punished, yes of course women deserved to be heard – it was just that getting involved with the Graffiti Girls was not good for her mental health. She'd spent the whole two weeks since they'd painted the gym terrified of her own shadow and feeling like she had 'graffiti artist' tattooed on her forehead. There had been four more articles in the local papers – one had offered a reward for anyone who could reveal the identity of the Graffiti Girls – and last Wednesday, they'd even had a mention on BBC Radio Scotland.

Marion continued to stand there, saying nothing. It wasn't that Susan didn't like the young woman exactly, but there was something strange about her reserve, the way she would appear at her elbow and stand there, perfectly comfortable in the silence that most other adults would feel the need to fill.

Susan tried to fill it. 'It's quiet today, isn't it?'

Marion nodded but volunteered nothing more.

It had been almost two years since she'd joined the library, and overall, Susan was glad the council had hired her. She'd had some doubts when she first met her, largely centring round the girl's taciturn manner and slow, almost lazy way of speaking, but as soon as she'd started talking about books – the books that had made her, that still influenced her, the ones she would recommend to friends, the ones she would take to a desert island (Susan's favourite conversation starter) – she knew she was talking to the real deal. She was a fellow book lover, someone who appreciated the importance, no, the absolute necessity of books. So she had no real complaints about Marion's professional capabilities, but as to building any sort of relationship with her, she was at a loss. Marion said so little, shared almost no personal information, nothing about her social life – if she had one – or what she did out of hours, apart from reading.

Still, Susan knew better than anyone that what really mattered was what happened inside the library, during opening hours. Marion drifted away and Susan surveyed the library with a small sigh of satisfaction. Even after all these years as a librarian, a place full of books was still a magical place to her and she knew that plenty of their regulars agreed. Take Simon, sitting over by Contemporary Fiction. He'd been coming into the library every Thursday for as long as Susan could remember. Always the same routine: pick up the *Daily Record* – Susan had tried to persuade him to try the *Guardian* but he wasn't having it ('my dad would turn in his grave if I changed my allegiance love,' he'd say) – then sit at the same table beneath the shiny print of the Coliseum and finish his paper almost dead on half eleven. Stretching, he'd wander over to the breakout area, pour himself a cup of tea and have a ten-minute chat with Roslyn, who'd be taking a break from whichever historical romance she was working her way through that week. Then there was Roy, he came every day except Monday, because that was his day for the bowls. He'd sit at the computer desk furthest away from the door and bash away at the keyboard for two hours at a time, filling out applications for jobs he never got. The girls from Morrisons along the way popped in throughout the day, often bringing in cakes and biscuits for her and Marion that were 'only just on the turn, shame to waste them', and making Susan laugh with their stories from the meat counter and what was happening in homewares. They had Bounce and Rhyme on Tuesdays and Wednesdays, and Susan loved seeing the chubby babies, delighting in the singing and nursery rhymes, and taking her back to when Fraser was that age and she'd been the most important person in his world. Quite often they had school kids come in, sometimes when Susan suspected they should be in class. She reckoned they learned more in a library than they ever would in school so she didn't say anything, except when they came in in groups of four or five and were too noisy for her regulars to concentrate.

She loved her job at the library. She was aware of her

reputation as being a stickler for the rules, and knew the new guy, Cameron thought she should lighten up a bit. But he'd been foisted upon her by the council as temporary cover for staff shortages and had only been qualified for five minutes so what did he know. Of course Fraser thought she was crazy to stay at the same job her whole working life. Sometimes she wondered what he'd say if she told him this was the same library in which she'd spent all her Saturdays when she was his age, and older. No doubt he'd think that was even more pathetic.

Her phone pinged and she bent to get it out of her bag. Normally she disapproved of mobile phones in the workplace. Apart from the noise, all they did was distract the staff, and Cameron in particular was too easily distracted already. She'd made a point of keeping her phone close this week, though, as Fraser was having a particularly tough time studying for his exams and she wanted to make sure she was there if he needed anything.

The text was from Carole. 'Still on 4 lunch?' Lenore looked up to check no one could see her texting then quickly typed, 'Yes. 12.45 Café Nisi x' and dropped the phone back into her bag.

'You could go for lunch now if you wanted,' said Marion, appearing again from nowhere as though on cue. 'Nobody'll miss you.'

'Early lunch is at half past, Marion,' Susan reminded her. 'Where's Cameron?' It struck her suddenly that she hadn't seen their new librarian for at least half an hour.

'Fag break.'

Susan rolled her eyes. 'I've already had to tell him twice he can only smoke on his tea breaks or lunch. Looks like I'll have to speak to him about it again.'

The long hand of the clock finally hit the six and Susan got up to put her jacket on. 'Make sure Cameron prints out those posters when he gets back.' 'If he ever does get back,' she added under her breath. She could see Marion heading towards the kettle as soon as the coast was clear and felt a tight little knot of exasperation forming in her belly. Breathing deeply, she tried to let it go; she was on her lunchbreak, after all.

There was a thin sun breaking through the clouds which, following the morning rain, created a striking rainbow across Cadzow Bridge to her left. The park below was coming into its own as it did every spring, the foliage returning, lush and strong, the spreading bramble bushes dotted with pink and white flowers, and the pathways filling up with walkers and groups of youths in their exercise gear, heading over to the sports grounds across the park. Hamilton was really quite beautiful in Susan's opinion, she'd never wanted to live anywhere else.

She, Carole, Lenore and Amy used to meet at the back gate by the old Science block every lunchtime and walk across this bridge to Lightbody's for apple turnovers or Marini's for chips. Lenore was always full of what had happened in English or Chemistry that morning, while Carole used the wall as a barre to practise her dance moves. Amy was usually foaming at the mouth about some injustice or other, perpetrated against herself, a classmate, or womankind in general. Susan would hum quietly in the background, half-listening in, half away in whichever world had been conjured up by the book she was reading that week.

She crossed the road at the music shop that Dennis and Carole used to spend all their time in once they'd started going out together. Susan had gone in once with Carole to buy Dennis music sheets for his birthday. Of course Carole had been completely in her element there but Susan had been cowed by the cool young guys hanging out by the keyboards at the back. It didn't matter since they only had eyes for Carole, which was fine by Susan who would rather have been swallowed up by the floor than be noticed by one of those guys. The charity shop next door was closed again. It was a shame because they seemed to have plenty of stock to sell, just not enough willing volunteers to stand there and sell it. She peered into the fish shop as she passed but the queue put her off dashing in to get Fraser a piece of salmon for his dinner. She'd read last week it was excellent for boosting brain power, so maybe she'd nip in on the way back. There was a queue outside Threads too, and Susan had to veer off the pavement into the road to avoid the women standing in pairs, chatting and laughing, the wait for new curtain material and knitting needles not dampening their mood.

As she turned into Quarry Street, she avoided looking up the lane where the gym was and focused straight ahead instead. She'd overheard two mums from last week's Bounce and Rhyme say it had been painted over already, but she still preferred to avoid looking at the scene of the crime. She spotted Carole turning right into Café Nisi. *Good*, she thought, *she'll get us a table*.

As always at lunchtimes, Café Nisi was packed. Susan squeezed by the queue at the counter and looked towards the open fire and the tables at the back to find Carole.

'Susan, over here.'

Susan smiled. Carole had this knack of procuring the best table in any restaurant, café or bar they went to. It was a standing joke among the girls when they went out that Carole should go ahead to secure their pitch for the evening before the rest of them arrived. Even Susan, with her complete disinterest in looks, was aware that Carole had always been the best-looking of the group, and today she looked even better than usual. Her hair was tied back from her face, in a shiny French plait that reached halfway down her back. She wore tiny pearl earrings and a white blouse with a high-necked mandarin collar, a gold chain resting flat against her always faintly tanned skin.

'You look nice,' said Susan, as she took off her jacket and sat down opposite Carole at the booth by the open fire, which wasn't lit today.

'Thank you, so do you,' said Carole automatically. 'Although you need some chapstick for your lips.'

Susan put her hand up to her face to hide her mouth. 'But really, you do look . . . great. Sort of fresh-faced, or less tired . . .?'

Carole laughed. 'Fresh-faced or less tired? Is that the best I can hope for now I've hit the big four-oh?' But she said this with the confidence of one who has always been feted for her looks and is still aware of their power. She touched her hand to her cheek. 'I've been for a facial this morning, actually. Must have worked.'

'Someone's got money to burn,' said Susan, as she picked up a menu from behind the glass dish of ketchup and mayonnaise sachets.

Carole shifted in her seat. 'Might as well enjoy the fruits of Dennis's labour. Anyway,' she said, bristling at the implication she was wasting her time and Dennis's money with fripperies, 'I know we only value work outside the home but I do work hard too, you know. I mean, it's great, all that time with the kids — well, that's not always so great, to be honest — but I do need time for myself too, to take care of myself, treat myself sometimes . . .'

She trailed off and Susan said quickly, 'You don't have to

justify it to me, Carole. Being a parent's the hardest job in the world, I should know. Of course you need to treat yourself.'

'And speaking of treating . . .' Carole reached into her bag and brought out a small, square package, with Susan's name on it. 'This is for you.' She passed it across the table.

'Why? My birthday was back in January and you got me that lovely notebook.'

'It's not for your birthday, it's just . . . because. Go on, open it.' Carole watched as her friend took great care to peel back the sellotape without tearing the wrapping paper.

'Rip it open like you mean it,' she laughed.

'No, this is lovely wrapping paper, I can reuse it. What's— Is it . . . is it Gucci?' Susan held up a fine gold necklace, the double G dangling from the edge of her palm.

'It stands for Graffiti Girls, get it – GG?' said Carole, before adding, 'Probably best not to hold it up like that, mind you.'

'Oh my God, Carole, did anyone see?' Susan's eyes darted round the café but the customers at the adjoining tables were too busy with their cappuccinos and panini to notice her and Carole.

'No, it's fine. Honestly, Susan, you're so jumpy, you might as well have "Guilty" tattooed on your forehead.'

'And that's exactly the reason I can't wear this, we'd be as well going to the police station now and admitting it.'

'I meant for you to wear it under your jumper. Look.' Carole pulled down the neck of her blouse far enough for Susan to see the same gold necklace with its treacherous GG lying flat against Carole's chest. 'I got us all one, because we're all part of this and it feels great, doesn't it?'

Susan placed her necklace delicately back in its box and

looked up at Carole. 'You got us all a gold necklace? Where's all this money coming from – is Dennis robbing banks now?'

Carole didn't answer because a young waiter had appeared at their table, ready to take their order. As usual, Susan might not have been there as the boy, who couldn't have been any older than Fraser, gave all his attention to Carole. She smiled up at the infatuated youth, well aware of the effect she was having on his raging teenage hormones.

When they'd ordered their tuna melt and ham and cheese toasties, Carole popped the box into Susan's bag and said, 'Take it, and make sure you're wearing it on our next mission.'

'I don't know if I can take any more, Carole, that's one of the reasons I wanted to see you today. It's keeping me up at night, worrying we might get caught.'

Carole waved her objections away. 'Let's not talk about that then. What have you been up to this week, have you seen Lenore?'

'No, she texted me to go out running with her. Can you imagine – me pounding the streets, my red curls and . . . everything else bouncing?'

'Why can't she go out running on her own?'

'She did, twice. The first time a car slowed down and two young guys shouted insults at her out the car windows, and the second time, she was running down by the Mausoleum and a guy shouted at her that she could stop the traffic with that face and threw a scrunched-up Red Bull can at her.'

'What is it with these men? We can't even go out exercising now? I hate to think what Amy would have to say on the subject.'

She sat back and looked around her. 'Still, good to hear she's out running and back to her old self. I think that Dave Bates business really upset her. But you know her better than any of us – is she really okay?'

'I wouldn't say I know her better,' said Susan, 'just longer.'

'You've been her best friend for as long as I can remember. When I first asked you round to mine to meet Amy, you insisted on bringing Lenore. You two have been best friends all through school, university, Tommy leaving . . .'

'Not quite,' said Susan, reaching up to push back her unmanageable curls which were threatening to trail into her ham and cheese toastie. 'We've never really spoken about it but actually I was quite hurt by the way she dumped me, all three of us in fact, when she went to uni. Even before that, in sixth year, remember we never saw her.'

'I can hardly remember sixth year now, I was too busy snogging Dennis and playing at being the groupie in the band to notice who else was around.'

'She told me once it was because she'd put on weight – which I don't understand at all. What difference would that make to seeing your friends?'

Carole stopped stirring her coffee. 'Has something happened between you two?'

'No, not at all. I just mean, me and Lenore have been friends since nursery, when the important thing was who you sat next to. Whoever that is automatically becomes your best friend, don't they, doesn't really matter if you're compatible or not. But I sometimes think if you hadn't met me at that dance class my mum dragged me to, and introduced me and Lenore to Amy, Lenore wouldn't have been interested in being my friend once we hit high school.'

'That's rubbish, Susan. We're all friends together, a group, a team, always have been.'

Susan was about to say more then decided this was not the place, and anyway it felt disloyal talking to Carole like this about Lenore. Maybe Carole was right, what did all that old history matter now?

'Anyway, she seemed okay after our last "mission".' Carole made air quotes round the last word, and Susan looked all round, shushing her.

'This is what I mean. I'm not like the rest of you, I can't see this stuff as some great adventure. I'm seriously worried we'll get caught.'

'Calm down,' said Carole, reaching over for her friend's hand. 'It's only a laugh, well, to me it is, but I think Amy really is on a mission.'

'That's exactly it, it's not a laugh to me – I'm a person who follows the rules, I'm a librarian, for God's sake, but somehow when we're all together, especially if Amy is in full flow, I seem to get swept along, doing these crazy things.'

'Amy's a born leader, isn't she?'

'And you're positively blooming on it too.' Susan looked enviously at Carole's glowing skin, her sparkling eyes.

'It's true, it's cheered me up no end, being part of something, feeling like we're making a change. Or at least, we're starting conversations anyway. Remember those women at the fundraiser? They're our fan club. Come on, you need to stop taking it all so seriously.'

Susan pushed away her empty plate. 'Maybe you're right.'

'I am right. Definitely.'

'Okay,' Susan laughed finally. 'I'm being stupid. Probably menopausal.'

'Ah ah ah,' teased Carole. 'What would Amy say to that?'

Susan raised her chin and put on a high-pitched voice that was nothing like Amy's gruff tone and said, 'The detrimental effects of the menopause on women's brain power is yet another lie perpetrated by men to persuade women past childbearing age that they are worthless.' She looked back at Carole. 'Something like that?'

Carole laughed so loudly that the man sitting at the next table craned his head round to see who was causing all the commotion.

'Can we help you?' said Carole sweetly, and the man immediately turned back to his coffee, contenting himself with a low tut and a shake of his almost bald head.

'It's nearly half one,' said Susan suddenly. 'I'll need to get back.'

'What's the rush? Are you not the boss of that whole place by now? I'm sure no one will notice if you're ten minutes late.'

'That's not how it works, Carole. I'm the Senior Librarian, I can't be seen taking extended lunch breaks. I'll need to dash. Let's organize something with the others next week?'

'Okay, suit yourself. I think I'll have another cappuccino,' said Carole, catching the eye of the young waiter immediately. 'Don't work too hard,' she called as Susan made her way through the still-hectic café to the door.

When Susan got back to the library, she was not surprised to find that Cameron was again missing in action. She set off to find him and tell him in no uncertain terms what she thought of his work ethic when she spotted him at the main door. *No doubt flirting with Linda again*, she thought. But as she walked through the reception area, she saw that Cameron was not with the young receptionist at the Town House; he was helping a pair of pensioners load their shopping trolleys on to a waiting bus.

'There you go, Terry,' he said as he lifted the first of the two large tartan shopping trolleys on to the bus. 'Yours next, Myra, you get on and I'll pass it up.'

'You're a wee doll, Cameron,' said the smallest of the two women, dropping the large print book she'd taken out of the library into her bag. 'But make sure you don't squash it now, it's got a big steak pie in it to take along to Irish Mary's do tonight.'

'Don't worry about that,' said Cameron. 'Get yourself a seat and leave the bags to me.'

'Thanks, Cameron,' called Terry from the bus. 'See you next week, son.'

Both women waved as the bus set off along the bridge towards Uddingston.

Cameron turned and stopped abruptly as he spotted Susan. 'Good for you,' she said as he walked past her. He didn't answer, but Susan was sure he was blushing as he headed back into the library. Maybe she'd misjudged him after all.

Their rapprochement did not last the afternoon. She'd left her post for a maximum of ten minutes to visit the loo and when she came back, Cameron was already lolling in her chair. Not that anybody had their own chair exactly but Susan sat on the one in the middle, directly facing the door, always had, and she'd left her cardigan on the back of it, in case there was any doubt. Pointedly, she said, 'Excuse me' and removed her cardigan from behind his back. She made sure he could see her placing her mobile in her bag, whilst staring at his iPhone sitting proudly in the middle of the counter.

'Phones away, Cameron,' she said finally when he didn't take the hint.

Cameron moved his phone slightly to the left and said, 'Is it always as quiet as this?', reclining even further in his chair and resting the tips of his boots on the counter.

'Some days are quieter than others, yes. Was it not like that at East Kilbride?'

'It was never exactly a rave but not a graveyard like this either. As soon as the sun comes out, everyone's got something better to do than come to the library. Even the computer nerds from Coding Club have found something more interesting to do.' He sniffed. 'Don't know how you can stand it.'

Marion sidled past the desk on her way to lunch, her eyes to the floor and her collar up to cover most of her face.

Cameron gave her the side-eye and continued talking to Susan. 'That's why I've decided to apply for another transfer.'

'Really? You just got here.' But there was nothing Susan would have liked more than for Cameron to leave so she didn't want to put him off.

'Information and Communication Officer at the council headquarters. Step up from the old Bounce and Rhyme, eh?'

Privately, Susan thought it was several steps up from his current pay grade but she didn't say so. 'In the meantime, you are employed here so we don't have our mobile—'

Her own phone beeped shrilly from the depths of her bag and Susan ignored Cameron's smirking as she dived for it. It could be Fraser.

It was a text from Carole. 'Lovely to cu @ lunch, nb 2 put ur necklace on, we're all GGs now. C x'.

Susan dropped the phone like it was hot metal and told Cameron briskly that she would be in the back preparing the Scratch lesson for that week's Coding Club if he needed her.

As she worked on the computer instructions for the kids to

code various instruments and put together a band, her mind was doing its own processing of all that had happened in the last few weeks. Being friends with Amy had always entailed getting swept into her crazy schemes but as she'd tried to explain to Carole, Susan wasn't like the rest of them. She'd always been much more reserved, and had to be cajoled into participating in whatever was going on. She was being honest with Carole when she'd wondered why the others were friends with her at all. Yet here they were, still friends all these years later, and even though Susan loved her friends very much, she was still fretting over the things they got her involved in.

And it wasn't as though she didn't have enough to fret over with Fraser at the moment, she thought, pausing to make herself a coffee and have a quick check out front that Cameron wasn't slacking and that no one desperately needed help with something only she could deal with. But no, it was still quiet and Susan returned to her post at the pc in the back.

Typing the Scratch instructions was second nature to her and her mind was free to wander as she worked. Seeing so much of the girls again, and especially the business with Lenore and that creep Dave Bates, had sent her hurtling back to the past, bringing to the fore things she hadn't thought about for years, things she'd done her best to bury.

After Lenore had returned from Leeds and they'd all met up again, they'd had some pretty wild nights out. Both Dennis and Tommy being on the scene by then meant it wasn't often that all four girls could go out together so when they did, they really enjoyed themselves, mostly led by Amy, who never seemed to want a partner, and was always more interested in the four of them having the best time they possibly could. Susan remembered nights when they'd been thrown out of the pub in the end, Amy refusing to leave till she'd finished her pint of cider and black, the others having to force her to put her jacket on and push her out the front door, pint glass still in hand.

Susan usually drank much less than the others but on one particular night, they'd been out since early, starting in the Bay Horse and working their way along the pubs in town from the George to the Libertine, and everywhere in between. She remembered being helped into a taxi at the end of the night by a very friendly young guy who'd insisted on buying her a drink half an hour earlier then hadn't left her side since. She suddenly felt unbelievably sleepy and wanted to be home and in bed immediately. She knew she had to tell her friends she was leaving but they were on the other side of the packed dance floor and seemed unreachable. But it was okay because the guy said not to worry, he would see her home safely.

As the cold air hit her, she wobbled dangerously on the cobbles outside the Libertine and had to prop herself up against the wall. She remembered counting the bricks and thinking she'd never noticed before how brightly coloured they were – a dazzling orange that hurt her eyes. She heard the nice guy arguing with the taxi driver who didn't want to take her in case she was sick on his leather upholstery.

'Don't worry,' said her knight in shining armour, 'I've got her.' Turning to Susan he said, 'What's your address?' as he swung her arm round his shoulders and bundled her into the taxi, the driver tutting and making faces at her in the rear-view mirror.

She must have been capable of giving the address of the little ground-floor flat in Earnock she'd been living in at the time because she woke up the next day in her own bed, her head splitting and both inner thighs unaccountably stiff and sore. Her phone was flashing the way it did when there were text messages waiting but she couldn't look at the bright screen, nor bear to pick up the phone which kept ringing insistently as she tried to sleep. She tossed and turned in bed all day, her sleep punctured by fractured images of the lovely guy who'd helped her home, doing strange, intimate things to her in her own flat. Why was he here though, had she invited him in, did they know each other from somewhere? At three o'clock, as the daylight was beginning to fade and the gloomy shadows were lengthening in her bedroom, Susan sat upright in bed, a spark of realization bursting into flames. She looked across the room at her jeans and cap-sleeved top from Next shimmering mockingly at her, she scrutinized the sheets beneath her, crispy and crackling in places with something unmistakable, and saw bruises like whispers on the tender skin between her legs, and knew without a shadow of a doubt. She told her concerned friends later she'd got home fine, to stop worrying, knowing that none of them would have put themselves in the same position she had, and kicking herself for being so stupid.

Fraser was born eight months and three weeks later, when she was almost twenty-seven and about to be promoted to Acting Senior Librarian. Of course, she didn't get the promotion when she announced her need for maternity leave. She told those who needed to know, including even her friends, that her pregnancy was the result of a one-night stand which, in a way, it was.

It seemed impossible to Susan that Fraser was now at the stage where he was sitting his Highers and planning what to do with his life. At times it seemed very unfair that he should be talking about heading off to Aberdeen or Dundee, or even – God forbid –

London to study and make a life for himself that didn't seem to include her at all. There were times when she wanted to scream at him, what about my life, my ambitions, all the things I gave up to have you? Instead, she'd force herself to smile encouragingly and even offer to help him fill in the application forms.

'Are you writing the coding instructions or a novel in there, Susan?' Cameron called through from the front desk. 'Believe it or not, we've got a rush through here, so a hand would be appreciated.'

'What? Sorry, yes, of course, I'll be right through. I'm finished here anyway.'

When she got home that evening, Fraser was lounging on the couch, with YouTube on the telly and a half-eaten cheese and coleslaw sandwich she'd made for him that morning and placed under clingfilm in the fridge, on a plate on his chest.

Susan reached over and snapped off the TV before she even said hello.

'Oy, I was watching that.'

'So I see.' She took the plate off his chest and stood over him. 'Weren't you supposed to be studying? Your exams are only a month away.'

Fraser swung his legs round and sat up to face her. 'I can't study every hour God sends, Mum.'

'Hardly that, Fraser. You spend more time with that girl than—'

'Why do you have to keep calling her that? Her name's Fiona, you know that full well.'

'Fiona then.' Susan waved her hand dismissively. 'You're spending far too much time with her and not enough time with your books. What on earth do you find to talk about with her anyway? She seems so . . .'

Fraser stood up so that he was towering over his mother, forcing Susan to acknowledge that however much she babied him, physically, Fraser was now a man and he could easily intimidate her if he chose to do so. Perhaps the same realization struck Fraser because he took a step back before speaking again.

'She seems so what?' he said. His voice remained dangerously low and Susan knew he was ready for yet another row. Squabbling and fighting was all they seemed to do these days, and he'd been such a sweet boy.

Susan's parents had got over their initial shock and had helped out as much as they could but for the most part, Susan and Fraser had been on their own all Fraser's life. After the cramped early years in Susan's flat, they moved to the starter home in the new estate they'd lived in ever since – when Fraser was a toddler, and needed outside space to play. He'd spent hours and hours in the garden on his red metal swing, and she'd been there with him, either pushing him 'higher, Mummy, higher' or later, sitting on the grass beside him while his little legs pumped hard and the swing flew through the air as he chattered on about Roblox and Power Rangers and all his new friends from nursery, whose names and favourite foods Susan knew almost as well as Fraser's.

She glanced behind Fraser and towards the back garden. The swing was still there, rusting and unloved at the bottom of the grass. She turned back to her glowering son, wondering if she'd been too soft on him, allowed bad behaviour to go unchecked where a better mother, or a father, might have curbed it. She tried again, smiling a little to soften her tone. 'I only meant, I can't think you'd have much in common? She spends most of her time posting pictures of herself on Instagram and talking about this model and that actress, none of whom I've ever heard of.'

'She has to spend a lot of time planning her career. What with the exercise regime and the dieting, and . . . and practising her walk and everything. Modelling is much harder than it looks, you know, Mum. You know nothing. You've hardly spoken two words to her, how would you know what she's like?'

That was true, thought Susan, she hadn't been very welcoming of the girl since Fraser had introduced her after Christmas, blushing and stumbling over his words.

'Look, Fraser, I don't want to argue with you tonight—'

'Could've fooled me,' muttered Fraser, his eyes to the floor.

'No, really I don't. I've had a hard day, and I've got a few things to worry about at the moment.'

She was momentarily pleased to see the old look of concern flit over her son's face but immediately slipped back into parent mode. 'Work stuff,' she assured him. 'Nothing important. How does steak pie sound for dinner? Fancy that?'

'I got up late. I just had that sandwich.'

Susan bit her lip so she wouldn't say anything else to annoy him. 'Okay then. I'll leave yours plated in the microwave, don't leave it in for longer than two minutes, otherwise the meat will get dry.'

Fraser made a face. 'You're going out again?'

If she hadn't been trying so hard not to start another row, Susan would have pointed out that he ignored her most of the time, so he had no right to be annoyed when she went out. Sometimes she liked that he felt that way, it made her feel she was still important to him, but other times it made her feel caged in, restless and ready for a life of her own again, one that didn't revolve round Fraser and his ambitions.

'It's only the Book Group,' she said. 'I'll be back by ten.'

As it turned out, she was home by eight forty-five, the group's meeting having been cut short in order to prevent all-out war between their longest-standing member, Mr Heggarty, and their newest member, Mabel, who was a student of English Literature from the nearby University of the West of Scotland. Susan had tried hard not to get involved even though she thought Mabel had a point and that perhaps Mr Heggarty's description of *Lolita* as a 'tender love story' between a mature and responsible academic and a 'perky young thing' was pushing it a bit.

'He's a nonce, pure and simple,' said Mabel, crossing her arms tightly across her chest to indicate her opinion on the matter was final.

'We don't stand for that language here, love,' said Mr Heggarty. 'Tell her, Susan.'

'Well, yes—' began Susan.

'And what about the way she acted, eh? Tempting the poor man till he couldn't resist—'

'What? Are you crazy? She was a schoolgirl. He even tried to kill off her mother so he could have his way with a twelve-year-old.'

'I'm pleased to see a book provoke such a reaction but—' Susan tried again.

'A well-developed schoolgirl who knew exactly what she was doing,' said Mr Heggarty, shaking his head and adding, 'Wee flirt' under his breath.

'What? Are you saying she was asking for it?'

'I'm saying some people might see it that way.' He looked round at his old ally and post-meeting drinking buddy Mr

Hailsham for support, and they both leaned back on their chairs, their trouser legs rising to reveal hairless white ankles.

'And that's where I have to draw the line, I'm afraid,' said Susan, standing up and gathering in the books. 'Next month, let's try and stay on less controversial territory. It's your choice next time, Mabel, and we're discussing . . . oh. *The Bluest Eye* by Toni Morrison, right.'

'Should be fun,' said Mabel, swinging her bag across her body and putting on her cycling helmet.

'Yes, indeed,' said Susan. 'I look forward to it,' her heart already sinking.

Less than twelve hours later, Susan was back in the library, seated through the back and sorting through the latest children's offerings. She smiled as she caught sight of some of Fraser's old favourites, *Kipper the Dog* – which had led to endless but fruitless requests for a puppy, and *The Tiger Who Came To Tea* – which they'd gone to see one Christmas at the Town House.

'Hey,' said Marion, as she plonked down another pile of brightly coloured hardback books on the desk in front of Susan.

Susan jumped, and Marion smiled, her almost black lipstick jarring against her teeth. 'Jumpy.'

'Why do you have to keep sneaking up on me like that?' said Susan, reaching down to pick up one of the books which had fallen to the floor. 'Where's Cameron? Is he at the front desk?' She craned her neck to see the front desk of the library which looked empty.

'He's away talking to the girls in the booking office. I think he's taken a fancy to Linda.'

'It's like working with an errant child,' said Susan. 'Here, you take over from me and I'll man the desk. Remember to date each book and mark it on the sheet.'

Marion rolled her eyes but sat down and picked up her pen.

The library was quiet, there was nothing on today until the Reading Group came in at four. Susan waved over to Roy who was crouched over the pc at his usual spot, his phone, keys and a pre-ordered copy of Neil Lancaster's latest on the desk at his side. She smiled at the two older women standing by the coffee urn, discussing animatedly the twists and turns in a Netflix show they'd both been binge-watching. There was still no sign of Cameron but he could be around somewhere helping customers again so Susan decided to give him the benefit of the doubt. She hung her cardigan over the back of the chair and sat down behind the front desk, satisfied that all was well for now in her little world of books and community.

Time for some housekeeping, she thought, as she saw the papers and lidless pens strewn over the desk which she liked to keep pristine. She was about to sweep the scrap paper into the bin when Cameron's name at the top of one sheet caught her eye. Then his address, followed by his current post. She realized it was his application form, printed out and lying on the front desk for all to see. She looked up and round the library. No one else had come in, the two women had moved to the magazine rack, and Roy was chewing his pen as he thought about what to type next. More importantly, there was no sign of Cameron or Marion, so she lifted the application form, which turned out to be three sheets of paper stapled together, and slid it across the desk with the tips of her fingers until it was in front of her. She glanced up again to make sure she wasn't being observed. Her heart racing like she was about to commit first-degree murder, she started to read Cameron's application. By the time she'd finished the first page, she was too angry to remain seated and her hair had escaped its loose band so that the curls swept across her reddened face.

She pushed the application back under the pile of papers where she'd found it and muttered to herself, 'Unbelievable, absolutely unbelievable.'

'What is?' said Marion, not waiting for a response as she spoke from behind the towering pile of children's books in her hands. 'Where do you want these?'

'I wouldn't mind so much if he was any good at his job, but all he does all day is watch stupid videos on his phone when he thinks I'm not looking, and then chat up Linda from the Town House the rest of the time. How is he worth so much more than me? Who decided that?'

The women had managed to snag their favourite table in a packed and noisy Jilts, having assembled hastily that same evening so that Susan could tell them what she'd learned from her afternoon's snooping. She sat back in despair as Carole and Lenore looked on sympathetically, urging her to drink more wine, eat some crisps. Amy's face was thunderous.

Susan sat forward again, the subject exercising her like a dog with a half-chewed bone. 'He's way less qualified than me – did I mention that? Then I find out he's on two pay grades higher than me. Meanwhile, I've got over twenty years' experience under my belt and I'm so good at my job. Sorry' – she looked up at the others apologetically – 'that sounds big-headed, but I am.'

'Don't apologize for telling the truth, Susan. Of course you're worth more than him. It's an outrage that he's earning more money than you, his superior in every way.'

Susan picked up her wine. 'Thanks, Amy. Trouble is, what can I do about it? How does someone like me, with no power, take on the bigwigs at the council, who have all the power?'

'That's the way they want you to think, don't you get it? For us to stay quiet, disappear and take our dried-up ovaries with us. Yes, Lenore, before you interrupt, I know yours are not dried-up, and the truth is, none of us are past it. Paying this Cameron more money than Susan is another symptom of the way society treats women as they get older. "Women of a certain age", ppff, what age is that, exactly? It's just women who want more, ask for more, that scares them. They think we want to ambush them, take their jobs, their freedoms, their privilege.'

'Don't we?' said Carole, thinking she for one would love some of Dennis's freedom and privilege.

'No,' said Amy. 'That's not it. We want . . . we want to make space, that's all. Space for us and our ambitions. Space to breathe away from the caring sharing nurturing Mother Earth image we're supposed to live up to. '

The women were quiet for a moment, each thinking over what Amy had said.

Carole spoke first. 'Susan, I know you said you didn't want to do any more but it seems to me this is an issue crying out for some public messaging, if you know what I mean?' She looked round at the rest of the group, Amy was already nodding.

'I don't know—' Susan began, gripping the stem of her glass, the very thought of another graffiti escapade making her hands clammy.

'So, what then?' said Amy sternly. 'You carry on doing all the work while Cameron sits back and earns twice what you do? Come on, Susan, you're better than that.'

Lenore put her hand on Amy's sleeve and said, 'Wait a minute, Amy, don't bully her. If she doesn't want to stand up for herself—'

'No, it's not . . . no, I do, I do want to stand up for myself. You're right.' She paused. 'You're all right, I know you are.' She tapped her fingers on the table and said, 'Okay, what's the plan this time?'

Amy smiled. 'It's obvious, isn't it? We graffiti the front walls of the library.'

The other three were horrified and shouted, 'No!' with one voice.

'Oy, keep it down, girls, there's dominoes being played over here,' came a voice from the other side of the bar.

'Oh, we are doing this,' said Amy, giving the man the finger at the same time. Turning back to her friends, she said, 'Why not? It's an old building, part of Hamilton's heritage, think of the stir it would cause.'

'No,' said Susan quietly. 'We can't graffiti the library.'

'But why not?' Amy insisted. 'Writing on buildings that people care about is the whole point of graffiti. People can see it and that means it affects communities, not just the owners of the property we write on. And we want the community to see it, don't we? I say the library is next.'

Susan slammed down her glass and the others jumped in surprise. 'We will not be defacing the library, Amy, and I'll tell you why. You mentioned community. The library is the hub of the community. I know people don't think of the library like that, it's just the place to go and get books but it's more than that, so much more. It's the place people can come and stay warm and see other people and yes, read books, but also drink coffee and connect and find out what's going on in their community and, here's the most important thing, it's all free. The library is the poor person's haven so we are *not* scrawling slogans on the walls of the library, and that's final.' She sat back and pressed her lips together to indicate that she would brook no argument on the matter.

'Susan's right,' said Carole. 'We can't deface the public library.'

The women were silent for a moment then Amy snapped her fingers. 'I've got it. The council offices on Almada Street. Very public, opposite the Water Palace so everyone will see it, and even better, they're the ones responsible for setting pay grades so who better to host a set of public messages about paying women what they're worth.' She turned to Susan. 'What do you think, could you agree to that?'

'It does make sense but – the council building? It's a bit out in the open, isn't it? Be hard to graffiti that without being seen.'

Amy made light of her concerns. 'Don't worry about that. We'll do it in the middle of the night, full Black Panther outfits, the works. Come on, what do you say?' She stood up and raised her glass. There was a long moment while the others thought about it then Lenore stood up and said, 'Why not, I'll do it.' Carole lifted her glass and said, 'In for a penny . . .'

Susan stood up last. 'Still getting us into trouble after all these years, Amy,' and clinked her glass against the others. 'Go on then, count me in.'

It was gone midnight by the time Susan got home and she was surprised to see the light still on in Fraser's bedroom.

That's my boy, she thought, as she hung up her jacket. *Putting in the hours at last.*

She looked up as she heard banging followed by giggling

coming from her son's room. She stood at the bottom of the stairs uncertainly and called up, 'Fraser? Everything okay?'

She heard Fraser say, 'Shit' followed by something else she couldn't make out and wondered if she should go up and check on him.

'Fraser?' she called again.

'Be down in a minute, Mum,' he said, his voice strangely high-pitched.

Susan went into the kitchen to make herself a cup of tea and drew a sharp breath when she saw the state of the place. She didn't ask much of Fraser in terms of household chores – in truth he did nothing at all to help around the house – but she did expect him to tidy up after himself if, by some miracle, he deigned to come down and make his own snacks. The surface was littered with empty crisp bags and biscuit crumbs, and the cold remains of a half-devoured slice of toast and jam. There was a greasy pan still sitting on the cooker, bits of bacon rind lying at the edge like maggots. She saw that the giant Lindt dark chocolate Easter egg she'd been saving to present him with on Easter Sunday was almost finished, the foil scrunched and discarded, the box a crumpled mess. 'What on earth's been going on?' she said aloud, as she swept all the rubbish from the counter into the pedal bin by the door. Before the rubbish reached the bin, she saw the red label of an empty quarter-bottle of vodka lying amidst the egg shells from the omelette she'd made them for dinner hours earlier.

'Hi, Mum,' said Fraser, stumbling against the door frame then righting himself, as he entered the kitchen. His cheeks were unusually flushed and Susan clicked her tongue at the dark stain across the chest of his polo shirt, marring his normally pristine appearance. 'Sorry about the mess, I got a bit hungry while I was studying. And you were out again so I had to make it myself,' he added, managing to make it all Susan's fault.

'I'm not as bothered about the mess as I am about the vodka bottle lying in the bin. Why would you drink—'

The front door slammed. Fraser started talking immediately. 'So did you have a good time tonight? Book club again, was it?'

Susan stared at him. 'Why are you shouting like that, Fraser? And I wasn't born yesterday. Did you have company here tonight? Was Fiona here again? When you were supposed to be studying?'

'No, I—'

'Don't lie to me!'

'Stop screaming like a banshee, woman, and I'll tell you.'

Susan bristled. 'Do not call me "woman", young man. I am your mother and you will show me some—'

'That's it. I've had enough, Mum,' shouted Fraser over the top of her. 'All I ever hear from you is "you need to study, Fraser", "It's your exams soon, Fraser"'. Susan was shocked at the way he was mocking her with that shrill whiny voice – she didn't sound like that, did she? 'You have no idea how hard I'm working. I need some downtime sometimes. Even you've been going out more than me recently.'

He moved closer so that he was standing over Susan now, looking down at her and breathing vodka fumes in her face. Susan blinked in disbelief that her own son – her precious, mannerly, doted-on Fraser – could act like this. But this time, she was angry too and refused to be intimidated.

'I've passed all *my* exams, Fraser,' she shouted, jabbing at her chest to make the point. 'I have *my* degree.'

'Yeah? And what good has it done you? Working all the hours God sends for peanuts, singing nursery rhymes with toddlers and providing a babysitting service for the weird and the lonely.'

Susan stepped back like she'd been wounded. 'It's . . . that's not what I do at all, I manage the library, it's important . . .'

Fraser swore softly under his breath but Susan heard it and flinched. 'We've had to struggle for money all my life, Mum. I've never had what everyone else has had, none of it. Not the Stone Islands, not the good phones, and not once, never have I had a pair of trainers I wasn't ashamed of. What's the point of me working hard to end up in the same position as you?'

Susan laid her hand flat to her chest and propped herself up against the counter.

'Look, I'm sorry,' said Fraser, not looking at her. 'I am trying hard at school, okay? I'll do fine in my exams but I need time off too. It's Friday night and I wanted to see Fiona. She came over and we had a laugh, we weren't doing anything wrong.'

Susan gestured to the vodka bottle in the bin.

'Nothing that all my pals haven't been doing since long before now anyway.' He looked behind him at the mess still on the counter. 'I'll clear that up tomorrow. I'm going to bed.'

Susan resisted the urge to say more and let Fraser head back upstairs. Ignoring the mess, she made herself some tea and sat quietly at the table. She was still sitting there hours later, and shivered as a pale pink light streamed into the kitchen. Gripping her empty teacup, it occurred to her that maybe her son was right and her inability to push for more recognition at work had done them both a disservice over the years. She got up stiffly and rinsed her cup under the tap. Amy was right about one thing – they were all worth a lot more in life than they were getting, in more than ways than one.

★

The women arranged to meet up again a couple of days later, in the middle of the night. Hamilton town centre was very quiet, and Almada Street, populated as it was mainly by offices, was like a grave. Susan had complained they didn't need to leave it quite so late but as Amy pointed out, the Almada chippy and the Indian takeaway on the opposite side of the road were both open till midnight, even on a Sunday, so they had to leave it till after that.

Susan parked her car round the corner, at the entrance to the old Bell College campus. The clock on her dashboard flashed 02.59 and she shivered as she switched off the engine and looked up and down the empty street. *Where is everyone?* she wondered, and rubbed her hands along her thighs to keep warm. Almost immediately, the headlights of Lenore's car flashed at her as she parked in front of Susan, jumping out and joining Susan in her car.

'Brrrr, nippy at this time of night, eh?'

'I'll put the heater back on.'

'You okay?' said Lenore, catching sight of Susan's ghostly pale face. Her unruly hair was being kept in check by a huge black bobble, but the scraped-back style emphasized the extreme pallor of her skin and the blueish shadows beneath her eyes. 'Your lips look sore. Looks like you need industrial strength Vaseline.'

'Thanks very much,' said Susan, touching her fingers to her dry lips, flakes of skin peeling off the bottom one. She turned to Lenore sharply. 'What are we doing here? In the middle of the night, about to commit a crime? At our age? And I'm a librarian!'

Lenore reached over and touched her friend's knee. 'Come on, it'll be fun. And even if it isn't, something has to be done. It's right what Amy says, we've been taking too much from too many quarters for too long. Ah, speak of the devil . . .'

'You're right about that,' muttered Susan but turned off her engine again and patted the back seat for her gloves, before getting out and joining Lenore on the pavement between their cars and Amy's work van.

Carole got out of the passenger seat of the van and stood beside them.

'Good evening, girls,' said Amy brightly, stamping her feet against the cold night air. 'We all ready for this?' She cast a critical eye at her motley crew and told them to jump in the back of the van.

'What?' said Susan. 'No, come on, let's get this over with.'

'Into the van please,' said Amy again, and when no one moved, she added, 'I'm assuming we want to do this without being caught, yes?'

They all bobbed their heads in agreement.

'In you go then,' said Amy, throwing open the back doors and closing them behind her after all four women were squashed into the van.

'You can't swing a cat in here, Amy,' said Lenore, the tallest of the four so having to bend over so her head didn't bang off the van roof.

Amy ignored her. 'Right. Susan, take one and pass the rest along to the others.' She handed Susan a bundle of black woollen balaclavas.

'What's this? A balaclava? Is that really necessary?' said Susan, holding one up for the others to see.

'Let me put it this way, your ginger curls are currently the only means of lighting in this van and yet we can all see perfectly. I think that speaks volumes as to why you in particular need to cover up with a balaclava.'

'Don't mind Amy,' said Carole. 'She's just jealous of your fabulous head of hair.'

'Definitely,' said Amy drily. 'And also take one of these each.' She handed out the small black face masks she used to cover her mouth when she was doing a particularly messy plumbing job.

'Amy, come on, are you kidding?' said Lenore.

'No, I'm not,' said Amy. 'I'm deadly serious. I've been doing my homework and I know there's no film in the CCTV cameras outside the council buildings. For once, the cuts have worked in our favour. But we don't know about the other side of the road. Any one of the premises there might be filming the street, so we can't take any chances.'

'You're scaring me now,' said Susan, her voice muffled behind her mask and balaclava.

'You don't need to be—' began Carole before she was interrupted by Lenore's shouts of 'Ow, what's that?'

They turned to see her holding up a large grey plunger. 'That plunger almost got stuck up my backside,' she said, holding up the instrument for the others to see.

'Wouldn't be the first time, would it?' said Amy, and the tension was eased as the others laughed so hard they would have fallen over each other if they hadn't been in such a confined space.

'Right, next,' said Amy, shushing them as she reached back into her tool bag.

'Oh Lord, what's coming next from her bag of tricks?'

'Ta-dah,' said Amy, holding up an extra-large spray can. 'I've got one of these for each of us. If we're going to do this, we're going to do it right. Never mind the old paintbrushes and the tiny canisters. Tonight, girls, we are going to give Banksy a run for his money.'

Carole studied the can she'd been handed. 'Neon Green,' she read, and looked over at Susan who was holding a can of Radiant Red.

'We're taking this to a whole new level, gang, so let's get going.'

Out on the street, Amy rested a set of stepladders on the pavement, and put her finger to her mouth to tell the girls to stop laughing and chatting while she went round the corner to check the coast was still clear.

'These leggings are killing me,' whispered Lenore to Carole as they waited.

'How do you mean?' said Carole, peering at her friend in the darkness.

'Look how tight they are. I've lost a bit of weight since that whole business with you-know-who, but maybe not as much as I thought when I ordered these size 10s.'

She turned round and bent at the waist a little so that Carole and Susan could see the black lycra stretched till it was almost translucent over her butt cheeks.

'Lenore, that's positively indecent,' said Susan. 'I can practically see your backside through those.'

'Let's hope the CCTV cameras are off then, otherwise someone's going to get an eyeful as you climb up those stepladders,' said Carole, setting the other two off again.

'Ssshhh,' hissed Amy, appearing round the corner like a ninja in her black combats, balaclava and mask over her mouth. 'Coast's clear, come on.'

The women tiptoed round the corner, tripping over and shushing each other loudly in their attempts to be quiet. They gathered at the bottom of the council steps, looking up at the huge expanse of white wall.

'Now then,' said Amy, looking all round to check the street was still empty. 'We need to be quick about this.'

Before anyone could say anything else, she reached up with her own spray can – Electric Blue – and sprayed, in the quick-drying bright blue paint:

A WOMAN NEEDS A MAN LIKE A FISH NEEDS A BICYCLE

'What on earth does that mean?' said Susan. 'What's that got to do with equal pay?'

'Nothing,' smiled Amy. 'I just fancied going old-school. Right, come on, you lot, make a name for yourselves.'

Susan placed the stepladder close to the wall, climbed to the top and scrawled in huge scarlet letters:

EQUAL PAY FOR EQUAL WORK

Breathless and hardly able to believe what she'd done when she saw the size of it, Susan giggled nervously. Carried on the cold breeze, the now-familiar turpentine smell of the paint hit her and she clutched her stomach. 'I think I'm going to be sick,' she said, stumbling back down the ladder.

'Rubbish,' said Amy. 'Brilliant work, Susan, I bet that felt good, didn't— Oh.' She turned away as Susan vomited loudly behind a bush. 'Or not. Come on, girls, hurry up,' she shouted at Carole and Lenore instead, who were both daubing the wall with slogans of their own, while Carole finished off with their signature calling card, **Graffiti Girls GG** and an emerald swirling underline for a last flourish.

'There,' she said, and stood back to admire their handiwork. In all, the whole exercise had taken them less than ten minutes.

Susan looked up from the bush and went even whiter. Most of the wall on the left-hand side of the building was now covered in a kaleidoscope of letters in blue, red and green. The bigger spray cans had proved to be much more effective in applying the paint to a larger surface area, and their previous efforts with the small spray cans and paintbrushes were minuscule in comparison with this feminist mural.

'Oh. My. God,' said Susan, stunned.

The others stood silently contemplating what they had done when Lenore said finally, 'Come on, we'd better not hang around.' She lifted up the spray can in her hand, and indicated the stepladders and their outfits. 'Short of phoning up the police to tell them we did it, we could hardly be in a more incriminating position.'

'You're right,' said Amy, snapping out of it. 'Gather up the stuff, everyone, and let's get out of here. Lenore, don't forget to pick up that empty can.'

Lenore bent to pick up the can at her feet and, as she did so, the others heard a renting sound from her leggings and Lenore felt an icy wind up her butt crack as her far-too-tight leggings ripped right up the middle seam.

Carole clutched Amy, the pair of them dissolving into fits of laughter as Lenore stood up, her hands behind her back as she desperately tried to cover the gaping hole over her backside.

'Do you mean to tell us that you weren't even wearing any underwear?' said Susan breathlessly, hiccupping and holding her hand over her mouth as she tried to smother her laughter.

'No, it gives you a line, doesn't it?' said Lenore, which made the others laugh even harder.

'Hey!'

The women froze.

'What the——!' A man dressed in the navy blue uniform of a

security guard was peering at them through the glass door of the council building.

'This is bad. This is very bad,' cried Susan as they gathered together all their stuff as fast as they could.

'This is really very bad,' repeated Susan, standing around, her hands in the air.

'Has anyone ever told you you'd be a great team leader, Susan? Really – inspirational in a crisis,' said Lenore.

'Never mind that now. Keep your masks on, girls, but *run*, come on,' shouted Amy, shoving the stepladders under her arm and scrabbling around in her pocket for the keys to the van.

They could hear the security guard behind them, shaking and shoogling the door, trying to turn the keys in the lock so that he could get out and chase them. Fortunately, having just woken up from his two-hour nap and still woozy from the extra nip of whisky in his coffee, he wasn't quite as quick as he might have been. By the time he managed to unlock both locks on each door and fling them open, the women had reached the safety of their vehicles, thrown everything they had with them into the van, and raced off in the other direction, hearts pounding as they headed for home.

The following Tuesday morning, Susan stared at herself in the mirror in the ladies' toilet at work. Her hair, even for her, was a mess – the corkscrew curls tighter and higher than usual so that she was wearing a helmet of orange bubbles. Her eyes were red-rimmed from worry and lack of sleep. Equally red and embattled were her poor lips which had been under almost constant attack from her two sharp front teeth since the Graffiti Girls had accomplished their latest mission.

She hadn't seen the other girls since Sunday night but she had visited the council buildings herself the previous afternoon to survey their handiwork and almost had a heart attack as she tried to stroll by nonchalantly. A small crowd of council workers in the same distinctive council shirts as her own had gathered in front of the building. There was a group of police officers, standing around in pairs, adding to the throng as well but it would have taken a football crowd for the graffiti to have been concealed from Susan's view. There, staring back at her in all their neon green and scarlet glory, were the phrases that had seemed so just when they were writing them large on the wall only the night before. Now, all Susan could think was how horrendous the previously pristine white building looked, and wonder at how she could have been part of such a thing.

'Look at that,' she heard one young girl say to her friend as, drawn by the crowd, they stopped to take a look.

'What does it say?' Her shorter friend stood on her tiptoes and peered through her John Lennon specs towards the building.

'Equal pay for equal – what's that last word?'

'Work,' said Susan automatically, her hand going to her mouth in panic. 'I mean, I'm guessing, that's the phrase isn't it, that's what you'd expect it to say . . .'

The girls looked at her for a moment then shrugged and walked on.

Susan stayed where she was, mesmerized by the police officers, who appeared to be searching the ground around the front of the building, gesturing to each other and making notes.

Oh God, thought Susan, *what if it was like one of those episodes of CSI where one of the officers was a young hot-shot transfer from another force, with something to prove?* He'd spot a footprint in the grass verge at the side of the path and take out some otoscope or ophthalmoscope or whatever they called that equipment, make an identical match of the footprint then go round everyone living in Hamilton and ask to see their trainers. And actually, she thought with horror, she was still wearing the same black Adidas trainers she'd had on the night before. Maybe there was a tracker dog somewhere that would sniff her out and come bounding over to where she was standing and—

'About time someone brought it up,' said a cheery-looking woman in the same sky-blue council blouse next to her.

'I'm sorry?' said Susan, biting her lip and tasting blood.

'I'm just saying, I've worked in the council since I left school and I know for a fact I'm still earning less than my wee brother and he started in refuse collection after me. That's not fair, is it? Well, *you* know . . .'

'What do you mean? Why would I know anything about it?' said Susan quickly, stubbing one toe behind the other trainer, wondering if her shoes had given her away.

The woman laughed. 'Because you work for the council as well?' She indicated Susan's own blue shirt.

'Oh yes, that's right.' She breathed out deeply with relief.

'That's all these Graffiti Girls are saying, you know. Be fair to us and we'll be fair to you. Otherwise, spray cans at the ready. I support them, don't you?'

Susan could feel her cheeks getting redder, and for once in her life was glad of the freckles that covered her entire face. 'I'm not sure, I think so but I don't know if vandalizing the building is the best way to go about it.'

'If folk won't listen when you ask them nicely, you need to do something extreme. And I don't know if you've ever tried to get the council bigwigs to listen to you but I have, and I'll tell you something – they're no more interested in paying us women the same as the men than they are in listening to our requests for flexible working so we can look after our kids, or paid leave so we can be there when they're not well, or anything else we ask them for. But when the men want time off, paid mind you, for their council snooker team tournaments, it's a different story then.' She turned back to the building and nodded approvingly. 'Good on the Graffiti Girls, I say, and I don't care who hears me say it either,' she added as two old men in bunnets and rain jackets shook their heads as they passed.

'You're probably right,' said Susan lamely. 'I'll need to get to work.' She'd marched off at high speed, turning back every so often to check whether she was being followed by Strathclyde's finest.

The day flew by as the library was busy with a steady stream of customers. They also had Bounce and Rhyme and Susan was able to forget her problems as she led the group of a dozen young mothers and their adorable, if loud, babies in rowing the boat merrily down the stream. She stopped worrying about the graffiti and thought about when Fraser was younger and she took him to every club going – from Bounce and Rhyme, to toddlers' groups and children's yoga classes in the church hall. They were always together, Fraser clinging to her side adoringly. She hadn't appreciated at the time how happy and carefree they'd been, just the two of them, and the biggest things she'd had to worry about was whether Fraser had had his five a day, and was getting enough sleep.

That evening, she got out the laundry basket to do the weekly wash. She was happy to have something to do to take her mind off everything but then, she'd never minded the household chores as much as the others seemed to. Carole was always complaining that Dennis didn't do his fair share – or maybe it was Amy complaining on Carole's behalf – and Lenore used to say the same about Tommy when they were together. Essentially, thought Susan, untangling a pair of Fraser's socks, if you didn't expect anyone else to help you with things, like she never had, you were never disappointed, were you. Men were overrated in many departments, in Susan's opinion, but in doing their share of the household chores perhaps most of all.

Fraser came into the kitchen to ask when tea would be ready.

'It's in the oven. Be about half an hour.'

Fraser propped himself against the counter, watching her. Things had been a bit tense since their row the other evening and Susan was treading gingerly lest he accuse her of overstepping boundaries again.

'Were you painting in your exercise gear?' he said, looking at the black leggings she was about to stuff into the machine.

Startled, Susan stood upright and said, 'What do you mean?'

'Your leggings – they're covered in red paint.' He pointed at the treacherous clothing in Susan's hand.

She looked down at the leggings and saw with horror that there was a long streak of red paint down the front of one leg, and several smaller splashes of the same colour along the backside.

'Oh God,' she said, stumbling against the washing machine.

Fraser laughed. 'You don't need to look so horrified, Mum. A bit of paint on your joggers isn't the end of the world, it's not as though you care what you look like when you go out. Call me when dinner's ready, okay?' he threw back over his shoulder as he left the room.

By Wednesday, Susan's lips were a mess and so was she. She was not cut out to be a felon and every time Cameron or Marion came anywhere in her vicinity she jumped like a scalded cat and apologized before they could tell her what it was they wanted.

She must have looked stressed when even Marion noticed and actually initiated the conversation. 'Something wrong?' she asked, as they sorted through the late returns together. 'You're acting like you've committed a bank heist—'

'Did someone say bank heist?' came a low voice from the other side of the counter. Susan jumped and her eyes widened as she took in the tall, official-looking police officer looming over the counter.

Instinctively, she grabbed the chain round her neck and folded her fist round the GG, kicking herself for forgetting to take the damn thing off.

'Just a joke, officer, obviously,' she stammered. 'Can we . . . is there something we can do for you?'

'Yes, I wanted to talk to you about the spate of vandalism we've seen in the area recently. You've heard about it, I take it, the graffiti on the council buildings and so on?'

Susan held one of her hands in the other to steady them, aware of Marion by her side staring at her quizzically.

She turned and addressed her. 'Maybe you could make Constable . . .?'

'Lown,' he supplied. 'PC Mark Lown, with the Community Liaison Group.'

Susan paled. 'Yes, maybe you could make PC Lown a cup of tea, Marion?'

Marion looked over at the policeman and he gave her a wide

smile and said, 'That'd be lovely, thank you, two sugars please.' She wandered through to the back without acknowledging either of them.

Susan shot an apologetic glance at PC Lown but he seemed unperturbed by the girl's surliness. 'Perhaps we could take a seat over there, Susan,' he said.

He knows my name! thought Susan, *I must be a suspect*, then remembered she was wearing her name badge on her shirt lapel. She told herself to calm down as she followed the police officer to the breakout table next to the Maps of the World.

'I'm not sure how I can help you,' she said, as soon as she sat down.

'The Community Liaison Group have produced these posters, and we would like to display as many as we can.' He unrolled the A4 sheets he was holding and Susan took a breath as she read:

Strathclyde Police
Vandalism and graffiti is destroying YOUR local area
If you know who is responsible please telephone
Crimestoppers on
0800 556 111
Help us to keep your community safe

Beneath the text, there was a picture of the building on Almada Street, the vivid green, red and blue graffiti hurting Susan's eyes. She could feel her cheeks firing up and hoped her freckles would cover it. Marion came over with PC Lown's tea and placed it soundlessly on the low table between them.

'Of course we'll put it up in the library, we have a noticeboard for public information notices.' Susan gestured over to the board filled with similar posters about council initiatives and coffee mornings to raise money for this or that charity.

'Thanks, we'd appreciate that. Obviously we'll also be putting it on Twitter and our Facebook page too but we want to get the message across as widely as possible. These women must be stopped before they deface any more of our local area.'

'Is it definitely . . . I mean do you know for sure it's women who are doing this graffiti?'

PC Lown sat back and took a sip of his tea. 'There's no doubt about it. The tone of their messages, for one thing, not to mention the fact they sign themselves off as the "Graffiti Girls". Look, see here.' He pointed to the picture in the poster where the words 'Graffiti Girls' and 'GG' could be seen quite clearly. Susan reached up and clutched her necklace.

'Mmm, yes, that does seem to indicate they *might* be women,' she said, glad that Marion hadn't bothered to bring out a cup of tea for her too as her hands were shaking so much she would have poured it all over herself.

'Okay,' said PC Lown briskly, gulping down the tea and standing up. 'I'll leave these posters with you, and if you hear of anything, or see anything at all, please feel free to contact me on this number.' He handed Susan a small card.

'I will. Of course I will,' said Susan. She stumbled against the edge of her chair as she stood up, and struggled to regain her balance as she had to keep one hand clenched round the GG at her neck.

'Careful,' said PC Lown, reaching out to steady her.

Cameron walked past and picked up the posters. 'Hmph,' he said. 'Graffiti Girls and their equal pay claims, my backside. What they forget is that men don't get time off to have babies and bring up children and ask for part-time hours so they can have it all.'

'That's certainly an opinion,' said PC Lown tactfully. 'But whatever we think of the fairness or otherwise of the system, defacing public property is not the way to go about changing things.'

Susan watched as he strode out of the library, and made up her mind not to say another word to Cameron for the rest of the day.

By the time Friday came around, Susan was a wreck and couldn't wait to meet up with Lenore and Amy for a drink after work. She started to pack up at five minutes to five and ignored Cameron's snide comments about clock-watching as she waited for the clock to strike the hour and set her free.

'I'm not cut out for this sort of thing, Amy,' she said, as she gripped her half-pint glass and downed three large mouthfuls of lager.

'Steady on, Susan,' laughed Amy. 'You don't need to drink it all in one go. Now, calm down a bit and tell us exactly what this policeman said to you.'

Susan put her glass down and wiped her top lip. 'Like I told Carole on the phone – where is Carole, by the way?'

Amy frowned. 'She's stuck in with the kids. I think Dennis thought it was his turn for a Friday night out. Just for a change. But go on, we'll fill her in later.'

Susan waited until a group of young guys in Berghaus jackets and baseball caps had passed then continued speaking fast in a low voice so that Amy and Lenore had to sit forward in their seats to hear her.

'It was Wednesday morning and I was sorting through the late returns with Marion. I mean, I was doing the majority of the work, Marion was hanging around saying nothing as usual, more of a hindrance than a help if I'm honest but— Sorry, yes, so there we were behind the counter half-hidden by the books when a huge face was looming over at us asking who had committed a bank robbery and—'

'Wait, what?' said Lenore. 'Who said anything about robbing banks, am I missing something?'

Susan waved her hand. 'No, the bank robbery's not important—'

'Sounds a helluva lot more important than spraying the truth on the council wall,' said Amy, opening her scampi fries and offering them around.

'Do you want me to tell you what happened or not?' said Susan tetchily.

'Please,' said Amy, gesturing that she should carry on.

'Right, well, turns out this policeman is from the Community team or some such thing and he's here to talk about the graffiti! Honestly, I don't know how I kept myself together.'

'Just as well you're always so calm in a crisis,' said Lenore, raising her eyebrows at Amy, who raised her glass in return. 'What was the name of this harbinger of doom?'

'PC Lown, I think, or Loan, something like that.'

Lenore stopped. 'PC Mark Lown? That's the same policeman that saved me. Was he tall?'

Susan shrugged.

Lenore persisted. 'Handsome? With lovely green eyes and—'

'I don't know, Lenore, I wasn't looking at him that closely. I was more interested in what he had to show me. He brought all these posters for us to put up in the library, look' – she reached into her bag – 'I sneaked one home so I could show you.' She passed the poster to Lenore.

Lenore read it and gave a low whistle before passing it to Amy. 'Looks like things are getting serious.'

Amy barely glanced at the poster before returning it to Susan, who stuffed it back into her bag. 'Come on, you must've seen a hundred of these posters online and stuck on to bus stops. Am I right?'

'Well, yeah . . .'

'And have you ever, I mean ever once, thought about calling the number to report something?'

Susan and Lenore thought about it then both agreed they would never take down the number and call it.

'Exactly, and nor will any other self-respecting member of the local community. What you guys seem to be forgetting is that people are on our side. The women of Scotland have been quiet too long, and not just South Lanarkshire by the way. Check this out.' Amy picked up her phone and scrolled for a bit before handing it to Susan. Lenore stretched and looked over Susan's shoulder.

'What are we looking at?' said Susan blankly.

'That's the local news site for Cambuslang, and if you scroll down a bit, you'll see Glasgow East. No doubt there's more examples but in both those places there's been a graffiti incident in the last two weeks. One of them, I think it was the Glasgow one, even scrawled beside it "Supporters of the Graffiti Girls". We've started something here, whether you like it or not. We've ignited the touch paper so of course there are going to be flames.

But don't worry, Susan, we won't let you get burned, everything will be fine, I promise.'

'Oh no, Amy, there you go again trying to draw me back into it. I'm telling you, I'm done with this, my blood pressure can't take it.' Susan sat back, trying to flatten her impossible hair with her palm, and rubbing her Vaselined lips together.

'We'll see,' said Amy, and stopped Susan as she was about to speak again. 'No, come on, it's Friday night in Jilts, let's change the subject. Who's got plans for the weekend?'

'This is it for me, after the week I've had,' said Susan. 'Then home for a very hot bubble bath and maybe even a wee glass of wine before I cook Fraser his tea.'

'How is Fraser anyway? I don't believe you've checked your phone more than six times tonight to check in on him.'

Susan told them about their argument the week before. 'He's right, you know, I need to try and let go a bit. And part of me is actually quite glad. I mean I'm out tonight and like you say, Lenore, I'm not really worried about him, I know he's with his girlfriend, playing Monopoly.'

Lenore and Amy exchanged a glance, a smile playing on Amy's lips.

'Monopoly?' she said, eyebrow arched.

'Yes, that's what he told me. They were playing Monopoly and she'd be gone by the time I get back. Not that I'd mind her staying for dinner, she doesn't eat anyway, part of her preparations for being a model, I suppose.'

Amy snorted. 'Preparations!'

'No, she's doing very well, apparently. It's not as easy as you think to be a model, you know,' said Susan, repeating what Fraser had told her.

'I'm sure,' said Amy. 'The ability to put one foot in front of the other whilst grimacing is vastly underrated.'

Susan tutted but she wasn't offended. In this case, Amy's opinion more or less mirrored her own. 'What about you, Lenore? Anything exciting planned?'

'The most exciting thing on my horizon this weekend is the Easter Sunday cross-country meet Carole invited us to. You haven't forgotten, I hope? Thomas is running the 5k, I think he's quite good.'

'Crap, I'd forgotten all about that,' said Amy.

'Love the way you're pretending to have so many more exciting things to do on Easter Sunday.'

Amy laughed. 'You're right. Okay, one more drink then I'm heading. My round, I believe?'

'Just a Diet Coke for me then,' said Lenore. 'I'm designated driver, remember.'

'Yeah, thanks for offering to take us home,' said Susan. 'Not like you not to have a wee wine on a Friday night.'

'It's amazing, isn't it? Turns out when you stop following a diet sheet like it's your religion, you don't need to save up all your alcohol units for a Friday night and drink till you drop. I can have whatever I want now, whenever I want it, like a normal person. And the weight's falling off me. Not that I'm that bothered about that any more,' she added, keen to avoid one of Amy's lectures on women being valued for what they do, not what they look like.

'Glad to hear it,' said Amy. 'Hurts to say it but maybe we can thank Master Bates in part for that, eh?'

'Ppff.' Lenore waved her hand. 'Haven't given him a thought for weeks. He got what was coming to him, thanks to the Graffiti Girls.'

Amy stood up and gave Susan's shoulder a quick pat as she went to the bar. 'Let's hope Susan eventually feels the same way.'

Easter Sunday dawned crisp and bright, perfect cross-country running weather. Susan was up early, putting the finishing touches to Fraser's annual Easter egg display on the kitchen table. When he was younger, she used to intersperse the chocolate eggs and bunnies with toys she'd bought from B&M or Poundstretchers – foam hammers, miniature figures from whichever show he was interested in that year, fluffy rabbits and, of course, books. Reluctantly, she no longer bought the toys – though she was tempted every year by the soft plushy animals – but she still made a beautiful display of different-sized eggs, mostly the sickly white chocolate Fraser had always been so fond of, as well as two or three books. Even those were becoming increasingly difficult to choose, in fact, she couldn't remember the last time she'd seen him with his nose in a book, but that was one tradition she couldn't let go of.

She checked her watch – almost eleven and he still wasn't up. Changed days from when he'd come in and bounce on her bed to wake her up before it was even light, so desperate was he to get downstairs and see what the Easter bunny had left for him. Susan sighed then decided she'd have to go if she was to make the rendezvous with the girls. She laid out a couple of hard-boiled eggs on a small blue plate with 'Happy Easter' emblazoned in yellow round the rim, and put the carton of orange juice, a small tumbler and his two daily vitamins by its side. 'There,' she said, feeling proud of herself for not going upstairs to wake him and present him with breakfast in bed. No one could say she wasn't letting go of the reins.

★

'Hey, Susan, over here,' shouted Lenore, waving as Susan parked her car in the field allocated for the purpose. Hamilton rugby club, which was hosting the day's event, was packed, lots of fit-looking girls and boys in their track gear warming up by the side of the pitch, as well as families dotted round, with the athletes' little brothers and sisters clutching their Easter bonnets for the parade later. The club had gone all-out as it usually did for its Easter all-sports event – there was a large, brightly coloured bouncy castle on the back field, which was already queued back to the clubhouse with impatient five-year-olds in their socks, there were tents offering everything from home baking and balloons to candles and cupcakes, as well as a hot dog and burgers stall, two different stands offering face painting and fake tattoos, and a photo booth. Surely Fraser would have loved this, thought Susan, annoyed at herself for not trying harder to make him come with her.

'How's it going, girls? I can't believe you made it before me, Amy, now I know I'm late.' She took the can of lemonade Carole held out to her.

'Excuse me,' said Amy. 'I don't know where this idea that I'm always late for everything stems from.'

'Well you're definitely not late, Susan,' said Carole. 'Thomas is in the third race and they haven't even started the first one yet.'

'I didn't know Thomas was so sporty,' said Susan. 'Where is he, warming up somewhere?'

'He's not really sporty,' admitted Carole. 'Not like Daniel anyway, he's never away from this place, even after he was injured when he was fifteen and ended up with a Meccano set on his knee for weeks. And if it's not rugby, it's football. He even took up boxing for a bit – after he saw a Conor McGregor

171

fight from Las Vegas and decided he wanted a bit of that female adoration.'

'Ppff, typical male,' said Amy.

'Watch what you're saying about my first-born son if you don't mind.' Carole turned to Susan. 'Did Fraser not fancy it then?'

'He would have loved to come but he's studying. He was knee-deep in his Chemistry notes when I left,' Susan lied.

There was a sudden rumpus at the side of the pitch. The women turned to see what the trouble was and saw Thomas and another boy in the centre of a group of four bigger boys, who were laughing and pointing at the pair in the middle.

'It's cross-country running, not cross-dressing,' shouted the boy closest to the women. His hair was shorn to his scalp, there was a faint moustache lining his upper lip, and he was dressed from head to toe in black Nike.

'And it's a men-only race, no fairies need apply,' shouted the boy next to him, shorter but built like a fire engine. The pair high-fived, as the other two boys in their circle laughed and jeered at the two hapless boys caught between them.

Carole put down her can of Coke and marched over to the scene, at the same time as a tall broad man stepped out of the crowd to join her.

'What exactly's going on here?' shouted Carole, reaching in to the circle and plucking out Thomas. Susan gaped when she got a good view of Carole's second son. Dressed in a pale green tracksuit and orange trainers with a red Nike swoosh, his hair was worn to his shoulders, and he looked to be wearing red lipstick – but surely not, thought Susan as she exchanged glances with Lenore and Amy.

'Boys, this is an Easter Sunday event for families and children. If you can't be civil to each other, please go home,' said the tall stranger, who Lenore and Susan both recognized as PC Mark Lown.

Susan's hand automatically reached to her chest to check her GG necklace was safely hidden inside her buttoned-up cardigan. She saw with horror that Carole's own necklace was swinging somewhere close to Thomas's face as she bent down to check he was okay, and hoped she was imagining the lingering look she saw Mark give to Carole's jewellery before she stood up and it fell back into the V of her top.

The boys were either intimidated by the adults' presence or decided it wasn't worth the hassle if parents were involved, and the stubble-headed ring leader inclined his head in the direction of the refreshments tent. As he and his gang started to leave, Mark grabbed him by his elbow and said, close to his face, 'You've been warned' before he let the boy go.

'Are you two okay?' He turned his attention to the two children left standing beside Carole.

'They're fine, thanks for helping though,' said Carole, putting her arm round Thomas and bringing him back to where the girls were standing. The other child trailed behind them.

'Sorry about that,' said Carole, forcing a smile. 'Boys will be boys.'

Thomas pulled away from under Carole's arm angrily. 'Me and Jaxx could've handled that ourselves, Mum, you've made things worse.'

'Jack? Is this . . .' Carole turned to Thomas's friend, who was even smaller than Thomas. He looked up at the women from under his long blond fringe, a gold earring dangling between his perfect ringlet curls. His own sports outfit was a tie-dye purplish top, cut deep under his arms, revealing his puny chest, and a pair of long, white Dolce and Gabbana shorts. Susan felt sure he was wearing eyeliner but thought she must be mistaken about that.

'Hello,' he said. 'I'm Jaxx, Tim-Tom's friend.'

'Tim—' began Carole before the loudspeaker broke into their conversation, announcing the first race.

'Come on,' said Thomas to Jaxx. 'Let's go and get warmed up for our race.'

The women watched as the pair sloped off down to the bottom pitch, Jaxx slipping on the loose, wet turf, and Thomas putting an arm round his skinny waist to help him up.

Carole stared after them, and the women were quiet for a few moments, Susan staring into her lemonade like it might provide her with a decent topic of conversation to break the awkward silence.

Finally, Lenore said, 'That was the same guy who helped me out with Dave Bates. He's the policeman who came to question Susan as well.'

'Don't say "question me", Lenore, that makes me sound like a suspect.'

'You know what I mean. He is handsome though, don't you think?'

Amy sniffed. 'If you like that sort of thing.'

'What do you mean – that sort of thing?'

'You know, beefcake. Brawn. Probably not much else.'

'He seemed nice,' said Carole vaguely before standing up a little straighter and adding, 'Right, come on, it's Easter Sunday and we're here to have a good time. And I need to find Archie and Glover, I haven't seen them since they ran off to queue for a hot dog. Let's mingle, girls,' and she marched off in the direction of the hot dog stand.

'I thought you did very well, Thomas,' said Lenore in the overly bright teacher's voice she reserved for pupils who were trying hard but couldn't quite cut the mustard.

'Thanks,' said Thomas shyly, pulling on his fringe and looking at the ground. 'Wasn't last anyway.'

'No, that was me,' piped up Jaxx beside him, seemingly unperturbed by his poor showing in the 5k, or by the incident with the older boys earlier.

Carole observed him with something bordering on distaste. 'You might have done better if you'd been less concerned with stopping every so often to pin back your hair, Jack.'

Thomas glared at her. 'It's Jaxx, Mum, I told you. Their name is Jaxx.'

'Sorry, I mean Jaxx.'

'Come on, let's get a burger before they're all gone,' said Thomas to Jaxx and the two boys headed off to the clubhouse.

'Not too long, Thomas, we're going home soon,' Carole shouted after them.

When they were out of hearing range she turned to the others and said, 'Is it just me? Jaxx? And that outfit? No wonder he and Thomas are getting bullied if he, sorry *they*, insist on dressing like a drag queen.'

'You can't say that kind of thing,' said Lenore. 'We get all sorts in our school, it's right that everyone is allowed to be themselves.'

'We'd never have got out alive if we'd dressed like that when we were at school.'

'Exactly. And that's not a good thing is it? Certainly not what we want for our children.'

'You're getting upset over nothing, Carole. It'll be a phase, you'll see,' added Susan.

'Easy for you to say. What if it was Fraser?'

Susan laughed. 'My Fraser would never—'

'Of course he wouldn't,' interrupted Amy in a tone dripping with sarcasm. 'We all know Fraser is a paragon of virtue.'

'I'm not sure I like your tone,' said Susan.

'Girls, girls,' put in Lenore. 'Come on, enjoy your hot dogs and let's not fall out among ourselves. Honour among hot – and the emphasis is on the word "hot" – felons, don't you think?'

'Ssshhh,' said Amy. 'We've got company.'

'Hello there, I thought it was you.'

Lenore turned to find the handsome policeman at her shoulder.

'Mark Lown? We met a few weeks back, outside the gym?' he said, smiling.

Taken by surprise, Lenore managed to drop her half-eaten hot dog, complete with extra ketchup, down her favourite cashmere sweater. A stain like a big red apple spread between her breasts.

'What a shame, you were enjoying that,' said Mark, his smile growing wider, then, seeing Lenore's face fall, 'That's a good thing, I like to see a woman who actually eats.'

'Lenore's your gal then,' said Amy, winking. 'Come on, girls, let's go and get Lenore another hot dog. Don't do anything we wouldn't do.'

Lenore said nothing as her friends rather obviously left her alone with Mark, but thought of plenty she'd have to say to them later.

'Sorry, perhaps I shouldn't have mentioned that in front of your friends? The night at the gym, I mean?'

'What? No, don't worry about that. Thanks again for coming to my rescue that night.'

'Don't mention it. Like I said, I don't know exactly what was happening but if you ever wanted to press charges . . .'

'Oh no, it was something and nothing, I've forgotten all about it now.'

Mark was quiet for a moment then said, 'You know, he had his gym graffitied shortly after that.'

Lenore's mouth fell open but she reached her hand up and twirled her hair, saying nothing.

'Yeah, weird really because the messages were all about the gym owner not respecting women, #MeToo, that sort of thing. Did you . . . hear anything about it?'

'I . . . I mean, I think I read something in the *Hamilton Advertiser*, something about his place being vandalized? Was it graffiti then? Oh well' – she forced a laugh – 'couldn't have happened to a nicer person, from what I hear.'

Mark didn't reply. He took a handkerchief from his pocket and offered it to her to clean up the ketchup stain. As she dabbed at her top, she wondered why he was staring so hard at her chest. *Not another weirdo surely*, she thought, then he said, 'That's a lovely necklace. Same as your friend was wearing today, and I think the librarian too?'

Lenore grabbed at her necklace and said, 'What, this? Oh yes, it's . . . it's Gucci, I believe. We all love Gucci – who doesn't love a bit of luxury – and yeah, we're still childish that way, all wearing the same thing . . .' Aware she was waffling, she couldn't seem to stop talking until she realized Mark was no longer listening to her but was staring past her instead, with a different expression on his face.

An extremely thin and beautiful woman was approaching them, exuding the body confidence of Naomi Campbell, as she clutched the hand of an equally attractive little boy, all bed head and mud streaking his cherubic cheeks in exactly the right places.

'We're going home now, Mark,' said the woman, glancing at Lenore momentarily but long enough to take in the ketchup stain, her dirty trainers, and Sunday afternoon, unmade-up face.

'Well done, Finn, you did great in the egg and spoon, son,' said Mark, ruffling the boy's already adorably ruffled hair.

The woman shot him a look, saying, 'I'm surprised you saw him, you seemed more interested in breaking up that scuffle with the hooligan element. Never off duty, eh, Mark?'

Lenore thought she saw a shadow flit across Mark's face but he was smiling again as he turned to her and said, 'This is my son, Finn. Say hi, Finn.'

The boy looked up at Lenore from under his lashes and tugged his mum's hand to go home.

'Tuesday evening, 5.30 p.m. Don't be late or he won't be there.'

'I'm never late—' Mark began to protest but the woman had already turned her back and proceeded to pick her way in her unsuitably wedged boots across the wet mud.

'Bye, Finn, see you Tuesday,' Mark called after them.

Lenore dug her toe awkwardly into the grass at her feet.

'Sorry, that was my wife, Annelise. Soon to be ex for reasons that were no doubt obvious.'

'I'm not sure you were entirely telling the truth when you

said you liked to see women eat,' ventured Lenore, recalling Annelise's stick-thin figure that suggested she had never eaten a hot dog in her life.

'I meant every word of it,' said Mark. 'I also said we were in the process of divorcing.'

'Here you go, be more careful with this one.' Her friends were back, with another hot dog for Lenore and one for Mark too.

'Thank you,' said Mark to Susan. 'And mustard too, lovely,' he said, cheersing the group with his hot dog.

'Have you . . . have you heard any more from the incident at the council? You know, the graffiti thing?' said Susan, ignoring Amy's laser-eyed stare.

'Nothing concrete as yet. Enquiries are ongoing,' said Mark, with a small smile. 'I think we are making some progress though.'

Susan's hand fluttered round her face as she nodded enthusiastically and said, 'Mmhhmm, mmhhmm.'

'Right, you still wanting a lift home, Lenore?' Amy cut the conversation dead. 'I'm heading off now.'

'Uh, yes, yes, thanks,' said Lenore, looking round for somewhere to dump her second half-eaten hot dog of the day. 'Thanks again for, you know, coming along that night when you did . . .' she said to Mark.

He waved away her thanks. 'Not at all. Nice to see you again.' He was aware of the other women gathered round, listening to every word, but ploughed on bravely. 'Maybe we'll see each other around, or I could give you my phone number if you . . .' He tailed off, waving his own half-eaten hot dog as he spoke.

'Yes, that'd be . . . I'd like that,' muttered Lenore, not looking at her friends as she swapped Mark's hot dog for her phone so that he could add his number to her contacts.

Mark seemed about to say more when Amy butted in to bring the conversation to an abrupt end. 'Come on, Lenore, I've got a burst radiator at half past four. Easter Sunday too – the things I'll do to get this business off the ground.'

'I need to get going as well,' said Carole, pulling her scarf up round her neck. 'Better gather up the gang. Haven't seen sight nor sound of Archie or Glover since they were trounced at the egg and spoon by that boy with the obnoxious mother. Thanks for coming, girls.' She waved as she walked off ahead of Amy and Lenore, leaving just Susan and Mark.

Susan waved them goodbye but was startled to see Mark watching her closely when she turned back round, the look on his face inscrutable. He seemed to be waiting for her to speak so she said the first thing that came into her head.

'You know, a lot of people are saying the Graffiti Girls – I think that's what they call themselves – are brilliant.'

'Oh?'

'Yes, I mean, I'm only repeating what I've heard, obviously, but I think plenty of people, women especially, are glad someone's speaking up on their behalf.'

'Depends on your point of view, I suppose. Graffiti's a crime, for one thing, but apart from that, cleaning up council property, anyone's property for that matter, costs a lot of money, but in the case of the council, that cost gets passed on to local residents. Or else the services will be cut and the ones that'll suffer the most are the ones who use them the most, like women and children, old folk too, I suppose.'

Susan faltered. 'I hadn't . . . I never thought of it like that. You might be right. But then again, why should women like me get paid less than men for doing the same job, just because we took some time out to have children?'

'Yeah, that's not fair, but you're okay now, your son's – how old did you say?'

'Sixteen.'

'Right, so you could apply for a more senior role now if you wanted to? Earn more money that way?'

'I suppose . . .' Susan realized she had never considered herself as material for promotion. The job that Cameron was applying for had come up before but it was several pay grades above her own and she'd never considered herself worthy but now, she thought, why the hell not? She was far more experienced than Cameron, and Mark was right, her son did need her less these days so she could concentrate on her own career, there was nothing stopping her.

'I'll need to get going myself,' said Mark, looking at his watch. 'Nice to see you.'

'Yes, and you,' said Susan, watching him with interest as he strode across the field, past the deflated bouncy castle and through the remnants of the home-baking stand. He stopped on the way to pick up discarded cupcakes and bits of greaseproof paper from the tablet, and put them in the bin.

By the time Susan had stopped off at Lidl on the way home, the house was already in darkness, the only sounds coming from upstairs the thumping and whining Fraser called music, and every so often, the high-pitched laughter of his girlfriend, Fiona.

Susan stood at the bottom of the stairs, calling up, 'Fraser, I'm home.'

The music stopped suddenly and Fraser's head appeared at his bedroom door. Both Susan and Fraser spoke at the same time.

'I wondered if—'

'Don't worry, Fiona's just leaving—'

'No, Fraser, wait. I wondered if Fiona might like to stay and have dinner with us. That's . . . if she's not got other plans?'

Fraser's eyes widened. 'Are you sure? It's Easter Sunday, I know you like it to be just us usually.'

'It's always just us, Fraser,' said Susan. 'It might be good to have some company for a change. And there's loads of roast beef, it's been in the slow cooker all day. Fiona can stick to the vegetables if she wants, models don't eat carbs, do they?' She turned back to the kitchen then stopped and added, 'And I was hoping maybe you could give me some advice later about putting together a new CV. My talents have been unrecognized at the library for too long – it's about time I applied for promotion.'

IV

Carole

CAROLE AND DENNIS SAT ON the hard seats outside the head teacher's office, Dennis shuffling and complaining about being treated like a kid himself. Carole ignored him. She'd barely spoken to him all weekend and she was still furious with him about Friday night.

Dennis had agreed to look after the kids for a change and she'd been out with some of the PTA mums till after eleven. When she got home, she was surprised not to see him lounging in his usual spot on the sofa in front of the television, a beer in his hand. She checked through in the front room too but there was no sign of him. She wondered if all the hours he'd been putting in at work lately were finally catching up with him and he'd gone to bed early.

Both the younger boys were sleeping, Glover still with a cartoon book called *The World of Reptiles* clutched to his chest. She peeled it from his fingers and pulled his pyjama top down over his tummy before she covered him properly with his duvet. 'Night night, sweetheart,' she whispered, before reaching over to kiss Archie who, even in sleep, seemed to be frowning and ill at ease with the world. If only she could keep them safe and happy at home for ever, she thought, not for the first time, as she took a last look at them both snoring softly, snug in their twin beds.

To her surprise, Daniel too was sleeping, sprawled on top of his bed in his T-shirt and boxer shorts, the lights from his pc still twinkling in the background. Carole stepped over his discarded trainers and yesterday's T-shirt and socks, and went over to close his curtains. Her oldest boy seemed to be able to sleep anywhere, anytime, regardless of the light coming from his pc, or the natural light that would flood into his room in the early hours of the following morning if she didn't keep closing his curtains for him. She kissed him lightly on his forehead, something he'd never let her do if he was awake, and whispered goodnight.

A faint light was coming from under Thomas's door. She tapped it softly before she went in, saying 'knock knock' as she did so.

As with his brother's bedroom, there was a lot going on in Thomas's room, but in a completely different way. Although the floor and surfaces were not littered with junk and dirty clothes the way they were in Daniel's bedroom, Thomas's room felt almost claustrophobic to Carole. The walls were covered in pictures cut from magazines, and there didn't seem to be any order to them. The ragged pictures of handsome teen pop idols – none of whose names she knew, so perhaps she was old after all – featured alongside primary-coloured shop-bought prints of guitars and skateboards, anime characters and the stars of what she assumed were his favourite TV shows – she'd long since stopped trying to keep up with what they were. There was barely a scrap of the original pale blue wall to be seen, just the odd patch visible through the yellowing sellotape. The effect was quite mesmerizing and Carole stood for a few seconds looking at it before she switched her attention to the bed.

Thomas was lying on top of his rumpled duvet, still in the soft green tracksuit bottoms and tie-dye pink and red swirled T-shirt he'd taken to wearing recently, despite the constant ribbing from his older brother and Dennis.

'Still awake, sweetheart?' said Carole, from the door.

Thomas didn't look up from his phone, but pointed to it instead to indicate he was talking to someone. Carole hesitated, she knew they all chatted on Snapchat and their various WhatsApp groups these days but she really didn't like the idea of Thomas chatting to who knows who in the middle of the night. It seemed intrusive somehow.

She walked over to his bed, and he looked up at her, annoyed. 'I'm on the phone,' he mouthed at her.

Undeterred, Carole sat on the edge of his bed. 'Who are you talking to?'

Thomas gave a dramatic sigh of the type they all seemed to learn in their teens. 'Just snapping Jaxx.'

Carole's lips thinned. She hadn't voiced her concerns about his friendship with Jaxx since the event last Sunday but now didn't seem the time to broach the subject. 'Okay, sweetheart, not too much longer then and put your phone down.' She smiled at him and reached across to ruffle his hair, which he'd grown long enough recently that it was becoming a bone of contention between her and Dennis, who did not appreciate his second son being mistaken for a girl. Something sparkly caught her eye and she saw a tiny silver sleeper in Thomas's left ear lobe.

'Thomas,' she said. 'When did you get that done? Why?'

Thomas scuttled under the yellow duvet, cupping his earlobe

with his palm so she couldn't see it. 'It's my choice, Mum, I can do what I like with my own body.'

'Calm down, Thomas, I know it is but . . . why would you want to wear an earring?'

'Why not?' he said huffily from under the cover. 'I'm talking to Jaxx now,' came his muffled voice.

Carole sighed and got up off the bed. 'Okay. We'll . . . talk about it in the morning. Night night. Love you,' she called from the door but Thomas didn't answer as he stayed hidden from sight under the duvet.

Carole wondered what Dennis would have to say about the earring. He couldn't say much, she reasoned, since he himself had worn a similar earring in both ears when he was with the band, and maintained the girls went wild for the look. Maybe there was a girl Thomas wanted to impress too, she thought, as she padded towards her own bedroom.

The bed was empty. Carole snapped the light on to double-check but there was no doubt about it – Dennis had gone out and left the children on their own at this time of night. He'd promised Carole she could have this one Friday night to go out herself so she hadn't even left Daniel in charge, which meant no one had been looking after the wee ones.

She was furious as she marched back downstairs to make herself a cup of tea and wait for Dennis to come home. As the kettle boiled, a treacherous voice whispered in her ear that nobody worked this late on a Friday night, however busy and important they were. Carole sipped her tea and wondered where her husband was and, more importantly, with whom.

★

Now they were having to attend this meeting at the school and the air between them still reeked of resentment.

'This place looks exactly the same as it did when we were here,' Dennis said, not caring or perhaps not noticing that Carole wasn't speaking.

It was true. The walls were still the same institutional grey and blue, and the mingled aromas of bleach, fried food and sweaty teenagers hadn't changed in over twenty years. Carole looked over at the children smiling back at her from the Achievements Wall, clutching their dance trophies and certificates for swimming 100 metres back crawl. Neither Thomas nor Daniel had their pictures on the wall, and the way things were going, both looked unlikely to achieve such heights – though there was every likelihood they'd see Daniel gurning at them from a mugshot at some point in the very near future. She was about to break her silence and say as much to Dennis when the office door opened and the school secretary popped her head round, and thanked them for their patience. 'Mr McLoughlin won't be long,' she said, without smiling.

'How can Lenore bear to work here?' said Carole, fanning her hot face with the thin blue scarf she'd twirled round her neck before they left, hoping it projected 'woman to be reckoned with'. 'Must be like never having left.'

'Aha, you're speaking at last. I knew you couldn't keep it up.' Dennis stretched out his legs and put his hands behind his head to show what he thought about being kept waiting outside the head teacher's office.

Carole tutted, but she was glad Dennis had agreed to come to the meeting with her. His sharp suit and general air of entitlement would give her the confidence she needed to stand up to the head teacher. She gave a start as she realized this, wondering when she'd become the sort of woman who needed her husband to back her up.

'No need to look so nervous, Carole. Relax, we're not on trial here, and for that matter, nor is Dan.'

Carole swung round. 'He's not on trial, Dennis, because he's already been charged and found guilty. What on earth was he thinking – beating up boys who are supposed to be his friends? One of them ended up with a fractured wrist apparently.'

'He's testing boundaries, that's all. Every teenage boy does it.'

'Where does he get it from, I wonder?'

It was Dennis's turn to swing round and face his wife. 'I hope you're not suggesting—'

The door opened again, and the secretary said the head would see them now.

'About time,' muttered Dennis, otherwise managing to hold his temper in check after Carole's warning glare.

Strong sunlight was streaming in the high window on the back wall behind Mr McLoughlin's desk, blinding Carole and Dennis, and putting them at an immediate disadvantage as they screwed up their eyes and looked around for a seat. But at least the sun wasn't discriminating – its rays were also catching the bald pate of the head teacher and making it shine and glisten, so it wasn't doing him any favours either.

Mr McLoughlin was typing behind his pc when they walked in, and he carried on doing so for a good minute while they stood there, awkwardly blinking in the full glare of the sunlight. Dennis coughed loudly twice and finally, Mr McLoughlin said, 'And save' and banged the save key of his pc with a flourish, before looking up.

Carole gave him her widest smile, her teeth flashing and the corners of her eyes crinkling, and smiled inwardly when she saw it hadn't lost its effect. Mr McLoughlin did a double-take as he took in Carole's beauty, incongruous amongst the battered office furniture and grimy walls of his office. He had to stop the smile from spreading across his own features by reminding himself of the reason this vision of blonde loveliness was in his office. He transferred his gaze to Dennis, and found it much easier to project the disdain he felt was appropriate to the situation.

'Please, sit.'

Carole, followed by a reluctant Dennis, took her seat in one of the low chairs opposite the desk. Mr McLoughlin was now looking down at them and he took this as his cue to begin listing the various misdemeanours chalked up next to their oldest son.

Dennis listened till the end then said, 'Daniel's a good boy, he loses his temper sometimes, that's all.'

'With all due respect—' began Mr McLoughlin, which Carole and Dennis both knew was more likely to be a sign of no respect at all, something which Carole also knew Dennis was not likely to take lying down.

'With *all* due respect, Mr McLoughlin,' said Dennis, in a voice dripping with insincerity, 'we've taken time out of our busy day to come here and listen to what you've had to say. I think we can agree to differ on interpretation but we do appreciate your time.'

Knowing when he was beaten, Mr McLoughlin put his hands up and rose from his desk to indicate the interview was over. Carole and Dennis struggled out of the low seats, Dennis giving his chair a swift backwards kick after he got on his feet. Mr McLoughlin frowned but recovered himself quickly.

'Boyoyoyo,' he laughed insincerely. 'So good to have had this talk, Mr Dungreavie, Carole.'

The use of her husband's surname and her own first name was not lost on Carole.

'I hope there won't be any further need to call you into the office. As you say, everyone is busy.'

Mr McLoughlin held his hand out to Dennis, which he took, after some hesitation. Carole held her hand out too but Mr McLoughlin didn't respond. Maybe he hadn't noticed as he was already halfway round his desk, opening the door of his office to usher them out. Since Dennis told her later that shaking the head teacher's hand had been like grasping at a wet fish, perhaps she wasn't missing anything.

Dennis didn't speak till they reached the school's main gates then he turned and said to Carole through tight lips, 'That laugh! Takes me back twenty-five years, and he's still an eejit. Don't ask me to come up to this school again.'

'What? Don't act like it's my fault we got a ticking-off from the head. It's Dan that's in trouble and he's *our* son, not just mine, *ours.*'

'Right, but you're his mother, you can do the school stuff, I should be at work.'

'I've got things to do too, you know. And I had to arrange for after-school care for Archie and Glover in case we're back late.'

'What do you want – a medal for doing your job?'

'What do you mean, "my job"? It's—' Carole stopped talking for a moment or so as a group of three curious schoolgirls eyed them from under their fringes, wondering what two adults were doing slinging insults at each other at the school gate. The tallest one in the middle put her hand to her mouth to stifle a giggle as Dennis glared at them until they turned away and carried on walking down the road.

'Look,' said Carole, changing tack. 'We've hardly seen each other for weeks, you're always working—'

'Yes, working, exactly. Earning money for the family so you don't have to.'

'I've never said I don't want to work, Dennis, if you would help out with the childcare a bit, but that's not the point. I was going to say why don't we make the most of this hour or so together and go and get a coffee at Zaccardelli's? When's the last time we did that?'

Dennis wavered, looking up the road at the cars streaming past on their way to the big Morrisons next to the school. Carole swung her hair and treated Dennis to one of her dimpled smiles. He gave way almost immediately. 'Okay then, but I need to go back to work straight after. I've a presentation first thing tomorrow morning that I need to make some headway on, and I'm drowning in admin crap, as usual.'

Carole hid her irritation at the manager speak. She could hardly remember the time before Dennis had talked like that – about the projects that were 'holed under the water', issues restricting the 'glide path' of whatever he was working on that month, cutting through the foliage to reach the 'root issues'. Maybe they all spoke like that in his office but she wished he wouldn't. Now wasn't the time to point it out though, she wanted so much for them to have one nice afternoon together with no kids.

They walked down the hill towards the Palace gardens, then cut up by the new flats on Aitken Road. The sun was high in the sky now, and there was an expectation of summer in the air.

This was a walk Carole and Dennis had done many times when they were at school. Often, Dennis would miss a class so his time off would coincide with Carole's free periods and they'd walk arm-in-arm along these pavements, practically skipping they were so happy to be in each other's company. That's what Amy forgot sometimes when she complained about Dennis and wondered why Carole was still with him. They had so much history together, quite apart from the children and the house and all the practical stuff that bound them together.

They weren't wrapped round each other any more but they were still walking close enough together that she was able to reach across and hold his hand. He looked down at her in surprise but didn't pull away. They walked in silence for a bit and she sneaked sideways looks at him every so often as they walked. Unlike many of their contemporaries, Dennis hadn't yet run to fat and his light blue shirt clung to his still-flat stomach appealingly. He wore his dark hair shorter round the sides now but still long and wavy on top, contrasting with the sharp, high cheekbones of his face, and emphasizing the unusual hazel-green of his eyes. In many ways, thought Carole, he hadn't changed from the boy she'd watched at the school Christmas show when she was a teenager.

Of course Dennis had been in a band, he'd been far too cool not to be. When they'd first met, Dennis was going through his vintage phase – shopping exclusively at charity shops and then only for baggy brown cardigans with pockets and oversized no-longer-white shirts with granddad collars and wide sleeves, pairing them with his prized soft black leather jacket. Carole thought he looked amazing, he was at that age, and in possession of that swagger, where he could wear anything and still look good. She'd watched him on stage from the back of the hall and knew she wanted him. She suspected Lenore fancied him too but Carole knew enough about her looks by then to know she could have any teenage boy she wanted, even the cool dude playing guitar in the sixth-year band. He'd passed through various style incarnations since then but was mostly in his office uniform these days, reserving his cigarette leg black jeans and tight-fitting black T-shirts for weekends. The long, tousled hair and silver earrings were long gone.

'Zaccardelli's, you said?' He broke into her thoughts and she smiled. Then he ruined it by reminding her, 'I can't stay long, I've got work to do.'

Carole didn't want to spoil the afternoon by saying that he always had work to do, so she kept the smile on her face and walked a bit closer to him.

They crossed Cadzow Bridge, the park below the bridge a sun-filled carpet of dandelions and spreading buttercups, the sky a warm turquoise. On the other side of the road was the Music Centre, the guitar and record shop they'd spent so much time in when they first started going out. The place had scared Carole at first – Big John would greet favoured customers from behind the counter, the strange smoky smell coming from the storeroom at the back making her feel like she was in a gangster movie. They'd spend hours there, Dennis looking longingly at the most expensive electric guitars, or playing idly on the Yamahas at the back. Meanwhile, Carole would pretend to look through the CDs, check out the badges and patches, and flip through posters of Nirvana and REM, all the while eyeing the older kids in their stonewashed jeans and Doc Martens as they came in and nodded to Big John.

One day she remembered in particular – Dennis had persuaded her to skip the last two periods of French and tear down to the Music Centre to pick up the twelve-inch version of 'It's No Good'. They'd put a deposit down on it the week before so they could get it on release day. As they sauntered out of the shop, Dennis gripping that all-important white and gold bag in one hand almost as tightly as he gripped Carole with the other, they thought they were the coolest kids in Scotland.

'You've had that smile on your face for the last ten minutes. Were you not at the same head teacher's meeting I was just at?' Dennis said, as he pulled a chair from under one of the tables at the back of the café. The place was crowded, filled with the young-mums-and-prams crowd, as well as the pensioners, here for a cup of sweet tea and a blether, or to treat themselves to one of Zaccardelli's famous vanilla ice-cream floats.

'Just enjoying being out with my handsome husband for a change,' she replied, taking off her jacket and folding it neatly on the bench beside her.

Dennis snorted as he pulled over the sticky plastic menu. 'Seems to me you've been out a fair bit recently,' he said, ignoring the compliment.

Carole resisted the urge to say at least she didn't go out and leave the children on their own, trying desperately to stay on neutral ground so that the afternoon wouldn't degenerate into yet another row. She scanned the menu in silence, though she already knew what she was having.

'A cappuccino please, and a fruit scone and butter,' she told the young waitress who came over with her tiny notepad and biro.

'Black coffee,' said Dennis curtly. Carole counted to three, knowing what would happen next. As the waitress put the menus back at the side of the table and walked away, Dennis called after her, 'Actually, get me a roll and sausage while you're at it.' *Every time*, thought Carole, but knew this was not the time to comment on it.

She sat forward and rested her arms on the table, which was still damp from the last swipe of the cloth the waitress had given it after its previous occupants had left. There was a mirror all along the left-hand wall so Carole was aware of her profile, and the reflection of an older guy in a smart suit, a couple of tables down, who was looking at her appreciatively. She glanced over at Dennis and was pleased to see he had caught it too. He reached across the table and put his hands on Carole's forearm possessively.

'What shall we do about Daniel?' she said to him, her face close enough to his that she could see the tired dark circles under his eyes, and the frown lines she knew so well forming an omega on his forehead, just visible beneath the dark curls of his fringe.

He pulled back and lounged against the chair, looking round the busy café. 'Seems to me we've got more of a problem with Thomas than Daniel,' he said finally, but not meeting her eye as he threw this out there.

'Look, it's a stage he's going through. You said yourself, you used to have an earring and enjoy wearing clothes that were a bit different. It didn't mean you were' – she leaned forward and whispered – 'gay. Quite the opposite, from what I recall,' she said, running her finger lightly along his forearm, but he wasn't to be distracted.

'Totally different, Carole, and you know it. Thomas is . . . well . . .' He raised his hands in the air and dropped them on the table, not knowing how to explain the unease he felt with his second son, especially now he too had met the famous Jaxx. 'And maybe I could even take the earring and the weird friends but now he tells me he's thinking of going vegetarian. He was lecturing me this morning on the benefits of kale. Next thing we know, he'll be eighteen and voting Tory.'

Carole laughed.

'I'm being serious though,' said Dennis.

'I know, and I know what you mean,' she said. 'I worry about him too but I think it's a phase and' – she stopped talking for a moment as the waitress came over with their order – 'I really think he'll grow out of it, especially when he gets tired of that Jack he insists on hanging out with.'

'You mean Jaaaaaxx,' drawled Dennis, sarcastically, his tone leaving Carole in no doubt as to how he felt about their son's new friend. 'I mean, what are that boy's – is it even a boy? – parents doing letting him out of the house like that – dressed like a Bee Gee in their *Saturday Night Fever* era? Do they want him to get beaten up? Do you know what Dan was telling me the other day – he had to go in and rescue Thomas when a bunch of first years – first years! – were threatening to beat him up because they caught him and Jaxx making a TikTok of ABBA in the back field.'

'I know, thank goodness for big brothers. ABBA!' said Carole, buttering her scone.

'But Dan can't be around every time. Thomas needs to learn how to stick up for himself.' He took a large bite of his roll.

'If only they could stay Archie and Glover's age for ever,' said Carole. 'Without Glover's snake obsession, obviously.'

Dennis didn't reply. They drank their coffee and watched the other customers come and go. Sitting at their silent table was like being in an empty rowing boat in the sea of chaos and noise that surrounded them, and it made Carole sad how little they had to say to each other when they weren't talking about their children. After all these years, it seemed they had said all there was to say.

'Remember we used to skive off school and sit here for hours with a plate of chips,' she tried again.

'As I remember it, you never wanted to skive off class. And after school, you were always dancing. I used to come here a lot with Vinny and Johnny Boy though, when we first started up the band.'

That wasn't Carole's memory at all. She remembered afternoons when they'd sit in one of the booths upstairs for hours, talking and laughing, just the two of them, never running out of things to say. She remembered too how they'd snog with the urgency only possessed by teenagers in love so that sometimes the manageress would come up and tell them acidly to book a hotel if they wanted to get up to that sort of thing, Zaccardelli's was not that kind of place. Carole would blush to the roots of her hair, and even Dennis would wriggle in his seat, whether out of embarrassment or to make sure the bulge in his trousers wasn't visible, Carole was never sure.

She was jolted out of her thoughts by the small drama unfolding at one of the other tables.

'I'm so sorry, sir,' she heard the waitress say in a panicked voice. She turned and saw the well-dressed man she'd noticed earlier standing over his table now, his face dark with anger as hot tea dripped from his sleeve.

'You stupid little . . .' he hissed, as he shook his arm and the liquid splashed the waitress in the face.

Dennis was on his feet immediately. 'She said sorry, so how about you act like a gentleman and leave it at that?'

The man took in Dennis's towering frame and teeth-gritted smile. 'Fair enough,' he said in a lower voice, 'but she'll need to pay for my suit to be dry-cleaned. It's Armani.'

Dennis smirked. 'I don't care if it's made of gold thread spun by the Queen of Sheba, this waitress is not paying your dry-cleaning bills to mop up a wee bit of tea, got it?'

The man pursed his lips and was about to say more when the manageress scurried over. 'Is there a problem here?'

A large tear fell down the waitress's face, the rest of the customers in the café gawping at the scene while pretending not to.

'No,' said the man finally, grabbing his wallet and phone from the table. 'Everything's fine, I was just leaving. I won't be paying for the tea. Obviously,' he added, desperate to score at least one small point, as he turned on his heel.

'Thank you,' said the waitress to Dennis. He handed her a napkin from the table for her to dry her face. 'The cup slipped from my hand,' she said.

'Never mind, love, let's clean up this table, eh?' said the manageress, after patting Dennis gratefully on the arm.

Dennis walked back to his own table and sat down opposite Carole, who said nothing.

'What?' he said, his jaw still tight after the exchange. 'You can't let bullies win, Carole.'

'I know,' she said, then after a pause, 'Your coffee's cold now, do you want another?'

'No, that's enough slacking for one day, I need to get back.' He slipped his arms into his navy suit jacket and got up to leave. 'Are you coming?'

'I think I'll have another cappuccino after all that excitement,' said Carole, looking round for the unfortunate waitress. 'Might as well make the most of a free afternoon. See you later. You'll be home for dinner?'

'I've had almost two hours off already, I'll do my best.'

Carole wanted to tell him he wasn't a brain surgeon and that the office could manage without him for half a day but she was scared to broach the subject in case he confirmed the nagging doubt she'd had for weeks now about whether he was actually putting in all the hours he claimed to, or whether there was something, or someone, else he wasn't telling her about.

After he'd gone, and her fresh coffee had been placed in front of her, Carole settled back in her seat and watched the other customers in the mirror. She glimpsed a skinny man with skin yellow like mustard and a tube attached to his cheek and running into his left nostril. His eye met hers and she raised her cup to her mouth to hide her embarrassment at being caught staring. Two tables along sat a young boy with a mullet. No one looked good in a mullet, thought Carole, and this one was ginger, no wonder he was on his own. The man at the next table looked up from his mug of tea, scratching the Celtic cross tattooed on his forearm, and gave her a half-smile. Carole smiled back but looked away immediately in case he took it as a sign to come over and join her. He shrugged, took a gulp of tea, and went back to his phone.

As her coffee cooled, the place went through a mid-afternoon lull and she was about to put her jacket on and leave when there was a racket at the front of the café. Shrieking and laughing, in came a group of young girls, about Thomas's age, maybe a little older, making enough noise to convince the other customers in the café that there were twenty girls coming in, rather than four.

'Eva, get your bag out the way and let me sit down.'

'Not my fault if your arse is too big for the bench,' countered the small blonde girl, tutting but moving her huge gym bag to the floor.

Two other girls, almost identical in their washed-out jeans and white crop-tops, sat down noisily opposite them, smoothing their already impossibly smooth hair and pouting into the long mirror. Satisfied with their appearance, three of the four started looking at their phones, whilst the other looked round for the waitress to make their order.

Carole couldn't take her eyes off them. The self-confidence, the assumption they had that they could be as loud as they wanted, that this was their world and they were not afraid of it. Had she and her friends ever been like that? Carole didn't think so.

'I just told them I was going, I mean I've been training for it all my life, of course I'm going to be part of the team,' the blonde was saying to the long-haired beauty opposite her.

'But London though, Eva, how will you even get there?'

The girl pouted. 'There's trains isn't there?'

Carole swirled round the cold froth at the bottom of her cup, and wondered how things might have been different if she too had adopted that cavalier attitude back in the day when she'd had the opportunity to do so.

She'd been the same sort of age as the girls in the café when she'd heard about the auditions for the dance school in East London. Her own Saturday morning dance teacher was adamant she try for a place and offered to talk to her parents for her.

'They want me to be a primary school teacher,' said Carole, shaking her head at her dance teacher's offer. 'But I'll talk to them.'

And she did manage to convince them to at least allow her to audition. They wanted to take her but Carole couldn't bear the idea of her mother fussing about her hair and what she was wearing, making sure she had a healthy breakfast, and planning the route to the audition with the zeal of an army major. It had taken some doing but she managed to persuade her parents to allow her to take the train to London with Amy, assuring them that they'd look after each other, and after all, they were seventeen years old and capable of making such a trip on their own. They weren't convinced at first but Carole's mum had met Lenore's mum in Tesco and when she'd told her Lenore was going to Leeds on her own for uni, she thought maybe they should allow their daughter the same freedom. Amy meanwhile told her dad they were going and that was it.

The train to London took four and a half hours but it felt much shorter. They managed to shake off Carole's parents – who'd wanted to stand on the platform waving at them till the train set off – and settled themselves in their table seats, with Diet Cokes and a giant Toblerone. They had a pile of magazines Carole's mum had bought for them, and a Walkman and a pair of headphones between them. Stations of unfamiliar places flew by outside their window and they chattered in high, excited voices until the announcer called out that they were in Euston. They packed up their stuff in a hurry and dashed across the station platform, coats flapping behind them, to find the correct Tube station and make their way to the Premier Inn in Stratford, booked by Carole's dad.

'Hey, look at this, we can make tea for ourselves in the morning,' said Carole, holding up the dinky white kettle and indicating the bowl filled with two sachets each of English Breakfast tea, Nescafé, and hot chocolate.

'Neither of us drinks tea.' Amy put her rucksack down on the end of the double bed. 'Which side do you want?' she said, not looking at Carole.

'Either,' said Carole, throwing her own bag on to the floor and running over to the window. 'Come on, let's get out and explore. We're in London!'

Despite being nearly summer, the rain didn't stop the whole two days they were there. London was for ever associated in both girls' minds with damp anoraks, crowds of people streaming in and out of Tube stations with wet umbrellas, and constantly taking cover from a downpour somewhere or other.

That first afternoon, they walked all along the South Bank, marvelling at the street performers and sheltering under a tree by the banks of the river. Later, they had chips and mushy peas at a café near the hotel.

'What shall we do tonight?' said Carole, pouring some vinegar on her mushy peas and scooping them up.

Amy made a face. 'Urgh, how can you eat that?' She pushed away her own plate and took a sip of Coke. 'I suppose we should get to bed early since your audition is at nine. That's what we came for, after all, your mum would kill me if I didn't get you there on time.'

Carole waved away mention of her mum but agreed. 'Come on then, let's go back to the hotel.'

The girls felt unbelievably grown-up, lounging on the double bed, watching *Friends* and feeling for once that they were living a life as exciting and full of possibility as the glamorous adults flat-sharing in New York.

At half past eleven, Amy turned to Carole to suggest they get into bed and try to sleep. She saw that Carole's eyes were shut and she was already half-asleep on top of the covers, her hair streaming across her flushed cheeks. Amy carefully peeled back the duvet underneath her sleeping friend and tucked her into the bed.

Half an hour later, Carole turned over. 'Amy, are you asleep?'

Amy was lying at the very edge of the bed, her body stiff as though she was pretending to be asleep rather than actually sleeping.

'Amy?' Carole whispered again, stretching her hand out to touch her friend's shoulder. 'Amy, are you awake?'

Amy didn't answer.

Carole wriggled over in the bed and curled her body round her friend's, spooning her. 'It's cold in here now, heat me up.' She snuggled into her shoulder, the warmth of her breasts against Amy's back, her knees pressing against the curved backs of her friend's.

Amy didn't move, didn't seem to be breathing even.

'Are you okay?' said Carole softly. 'Are you too tired to talk?'

'No,' said Amy, in a strange voice. 'I just . . . you should probably sleep before your big day.'

'Yeah, I know, but I'm too nervous to sleep. And I'm worried too — what if I get in?'

Amy turned round to face her, startled by the closeness of Carole's face to hers, her eyes on a level with her own. 'What do you mean?' She whispered too, more because of the dark and heat of the night inviting confidences rather than for fear of disturbing other guests. 'Isn't that what you want? To get into the dance school and be a dancer?'

Carole sat up suddenly, pulling the duvet off Amy as she did so. Amy tried not to stare at Carole's breasts, pressed against the thin T-shirt she wore to sleep in.

'That's just it. What if I do get in? I'd hardly get to see Dennis, and who'd keep an eye on him to make sure he doesn't get into any fights? And his band's taking off, you know, they're going to be really famous and all the girls will be after him and oh Amy, what if he forgets all about me?'

'Are you kidding – him forget about you? You're the most beautiful girl in the world, he can't believe his luck he's managed to hold on to you for this long.'

'You would say that, you're my best friend.'

They were both quiet for a moment then Carole said, 'Would you come and visit me if I lived here?'

'Of course I would,' said Amy, smiling in the dark. 'Try and stop me.'

'You're such a good friend. Thanks for coming with me to London.' Carole lay back down and pulled Amy's arm up so that she could snuggle under it. Amy kept a slight distance between them but she didn't pull away.

The next morning, they were at the auditions for nine o'clock sharp. The place was buzzing with girls – mainly girls, there was the odd boy – stretching and warming up their long limbs, or standing nervously in little powwows with whoever had accompanied them.

'Don't go, Amy,' whispered Carole to her friend.

'Don't be daft,' said Amy, gently taking Carole's hand off her arm. 'You'll be brilliant. And I'll be here waiting for you at two when it's finished, promise.'

Carole watched until Amy disappeared through the main doors and out into the still-damp London streets. She pushed her sports bag a little higher up her shoulder, raised her chin and walked up the main staircase to take her seat outside the audition room.

'Carole Moore?' A man stood at the door with a clipboard in his hand. He was wearing a multicoloured stripey jumper and had his hair tied up in a top knot. 'Carole Moore please?' he called again.

'That's me,' said Carole, jumping up and knocking over the bag of the hopeful next to her as she did so. The girl said, 'Watch it,' and Carole muttered an awkward apology.

'This way please,' said the man, holding the door open for Carole.

The audition room was small, not much bigger than their living room at home. One wall was entirely mirrors, with a wooden barre at waist height. In front of her was a narrow table at which was seated another man, older and wearing thick-framed black glasses that he was looking over the top of. An elegant woman of around forty or so sat to his right. Her hair was pulled back into a tight low bun which showed off her long neck and high cheekbones. Carole thought she looked like one of those women you see in a marketing campaign for Burberry's winter collection, or like someone who should be sipping dry sherry before the gong goes for dinner in a stately home. When she looked up, Carole saw that she had a large mole above her top lip, like Cindy Crawford. She shifted her weight from one leg to the other, as the woman let her eyes travel slowly from Carole's face down to her feet and back up again. She immediately felt stumpy-legged and coarse, and wondered, not for the first time, what on earth she was doing there.

Back home, two weeks later, Amy couldn't understand why she'd turned down their offer of a place. 'But why do you want to stay in Hamilton?' she'd said. 'I'm sure the Glasgow School of Dance is okay but it can't hold a candle to London.'

Carole refused to be swayed. It wasn't that Dennis had persuaded her not to go – whatever Amy said – but he had been brutally honest with her about his intentions to go to Glasgow Uni and the fact that he did not intend to spend his weekends on the Megabus to London. So in the end she'd stayed. She did well on her course, but when she and Dennis moved in together, and he started to earn more money than their own parents even, she'd never tried that hard to find a job. After she'd got pregnant with Daniel, any talk of her going back to study or looking for a job was forgotten. She was a mum to one, then two, and eventually four children. Life was busy for years and for the most part, Carole was happy to play second fiddle to the force of nature that was Dennis, but sometimes, when Dennis was at work and the boys at school, and she sat in her huge, white kitchen in the empty ocean of a Wednesday afternoon, she'd marvel at how she'd let it happen. How could a young woman who'd been as beautiful, as talented as she'd been, so full of ambition and plans for a life of her own, just disappear into the background of other people's lives like that, her only purpose to accommodate and facilitate their dreams? The feeling of being useless as a shadow, and as insubstantial as one too, had crept up on her so insidiously that Carole didn't know where or how it had begun, but it was a feeling that grew stronger with every passing year.

'Can I get you something else, or do you want the bill?' the waitress asked pointedly, swiping the already clean table with her damp cloth as she did so. Carole noticed it was a different waitress from before, she must have been daydreaming longer than she'd thought.

'Oh yes, sorry, just the bill please,' said Carole, glancing round and seeing the four young girls had gone already. The only customers left in the café, besides her, were an old couple in matching Trespass anoraks and an exhausted-looking woman she vaguely recognized from the tills at Asda, hunched over a mug of tea. She tapped her card on the machine the waitress brought to the table and peered through the window to see a light drizzle spattering the pavement. She tucked her hair inside her hood and started the walk home on her own in the rain.

'Why do I have to go to bed at the same time as him? He's a whole year younger than me,' whined Archie, as Carole told them both to go and brush their teeth.

It was later that evening and Dennis still wasn't home. Carole had made chicken nuggets and chips for the younger boys, ordered the older two an enormous stuffed pizza each from Hank Marvin via JustEat, and spent the rest of the evening buffing the bottom oven till it shone. She rarely used it, but still.

'Nine o'clock is bedtime, Archie, no arguments.'

'Wait, I forgot to show you my baking,' said Archie suddenly turning round on the stair.

'Archie . . .'

'No, honest, let me get it out my bag.' He ran through to the kitchen where his and Glover's bags were lying in a heap beside the beanbags. Carole scanned her phone for messages from Dennis, shouting back to Glover to get into bed and she'd be up shortly.

'Can I have a snake—'

'No snakes. Get into bed.' She followed Archie back into the kitchen.

'Here they are,' said Archie proudly, handing over a squashed and greasy package, sticky in Carole's hands.

She opened it and said, 'Biscuits – clever you!'

'They're cupcakes,' he said. 'Taste one.'

'Yes, of course they are,' said Carole quickly, peeling one of the flat, dry rounds from the greaseproof paper and taking a small bite. She gagged and said, 'Wow, they're delicious.'

'Honest? Because Mrs Smith said they were so bad I didn't have to pay the usual one pound for the ingredients.'

'What? She must have no taste buds then because these are so delicious that I am going to force myself to leave them all for Daddy even though I really want to eat them all.'

Archie's face was pink with pleasure and he high-fived his mum. 'I knew it. Everyone else's were all puffy and fluffy, not like mine at all.'

'They're perfect, Archie. Now up you go and brush your teeth and I'll come and tuck you in in a minute.'

Carole watched him hop up the stairs two at a time and decided she would blank Mrs Smith completely at the next PTA meeting.

She settled the younger two down for the night, noting that

Daniel and Thomas both had their bedroom doors resolutely shut as she walked back downstairs. She turned on a small lamp in the living room and thought about switching on the TV to counter the silence, but decided against it. Settling herself into the deep, plush cushions of their new sofa, she checked her phone again for a text or a missed call from Dennis. There was a message from Amy asking if she wanted to meet her for breakfast at Costa some time that week, and one from Lenore, thanking her for the boys' old school uniforms she'd donated to the school. Nothing from Dennis.

She let her eyes drift round the room, pleased with the sheen she'd managed to achieve on the coffee table and making a mental note that the irises in the vase on the fireplace needed changing. She tapped her fingers on her phone screen again — still no text from Dennis — and finally switched on the TV. She was drawn in by a programme about human attraction and blind dates, and thought maybe it was her fault she and Dennis weren't connecting any more. After all, when was the last time *she* had pranced around in frothy lingerie or they'd had a candlelit dinner just the two of them? Still no texts from Dennis by the time she was brushing her teeth, and she was asleep by the time he got home and crept into bed beside her.

She was still thinking about the programme when she dropped the boys at school the following morning. Instead of going back home, she headed to Sainsburys to buy salmon and salad, and a good bottle of white wine. She planned to set it all out beautifully in the dining room with candles and a tablecloth, and had visions of her and Dennis eating and drinking alone together, after the younger two were in bed, and Daniel and Thomas were up in their rooms, gaming or whatever it was they did these days.

They would talk and reconnect, Carole would listen to Dennis's stories of colleagues' slights and she'd remind him of why he was better than them and should ignore the lot of them. He'd ask her about her day, and what she'd been up to, and she might even tell him about the Graffiti Girls, and watch his face shine with admiration as she told him about the good they were doing, the issues they were highlighting, and how local women and even women further afield than South Lanarkshire were supporting them. Full of good food and wine, they'd go to bed, arms twisted round each other and laughing on their way upstairs to make love like they used to. She was imagining this scene as she waited at the red light, and realized with a start that she couldn't even remember the last time she'd seen Dennis naked.

By ten that night, she'd drunk most of the wine and there was no sign of Dennis. Where was he, and more importantly, who was he with? At eleven, she was pacing the kitchen, furious with him for spoiling her plans. An hour later, she started to worry. Where the hell was he, could something have happened to him? He finally picked up the phone at half past midnight. She could hear his breathy voice, hoarse with wine and good times without her.

'Where are you? And don't say work because I can tell you've been out drinking.' Even as she said the words, she hated herself for the way she sounded.

'Calm down, Carole. I told you . . . this morning, or yesterday, I'm sure I did. We had a late-night conference call with the American lot and it went brilliantly, so we're having a few beers to celebrate. Why are you still up anyway?'

'Because . . . I was waiting for you to come home but you're always working. Supposedly,' she added dangerously.

'You're right.' Dennis raised his voice now. 'I am always working, and what do you think I'm working for? It's all for you and the kids, so you can have all the new sofas and coats and golf memberships and whatever else you want. You should be pleased I work so hard, it means you don't have to!'

Carole was too angry to reply and threw her phone across the kitchen instead, closely followed by the empty wine bottle. She watched as the shards of glass bounced off the tiles, hitting the cupboard doors and landing in the vegetable rack.

It took her half an hour to pick up the jagged fragments of glass and Dennis still wasn't home by the time she'd finished. She made herself a coffee, pouring a large measure of Baileys into it, and sat at the kitchen surface, sipping the hot sweet drink and staring round her beautiful, pristine kitchen. It was true – Dennis earned plenty of money and he never complained about how much she spent, or what she spent it on. It was just that sometimes it would be nice to spend some of it with him, maybe going out for a meal or a weekend break somewhere now the boys were older. And another thing that had been bothering her recently was how often he told her she didn't need to work, she should just spend his money. That might be true, but she *wanted* to work, wanted that feeling Dennis must have – of working hard, getting better at something, putting the effort in, learning, achieving something. Looking after the kids was wonderful, the best job ever, she'd tell anyone who asked, but it was different to being out there in the world achieving things for herself. She knew none of her friends would have settled for such a small life, and hated herself for being so weak.

And it hadn't always been that way. When they were at school, Carole had been the one endlessly at dance practice, rehearsing until her feet and thighs ached with the effort. Dennis had had the band, of course, but as soon as he realized they were not going to be ousting Pulp any time soon, he immediately pulled out and focused all his attention on his studies. He'd always been an all-or-nothing kind of person – which was fine when he was all about Carole but not so great when she was in the debit column, which was where she found herself now.

She remembered the days they'd meet straight from uni and college, counting the hours till they saw each other. More often than not, she'd have to calm Dennis down as his nostrils would be flaring as he told her about whoever had crossed him that day. Her friends, especially Amy, were unimpressed by his hair-trigger temper but they didn't see the other side of him – the tender side that made him willing to spend hours, days sometimes, making her the perfect mix tape, or the way they clung to each other and swayed together to those tapes in her attic bedroom, her head on his shoulder while he spoke to her of love in soft, whispering tones, the rain pattering against the tiny window in the roof. What had happened to that young couple? she wondered, as she sat alone in her kitchen, the boys asleep upstairs and the fridge thrumming quietly in the background.

It was gone two in the morning when Dennis stumbled in, his face red and his top button undone, his tie hanging out of his jacket pocket. He dropped his keys and phone on the surface and said, 'I'm going to bed,' without looking at her.

'Wait, Dennis, I—'

Dennis waved his hand at her without turning round. 'I'm tired, Carole, I've been out of the house since before light this morning. Leave it, okay.'

Carole watched him walk away, then glanced back to the counter. His phone lay in front of her, dangerously close, like a landmine. She stretched her fingers towards it then pulled her hand back.

'Dennis, please, wait,' she called after him, getting up from her seat and following him to the bottom of the stair.

He stopped on the second stair for a moment, then turned and held out his hand to her.

She took it and leaned towards him. 'I'm sorry for shouting. I was worried about you.'

'I'm sorry too,' he whispered into her hair. 'Your hair smells like home,' he said, twirling strands of it round his fingers.

Carole smiled. 'I love you, you know that?'

'Do you?' he murmured, without looking at her. Before she could reply, he lifted her off her feet, and carried her up the stairs and into their bedroom. 'And before you say it, I am not waiting while you light the candle,' he said sternly as he closed the door behind them with his foot and threw her, laughing, on to the bed.

It was the following Saturday afternoon and for the first time since Carole could remember, all her boys were busy doing one thing or another and she was free to go into town with her friends and enjoy herself, even though Dennis was also out working, he said. For once, it had been Susan's idea to meet up. She'd called mid-week with her news.

'I got the job!'

Carole sat on the stairs with her phone, settling back to hear all the details. She was delighted for her friend who she'd long thought was due for promotion, having been underpaid, and unappreciated for the most part, for years.

'Well done, Susan, I'm so pleased for you. But not surprised, not in the least.'

'Thanks, Carole. I've said I'll stay on at the library till they find someone to replace me. We're even more short-staffed than ever – Cameron took the huff and left and as soon as he heard they'd given the job to me. I can't believe it – Senior Communications Officer! It was Fraser that suggested we go out to celebrate.' She paused. 'And I don't think it's because he and Fiona want the house to themselves on Saturday. I don't care anyway because I want to go out and celebrate. I deserve it.'

'Course you do,' said Carole. 'What time were you thinking? I'll need to check Dennis is here to babysit' – she suddenly heard Amy chiding her – 'I mean, look after the boys.'

As it turned out, Archie and Glover had a Saturday rugby camp – less about rugby training and more to do with making sure they had the numbers up for the annual photograph so the club could secure next year's funding. Carole didn't care, it was a day's free childcare and she wasn't about to complain. Thomas was spending the day at Jaxx's house, as to what they would be doing there Carole preferred not to think about too closely but she'd spoken to Jaxx's mother and she knew he'd be fine. Dan had muttered something about a golfing day at the club in Bothwell Dennis had recently splashed out on joining, and suddenly, Carole was free to spend the day however she chose.

She strolled along Argyle Street, conscious of the pale early-summer sun on her skin, and feeling the lightness only experienced by long-time mothers who suddenly find themselves child-free and able to swing their arms, stop where they please, linger over shop windows and generally behave like the free adults they'd been before the children came along. She kept her phone in her hand, glancing at it frequently in case one of the kids should need her. She still had almost an hour before meeting the others in Princes Square so a quick detour into the House of Fraser, she thought, and maybe spend some of that money Dennis was always on about earning.

'Cheers, everyone, and especially to you, Susan. Here's to the new job!' said Amy, raising her glass of prosecco to her friend before downing almost all of it in one gulp.

'Steady on, Amy,' said Lenore, laughing. 'We're here for the afternoon, you know.'

'What?' said Amy, topping up her glass. 'We're out to celebrate, come on, switch off the calorie counter and start enjoying yourself for once.'

Susan stepped in before Lenore could reply. 'Yeah, thanks for coming out, everyone, we should do this more often.'

'I'm always available,' said Amy. 'It's you guys with the kids and husbands that hold us back.' She looked at Carole pointedly as she said this.

'Don't start, we're all out to celebrate Susan's new job, so well done, Susan.' Carole clinked her glass against Susan's who was sitting beside her, her cheeks already pink with the unaccustomed afternoon alcohol, her ginger curls coming loose from their band.

'Thanks, everyone. Here's to big futures for all of us.'

The afternoon wore on and Carole drank more than she had for a long time. She kept checking her phone but none of the boys needed her. And of course Dennis hadn't called to ask if she was enjoying herself. She remembered when they were younger the days when he'd call her every half hour or so, worried that someone else would take her eye and she'd leave him. Now he couldn't care less where she went or with whom, as long as it didn't mean he had to look after the kids. And even though she moaned about being at everyone's beck and call, she found that when no one in her family needed her, she didn't like that either because if Dennis didn't need her to look after him, and the kids didn't need her to mother them, then . . . what was the point of her at all? She could feel the tears welling up in her eyes and bent down to her bag to find a tissue. What on earth was the matter with her?

'What's up with you?' asked Amy quietly. 'You don't seem as pleased to be out on a Saturday afternoon as I thought you'd be. Still prefer being on the leash to being on the lash?'

'I really wish you'd stop saying that, Amy. I'm not a caged animal, I do exactly what I want to do. It's just . . .' She trailed off and looked round the bar, full now with large groups mainly of women, mouths wide with laughter, the afternoon prosecco and freedom and being with their fellow women quickly going to their heads.

'What then, tell us?' said Amy, shushing Lenore and Susan who were trying to remember the words of an Echo and the Bunnymen song they'd liked at school.

Carole looked up and saw they were all waiting for her to speak.

'We've led such a little life, all of us, I mean. Haven't we?' She looked round at the others, Susan with her glass of prosecco halfway to her mouth, Lenore pausing as she reached into her bag for her lipstick, and Amy motionless as she stared at Carole, willing her to continue.

'What I mean is, we're none of us desperately unhappy. Susan, you've got your new job; your business is taking off now, Amy;

and Lenore, you've got your mojo back after Tommy leaving and everything. We're all doing okay but, well, it's not what we hoped for when we were at school, is it?' She picked up her glass and swallowed the rest of the fizzy wine, pushing it towards Amy for a refill.

'As long as Fraser's happy, I'm okay,' said Susan, but uncertainly, as though she knew she was being disingenuous.

'And I'm . . . happy enough,' said Lenore, trying not to see the young couple in the corner booth, the guy clearly besotted with his girlfriend who was texting and taking selfies while he desperately tried to get her attention. There was no disguising where the power lay in that relationship.

'Would you listen to us?' said Amy, dropping her glass on to the table so that the remainder of her prosecco sloshed out onto the coaster beneath it. 'Okay. Happy enough. Not dying, for Christ's sake, as if that's all we can hope for. No, Carole's right. If we were to measure where we spend most of our lives, we are all within an average four-mile radius of where we went to school more than two decades ago, and that's only because Lenore went rogue and moved up the road to Silvertonhill.'

'Eh, excuse me, I also lived in Leeds for four years when I went to uni,' put in Lenore.

'Oh, that's right, I'd forgotten you'd scaled the heights, the faraway downs of West Yorkshire, no less.'

'Well, still . . .'

'Yes, I know what you mean, but you see Carole's point.'

'I don't know why you're complaining, Carole,' said Susan. 'You lead a pretty charmed life from where I'm standing. With your looks, you always have.' She laughed but stopped suddenly when she saw that Carole wasn't laughing with her.

'Is that all I am to you? Good-looking Carole, with the blonde hair and the rich husband?'

'No, sorry, I didn't mean—'

'Look, I know what you're saying, Susan, and it's my own fault for letting it happen. I've always been complimented on my looks – that feels big-headed saying it out loud but it's true – but the thing is, that's meant I never felt the need to do anything else. Being Dennis's good-looking wife was my role, my job, and I was good at it. But what about now – in my forties and my looks are going? And anyway, what if I want to be something more than that? What am I supposed to do then?'

The women were all quiet for a few moments till Carole spoke again. 'I honestly feel like I've been sleepwalking for the last twenty years, almost, and it's taken the Graffiti Girls to wake me up and make me realize I need more from life.'

'Ssshhh,' said Susan, turning all around, but the bar was so noisy and everyone else so absorbed in their own private dramas, there was no need to worry about anyone listening in to their conversation.

'Do you remember when we were at school?' Carole asked her friends.

'I remember us all getting the Rachel cut and Dennis coming in in sixth year with that gigantic mobile phone attached to his belt,' said Lenore, but none of the others laughed. 'Sorry,' she said. 'Trying to lighten things up. Go on, Carole.'

'Remember how we planned to go travelling first – to Paris as au pairs maybe, then pick grapes in Capri, and drink beer at the festival in Munich. And the men, remember all the men we were going to meet? Not you, Amy, you had different plans to escape and live free. But look at us. It all came to nothing, all those dreams, the big plans. Do you ever think maybe that's why we were all so keen to get on board with Amy's graffiti plan in the first place? We were dying to be involved in something bigger than ourselves, for the first time since we were at school.'

'Wow, well said, Carole. What's brought all this on?' Amy was staring at her old friend with undisguised admiration.

'I'm pretty certain Dennis is having an affair,' Carole said suddenly, swirling the prosecco round the bowl of her glass. This was the first time she'd said the words out loud and as she did so, she knew it was true. They might have the odd good night like they'd had last week, but most of the time they were like ships passing in the night, her life taken up with childcare and the house, Dennis absorbed in his work – or so he said.

Lenore was first to sympathize. 'Carole, I'm so sorry, I know how that feels. Like you're . . . not good enough or something.'

'Absolutely no way is Carole not good enough for that sexist brute. Doesn't give a damn about any*one* but himself or any*thing* but money. And that temper – he's always been a thug.' Amy was incandescent with rage on her friend's behalf.

'He's not a thug, Amy, but . . . thanks, girls. It actually feels good to say it after months of thinking it.'

They were all quiet for a bit till Amy, characteristically, was the first to rally.

'Right. Sounds like we need another mission to make sure we're all still alive.' She raised her glass round to each member of the group. 'Who's up for it?'

'Nope, definitely not, count me out,' said Susan immediately, sitting back and folding her arms. 'There is no way you're talking me into that again. They've only just stopped talking about the council building being defaced and you want to go again? Are you mad?'

'No, listen, Susan. We've started something with the Graffiti Girls, whether you like it or not. We've made people think – it's for other women too, not just us. We need to keep the pressure on—'

But Susan was not in the mood to listen. 'It's all right for you, Amy. You've always been the outcast—'

'Thanks very much.'

'The rebel then, you know what I mean, always raging against parents, teachers, whoever. But we're not like that. Me, Lenore and Carole, we stick to the rules, we live by them. That's why it's so much harder for us than it is for you to vandalize—'

'Graffiti—'

'No, Amy, let's tell it like it is for once – it's vandalism, and even though it feels refreshing, thrilling, fun even at the time, when I get home and think about what we've done, it makes me ill. I can't eat or sleep, can't think about anything else. I can't keep doing it.' Susan sat back, out of breath and red in the face with the effort of standing up to the group's natural leader.

Amy was quiet for a moment then said softly, 'What's the alternative?'

'What do you mean?' asked Lenore.

'It seems to me we can carry on shouting, "We're here, we're over forty but we're still here. We won't be ignored, we won't be put on the sidelines, we won't be airbrushed out of the picture." It's about shouting loud and proud, these are our stories and they matter. They fucking matter.' Susan winced but

222

Amy carried on. 'Or else we can say nothing and disappear.' She looked up at the group. 'I think the answer's pretty clear, don't you?'

That Tuesday evening, Carole pulled on her stretchy black leggings and an old black Adidas hoodie of Dan's. She scraped her hair into a tight ponytail on top of her head, and washed her face of the remnants of the day's lipstick and eyeliner. Before going downstairs to wait on Amy, she had a last check on Archie and Glover. To her surprise, Archie was still awake, lying on his back on top of his duvet with his eyes wide open and staring at the ceiling.

She sat on the edge of his bed. 'How are you doing there, buddy?' she said, stroking his still-blond hair back from his forehead. She knew it would turn to the dark brown of his older brothers before long and thought again that she must take more photos of him before that happened.

'I'm okay,' said Archie, before turning to face her, a small tear running down his cheek.

'Archie, what on earth's the matter, sweetheart?'

'Nothing. It's just . . . I'm no good at anything at school.'

'What on earth do you mean? You're good at everything at school.'

'I'm not good at cross-country running. I came in last today. And I tried so hard.'

'Oh, Archie,' said Carole, touching his shoulder, and kicking herself for forgetting to ask him how he'd got on at his sports showcase day. 'But I bet you did better in the penalty shoot-outs, didn't you, because you are very good at—'

'I didn't score any. I was last at those too. Even Anne-Marie

Wilson scored one and she's fat. Even fatter than you *and* she can't run.'

'Oh. Well . . .' Carole was at a loss for a moment then rallied. 'But remember your cupcakes! You're the very best cupcake maker I know.'

Archie sat up in bed and smiled. 'That's right, I forgot about my cupcakes. You really liked them, didn't you?'

'I really did, Archie,' said Carole. 'Now, it's time for sleeping, young man. Come on, tomorrow's a new day and you want to be bright and ready for it, don't you?'

'Can I sleep in Glover's bed?'

'Archie, there isn't much room for both of you.'

'Pleeeeease.'

'Go on then.'

Archie jumped over to his brother's bed, and curled himself around Glover, his chubby fingers resting on his brother's shoulder. 'Night night,' said Carole, turning out the Star Wars lamp on the table between the beds and thinking how lucky the boys were to have each other – even if they fought like alley cats most of the time. Archie dipped his pointy little chin under the duvet and didn't reply.

She rapped Thomas's door next but he screeched, 'Don't come in' before she could open it. 'Sorry, Thomas,' she called through the closed door. 'Just to say that's me leaving to go out with the girls for an hour or so. Dan's in charge so do what he says, okay?'

'As if,' was Thomas's reply, and Carole thought about going in to press the point, but changed her mind. 'I won't be long,' she said and headed to Dan's room.

The smell of feet was overpowering. Daniel was going

through a phase of wearing rubber gym shoes which would have been cheap had it not been for the discreet label on the side of each shoe. They made his feet stink.

'For God's sake, Daniel, how can you study in a bedroom like this?' she said, almost tripping over a Domino's pizza box lying directly in front of the door, and eyeing the scrunched-up Red Bull cans littering his desk and piles of boxer shorts and inside-out T-shirts spread across his carpet.

'I'm working, Mum.' Dan didn't turn his face from the screen, his hand never moving from the mouse, his index finger poised over the controls.

Carole stared at him, hating the way the balance of power between them had shifted, and hating herself more for feeling that way. She was scared to tell him off for his messy room, or for anything at all these days, in case he packed his bags and moved in with one of his pals. And she could already sense the same changes happening with Thomas. She remembered when an invitation from her to go to Pizza Express at the Fort would be the apex of either boy's week. Now they couldn't care less if they saw her from one week to the next, as long as their meals were cooked and their clothes hung up neatly in their wardrobes. She remembered all those sad old ladies sitting on their own in the Asda café, eking out a cup of tea and a scone, as they looked on longingly at her and her toddlers and told her, 'Enjoy it, it passes in the blink of an eye.' She'd wanted to strangle them at the time but it turned out they were right after all.

'Why are you still standing there?' Dan said, his shoulders twitching. 'I thought you were going out?'

'I am,' said Carole. 'Dad's . . . working late again. He'll be home very soon so keep an ear out for—'

Daniel muttered, 'My social battery's completely out of charge, Mum,' and shooed her away with his hand without looking up from his pc.

Carole gave up and went downstairs to wait for Amy.

'Okay, everyone, we're all here,' said Amy, eyeing her little crew appreciatively. How far they'd come in just a few months – each woman dressed from head to toe in black, hair tied back, their face masks at the ready, and a can of lurid spray paint in their hands.

'Get on with it, Captain,' said Lenore. 'Love to hear how you're going to manage this one.'

'My thought exactly,' said Susan, her voice high and thin, as she looked all round them. 'The bar's still open, Amy, have we really thought this through?'

Amy could understand her friends' nerves. They'd hit upon the idea of targeting Jilts, the bar they'd all been coming to for years on and off since school. It was a well-known haunt for underage drinkers and they'd had some fantastic times there. But as they'd talked, they remembered they'd had some terrible times there too. Like the time Lenore couldn't get a taxi and those two skinheads had trailed her all the way along Quarry Street, telling her they liked a woman who was 'a handful'. Or the time the tall guy in an Oasis live tour T-shirt and jeans with more rips than denim had cornered Carole outside the ladies' toilets, whispering in her ear could he touch her hair and how he bet her lips were soft. Or the two guys who'd flanked Susan on the dance floor, each rubbing against the side of her body but with smiles and dance moves that made her seem like the unreasonable one when she complained about it. Or the countless times one or other of them had been cowed by groups of guys catcalling, staring them down, whistling, following them down the street, sometimes hurling insults, more often what they thought were compliments, and failing to see that that didn't make it any less frightening or humiliating. All of it was helped along by the alcohol they drank in places like Jilts so it was the perfect place to target. And of course, Carole and Dennis had spent many an hour snuggled up in the corner, downing cheap beer, and snogging. And since Dennis and his affair were responsible for Carole's current state of unhappiness, Jilts was really the only choice.

Amy understood the girls' reticence though. It was a few minutes to ten, the bar was open and even though it was fairly quiet mid-week, it was still a risk. But one worth taking, Amy thought.

'Right, we're going to keep it simple tonight. No ladders, just a small tin of spray paint each and we all write one slogan, big as you can, but as fast as you can. Got it?'

The other women nodded, Susan's eyes still darting all round, but Lenore and Carole intent on Amy, keen to follow her every instruction.

Amy continued. 'Here's how we're going to do it. There's a lane at the back of the pub, see it, where they keep all the bins?'

The others strained to see where Amy was pointing.

'I did a bit of a recce here last night and the only person who comes out to that lane is Big Nacho, the bouncer, who stands out there and has a fag break every half hour. He's like clockwork. Nine o'clock. Half nine. Ten o'clock. That means we have a half-hour window to get the job done, starting from' – Amy indicated the back doorway and they all saw a stocky man, dressed in too-tight jeans and a fake Gucci T-shirt, push open the fire door and strike a match against the wall and light up his cigarette – 'the minute he finishes that fag.'

At half past ten, Big Nacho pushed open the fire door again, cigarette and box of matches in one hand, a half-drunk cup of milky coffee in the other. He put his cup on the ground, lit his cigarette and inhaled, thinking how fresh the air was outside compared to the soupy indoor aromas of Eau Sauvage, pee from the stained trough in the gents' toilets and, at this time of the night, sheer desperation. He blew out and turned away from the alley and back to the pub. His unsmoked cigarette fell from his hand. 'What the—?'

The entire wall was covered in blue, red and green scrawl. Huge, gaudy letters, most of them at his eye level or lower.

WOMEN DO NOT EXIST TO SERVE YOU

GREAT TITS IS NOT A COMPLIMENT

DON'T BE THAT GUY

NO SHELF LIFE FOR WOMEN. 40 AND—

'What the hell does that say?' muttered Big Nacho. 'FA— FAB—' He stooped to get a closer look at the green scrawl at the very bottom of the wall. **40 AND FABULOUS, SIGNED THE GRAFFITI GIRLS GG**. Big Nacho's face went so red an innocent bystander might have thought it was about to explode. 'Forty and fabulous. Old hags! I'll give them fabulous. Fabulous? How fucking dare they? Who do these women think they are?' He stomped back into the bar to call the police, kicking the remains of his stone-cold coffee down the alleyway as he did so.

The June Gala Day was the first time the women had been out together since they'd graffitied Jilts a couple of weeks earlier. Although the incident had been deemed newsworthy enough for BBC Scotland's six o'clock news, there had been little more said about it in the local press, so they were all beginning to believe Amy that the Graffiti Girls had successfully completed another mission.

The parade was ushered in with the driving rain that usually accompanied the event. The howling winds were blowing hard enough to give the organizers cause for concern that the massive floats might topple on the unfortunate waiting crowd. But it was the same every year, and unless you counted that one boy who streaked across Quarry Street and straight into the path of the Gala Queen's float, causing minimum injury to himself and fortunately none to the hapless Gala Queen, they'd never yet caused personal injury, far less loss of life.

'We'll be absolutely fine,' said Norah, the local councillor in charge of the event.

'All right for her to say,' muttered Lenore, trying desperately to keep her hair, which she'd had done at the hairdresser's only that morning, in some semblance of a style.

'Did you not bring an umbrella?' said Susan, whose own hair was hanging in sopping wet ringlets round her shoulders despite her best attempts to keep Fraser's navy golf umbrella upright in the gale.

'Aha,' said Amy, triumphantly. 'This is where hairstyles like mine come into their own.' She spun round to show the others how the rain bounced off her shaven head, doing little to disturb the half-inch of hair all over.

'Bit of a price to pay, mind you.'

'What—'

'Never mind that,' said Susan before Lenore and Amy could get into it. 'Where's Carole? I thought we were supposed to be meeting here at eleven.'

They all looked through the streaming crowds but couldn't see Carole. Despite the weather, the event was well-patronized, as it was every year, and soggy groups of children of all ages, their parents, neighbours, teachers and local councillors all chattered loudly, waiting for the parade to begin.

Norah blew a whistle and picked up the megaphone. 'Good morning, ladies and gentlemen,' she boomed. 'And welcome to the Hamilton Gala Day parade. Today, as every year, we have a cornucopia of visual delights for you to feast your eyes on—'

'Hurry up and get started so we can go home and dry off,' muttered Amy, rubbing her hands pointlessly down her sopping jeans.

Beside them stood a small group of women Lenore recognized as mothers from the school. Three of them were sheltering under a giant golfing umbrella and their conversation was loud and indignant.

'Don't get me wrong,' said the tall woman in a blue North Face jacket closest to Lenore. 'I agree with what they've been saying up till now. Someone has to let these men know they can't behave like that, but vandalizing the local pub isn't the way to do it. I've been going there since I was sixteen!'

'I know,' agreed the woman next to her, heaving her canvas

M & S tote bag further up her shoulder. 'These men are entitled, yeah, but I'd say it's pretty damn entitled to be ruining private property like that.'

'Dorothy said she's hardly been able to make it pay since she took it over a couple of years ago, and this might be the thing that pushes her under. They're talking almost a thousand pounds to repaint that outside wall, that's a lot of money.'

Lenore, Amy and Susan eyed each other, saying nothing.

'How that's supporting women, sending Dorothy into bankruptcy, I don't know,' said the first woman, sniffing and looking across at the start line to see if there was any sign of the floats moving yet.

'And they're off,' shouted Norah, as the first floats began making their way across Cadzow Bridge.

'Hello everyone, sorry I'm late.'

'Hi, Car—' Amy turned to Carole, who'd appeared suddenly behind them. 'Carole, what on earth's the matter?'

Carole's eyes were heavy, the shadows beneath them purple and puffy. Her usually luminous skin was pale and flaky-dry, drips of rainwater from her umbrella streaming down her face making it look like she was crying.

'Nothing's wrong. Except . . . everything,' said Carole, her eyes tearing up so that it seemed like her whole face was underwater.

In front of them, the floats drove by, honking their horns and generally making as much noise as possible so that Amy gestured to Carole to wait till the parade had passed before talking. They watched in silence as Japan came first – the red crepe paper of the lanterns and the rising sun streaming down the costumes of the geishas on the float so that it looked like a murder scene – probably not the effect they'd been aiming for. That was followed by USA – complete with red, white and blue balloons and gun-toting cowgirls flinging their lassoes and shouting 'yee-hah' at the top of their lungs.

'No one can accuse Hamilton of pandering to stereotypes,' whispered Susan to Lenore, as the Scotland float passed to uproarious cheers, the giant saltire waving madly in the wind, and the lone piper doing his best to be heard amidst the honking and cheering. The Gala Queen sat atop a large throne, which was perched precariously at the front of the float. She was alternately waving and pushing back her hair which streamed into her face and threatened to topple her crown. Her pink sash was sodden. Sitting cross-legged on the back, dressed in their cub shirts and kilts, were Archie and Glover who, along with the rest of their cub pack, were counting down the minutes till they could get off the float and run back to the scout hall for hot chocolate and Tunnock's.

Amy felt for Carole as she pasted on a fake smile and waved at her boys. 'Come on,' she said. 'That's enough supporting the local cause for one day, let's go and get a coffee. You look like you need one. And the rest of the Graffiti Girls could do with cheering up too, I think.'

'There you go – large cappuccino, extra chocolate, and a pain au chocolat. Enough sugar there to cure any ill.'

'Thanks, Amy, I'm fine anyway. Honestly, what a lot of fuss I'm making about nothing.' Carole scrunched up the tissue she'd been holding and picked up her coffee, looking at Susan and Lenore apologetically.

No one said anything while Carole sipped her coffee and put her cup back down on the table. She looked round the café, busy with customers as bedraggled and forlorn as she was, at a loss to explain how she felt.

'Is it Dennis?' said Amy. 'Is it that arsehole, because if it is—'

'He's definitely having an affair.' Carole pushed her hair back from her face, determined not to start crying again. 'I know he is. Too many late nights, all these unexplained absences, urgent telephone calls in the night, for it to be anything else.' She glanced up at Amy. 'And I know you don't like him, never have' – Amy sniffed but didn't deny it – 'but . . . but I love him. I mean, I really love him. And there's no need to make that face—'

'Sorry.'

'That's the way it is. And the thought of him with another woman, well . . .' Her nose started to redden again, and Amy thrust the unused napkins in her hand.

'Thanks.' Carole blew her nose loudly.

After a moment, ever-practical, Amy said, 'What are you going to do about it then?'

'Do?'

'Does he know you know, for one thing? Have you confronted him about it?'

'Not yet, I'm still thinking what to say for the best. But you know what' – Carole threw down the damp napkin so that it narrowly avoided her pastry – 'if this had happened last year, I'd have been in pieces. What would I do without him, we've been together since school, he's my whole world, all that crap. But now? Since the Graffiti Girls, you know what, Amy, you're right – we're worth more than this. If he's found someone else, well, it hurts but I'm only in my forties, I'm young enough to start all over again if I want. And maybe now's the time for me to have the career I always wanted but somehow having kids managed to derail. It's a new beginning, that's what it is.' She rubbed her nose. 'Isn't it?'

'Absolutely,' said Amy firmly, though as she glanced at Carole, her nose huge and red, shoulders slumped, pastry crumbs on her shirt and chocolate round her mouth, then along to Susan, her lips ragged as they often were these days, her hands twitching with nervous energy, she wondered not only what on earth she'd started, but also if they'd have the strength to see it through. She truly believed everything she'd said about women being worth more than they were getting in life, and if the Graffiti Girls had convinced Carole she still had the time and the right to make different, *better* choices, that was surely something to celebrate. She gulped down the sweet coffee and tried to ignore the seeds of doubt those women in the crowd had sown about a turning tide of opinion and the possibility that local people might have had enough of seeing their town defaced, however much they agreed with the messages scrawled across the walls.

Carole looked up at the clock, although barely five minutes had elapsed since the last time she checked and it had said 1.17 a.m. The younger boys had been sleeping for hours, exhausted after the excitement of the Gala Day, and even Thomas had thrown his phone aside and lay, mouth open, snoring gently on top of his Madonna duvet the last time Carole had gone up to check. Dan was out with some friends and had texted that he was staying over and not to wait up.

Carole checked her phone again but there was nothing from Dennis. He'd said he was going on a work night out – the company's annual bonding and back-slapping trip, he'd said with a smirk. He'd given her all the details – into town, along to the quay for a dinner boat down the Clyde with the rest of his company. But that was how it worked, wasn't it? When these men were having their affairs, they told more elaborate lies, gave you more details than ever so you wouldn't suspect. Well Carole suspected all right. She thought about calling Amy to talk things through but she knew her friend would be all righteous indignation on her behalf and frankly, she didn't need any encouragement to think the worst of her husband.

'Where the hell is he?' she wondered aloud, checking her phone fruitlessly one more time. She got up from Dennis's usual spot on the sofa, drained the rest of her wine into the sink and put her glass into the dishwasher. A last glance at her phone before she gave up, turned out the overhead light, and started to go upstairs to bed.

There was a banging at the front door. Dan had clearly changed his mind about coming home and had forgotten his keys again. *Or lost them*, thought Carole, tutting as she went back downstairs to open the door.

As she did so, the door suddenly gave way and in fell Dennis, flat on his face on to the hall carpet, one hand still clutching a half-empty bottle of red wine.

'Don't you dare spill that wine on my white carpet, Dennis Dungreavie.' Carole dashed forward to take the bottle from him, but Dennis, despite his drunken state, still had enough presence of mind to know he did not want to give up his booze.

'Leave that,' he slurred. 'It's mine.' Awkwardly, he pulled himself up off the floor, one hand pushing against the carpet, the other holding fast to his wine bottle. Only when he was fully upright did Carole see his face.

'Dennis, what on earth's happened to your eye? And your

cheek? Have you been fighting?' She tried to cradle his swollen, bleeding cheek with her palm but he pushed her away roughly.

'It's nothing,' he said. 'Go to bed.' He staggered through to the kitchen and propped himself up against the kitchen counter.

Carole saw that he was limping on his right foot, and his suit trousers were torn at the knee. She followed him to the kitchen, turned the light back on and waited for him to speak.

Whether because of the bright light in his face, or Carole's concern, Dennis seemed to sober up pretty quickly.

'I'll make you a coffee,' said Carole, snapping on the kettle and reaching into the cupboard opposite where Dennis stood to get the mugs.

Dennis didn't answer but left his bottle of wine and took a seat at the counter. Carole could hear him breathing heavily and muttering under his breath.

She handed him a coffee strong enough to set him right, and stood facing him.

'We need to talk, Dennis,' she said finally, hating herself for such a clichéd opener but not knowing how else to bring it up.

'Not now, Carole, I've got too much on my mind. It's . . . things that don't concern you.'

Carole slapped her hand against the cold surface. 'Don't concern me? What the hell does that mean? We've been together for over twenty years, Dennis, there's nothing in your life that doesn't concern me.'

He looked at her in surprise. 'What's got into you? Why do you care if I'm late back, seems like you're never here these days anyway, always out with your pals, at bootcamp, or whatever it is.'

'Never here?' Carole's voice rose an octave. 'Never here? Are you kidding me? I'm never anywhere *but* here. You're the one that's out all hours, Dennis, so why don't you come clean and tell me now – who is she?'

'Who?'

'Come off it, this woman you're seeing. You might as well tell me who she is because I know there's someone else.'

Dennis put down his cup and started to laugh. 'Another woman? Now *you're* kidding. When on earth would I have time to see another woman? I'm working all the hours God sends, I'm never away from that office and this' – he gestured to his injured face – 'this is the thanks I get.'

'What do you mean?'

Dennis slouched over his coffee cup, the steam billowing in his face and making him sweat. A line of watery blood streamed from the corner of his injured eye. Carole waited, and slowly, he relayed the events of his evening.

The night had started off well. The driving rain from earlier in the day had stopped suddenly, and the warmer weather they should have been having in June made a belated appearance. In fact, by the time Dennis reached the quay, it was like a sultry midsummer evening – the perfect weather to set off the firm's annual summer booze-cruise down the Clyde, this time planned as an even more elaborate event to celebrate the winning of a new client – the largest pension fund in the US, an addition that would almost double the firm's assets under management. Fresh money was always worth celebrating, thought Dennis wryly.

'Glass of fizz, sir?' A girl dressed as a Playboy bunny, decked out in pink furry ears and not much else, handed Dennis a flute of champagne as he stepped on to the river boat. He took a sip and looked over at his companions for the evening. His fellow bankers postured round the boat, all greased-back hair and fuchsia pink ties, calling each other 'Amigo' and slapping each other on the back. Dennis wondered why he'd come. One of his colleagues on the European desk waved over to him and held up his glass. He waved back but didn't join him since he was surrounded by a group of fund managers whose extravagant gesturing and loud voices suggested they were already drunk and planning on being even more obnoxious than they were sober.

Dennis made his way up to the top deck, looking for a quiet spot to sit and drink himself into a better mood. He was thinking about Carole, and how different she'd seemed recently, more like the feisty girl he'd married. They'd been together for so long, it was easy to forget how beautiful she was, but then she'd come downstairs ready for a night out – and there'd been more of those nights out recently, he'd noticed – and he'd be enthralled by her all over again. And yet, they seemed to be growing further apart, so much so that he'd started to wonder if it really was her friends she was seeing on these nights out, or . . . Dennis pushed the thought away, he refused to contemplate the idea of his wife with someone else. He'd started to avoid her, working longer and longer hours, hardly seeing her some days rather than give her the opportunity to tell him she was leaving. When they were together, she only wanted to talk about the children, never him. He missed the days when all they could think about was when they would next be together, crawling all over each other, backs arching, tongues seeking, limbs meshing over and over in their tiny first flat on Caird Street. He downed the champagne left in his glass and looked around for someone to refill it.

An hour later, he was sitting in the same position, and still resolutely sober despite the countless glasses of champagne that had been passed to him by the various hostesses. Groups of men – and it struck Dennis for the first time, that it was all men – milled around him. They gathered in groups of four or five, splinters of conversation cutting into his solitude and falling to the ground like broken glass, reminding him that human nature is pretty shabby stuff.

'Of course I said to him, if you insist on paying more than minimum wage – even to the cleaners, mark you – you deserve to go under.'

'It's nothing serious, I'm far too young to get caught by a woman, especially a gold-digging bitch like her.'

'Did you see what she was wearing? Like fucking Lara Croft digging for treasure. She deserved all she got, slag.'

'More champagne over here, darling. You're slacking a bit.'

'Two million, that's what he paid for it. Don't tell him I told you.'

'Money makes the world go round, old man, and long may it be so. Cheers Amigo.'

Dusk was coming as the crew tied up the boat, having made their way down the river, past the Tall Ship, and the BBC buildings, and the towering warships under construction in Govan. Dennis could see the tired pink bunnies fixing their hair and pulling their absurdly tiny shorts a little lower on their legs. Why was it that whenever grown men partied together, all of them fully covered in their suits and slackened ties, nevertheless they required half-dressed women to mill around, serving them like geishas? Dennis lifted his glass again and saw that it was empty. He decided he'd had enough and went to retrieve his jacket, pushing past a group of drunken traders from the North

America desk. He'd been thinking about Carole all night, and how lucky he was to have her, and wondering if it was too late to try and put right whatever had gone wrong between them.

'Leaving already, Dennis?' called Charles, a senior manager he particularly detested, from the bar. Charles was standing very close to one of the hostesses, swaying slightly so that she had to keep pushing him back to steady him. Dennis looked at him closely – his eyes were glassy and staring at some point in the middle distance.

'Yup, that's enough for me, thanks,' Dennis replied over his shoulder as he looked through the rack of almost identical Hugo Boss jackets for his own.

'Stay and have a drink with . . . what did you say your name was again?' Charles breathed into the hostess's face, his wispy facial hair close to her cheek. She backed away, her smile a grimace as she tried to hold the tray of glasses straight and also keep her distance.

'Hollie. It's Hollie, sir.'

'Ah yes, Hollie Sir.' Charles brayed at his own joke. 'Well Hollie Sir, did anyone tell you you're the prettiest girl on this boat?'

Dennis glanced over again and saw Charles put his arm round the girl so that his hand reached down and hovered over her right breast. She swerved away from him and the whole tray of glasses filled with champagne clattered to the floor. Charles laughed as she looked in dismay at the broken glass floating around in the still-fizzing Moët. He swayed forward again, and as she bent to retrieve pieces of broken glass, he slapped her bottom so hard that she fell onto the deck, screaming as her knees and palms met the shards of glass. A group of trainee fund managers clustered close by laughed and shouted what a waste of champagne and someone should get the waitress to lick it up.

Charles hit the deck faster than Hollie had done. Dennis had hit his whiskered cheek with his closed fist and he watched the blood trickle from his nose and the panic seep through his sagging academic's body.

Dennis could hear shouting from either side, and was aware of Hollie crawling over the broken glass to get out of the way. He bent closer to the ground and jabbed Charles hard, far harder than Charles had slapped Hollie, the squelch of muscle and blood against his knuckles. He started to punch him again, twice, three times, more.

'Fuck's sake, Dennis, stop!'

'Someone call the police.'

'He's going to kill him.'

Dennis watched Charles squirm his way across the deck and let him get almost to the safety of the bar before he lunged forward and kicked him like a dog in the softness of his belly. Blood spurted from his teeth as he curled up in pain. Two of the junior fund managers from Charles's team piled in and one socked Dennis in the eye, the other landed a kick to his thigh before he managed to throw them both off and storm off the boat.

Carole stared at him.

Dennis raised his hands. 'So this is who you married, Carole. A thug basically. Who can't control his temper. You should have listened to your pals after all. Right?'

'Was Charles drunk too?'

'Out of his face,' snapped Dennis. 'Like the rest of them.

They're a disgrace, Carole, honestly. Talk about me having anger management issues? They're the ones behaving like louts to those waitresses. I'm sick of it, sick of being part of it.'

'Will they . . . I mean, will Charles bring charges? Assault maybe?'

'Doubt it. The last thing the firm wants is to bring attention to the drunken exploits of a bunch of rich, coked-up wanker-bankers carousing their way down the Clyde.'

Carole hesitated then moved closer to Dennis. She touched his face again and this time he didn't push her away. She ran her fingers from his swollen eye down his cheek and held his chin. 'I've never thought you were a thug, Dennis. Not once. I just . . . I miss the way things were when we were younger. I thought . . . maybe you were having an affair with someone good-looking and ambitious, like I used to be . . . until the kids came along, and everything changed.'

Dennis gave a grim laugh. 'Me? Having an affair? As if. I'm always working, Carole, always because . . . I know what you gave up for me, the dancing, your own life, for me and the children. I thought . . . if I could give you everything, you would stop regretting it.'

'It was my choice not to go to London. You never forced me.'

'No, but . . .' Dennis reached down and gripped Carole's hand in his own much bigger hand, placing it against his chest. 'I'm sorry if it seems like I take you for granted. I know you're the person that keeps this family together, and I know it can't be easy for you – looking after all of us.'

'Thank you. That means a lot. Especially since it seems like you're never here to notice what I'm doing, never mind appreciate it.'

'You're right, I have been working too much recently.' He gave her a rueful smile. 'I suppose I thought that would give me less time to think about what's happening here, with us. I thought . . . you might be seeing someone, you've been out so much recently, and you seem . . . different?'

'Maybe I am different, and maybe I'll tell you more about that one day. But for now, I can tell you, there's no one else. It's been you and me for so long, I can't imagine it any other way. And look what we've built together – all this, and the boys. Not bad for two kids from Hamilton, is it?'

'Not bad at all,' said Dennis softly, his eyes on her mouth as he spoke.

Cupping his injured face gently, she moved closer to him and kissed his mouth.

'Carole, I—'

The front door clicked open and Dan strolled in, throwing his keys in the air. He stopped mid-throw and the keys landed with a clatter on the hall floor. He stared at his parents and said, 'What's happening here then? Have I walked onto the set of *Love, Actually*, or something?'

Dennis laughed, his face reddening as though he'd been caught out being romantic by his oldest son and ally. 'Never you mind, where have you been till this time?'

'I told Mum. I was staying at Mordecai's but jeez, their house is cold. I woke up at one, lying on his couch, shivering under his dad's old overcoat, so I thought "Fuck this—"'

'Oy, language,' said Dennis.

'Never mind that,' said Daniel, coming into the kitchen and seeing his father close up. 'What's happened to your face? Your eye's, like, practically sliding down your cheek.'

'We can talk about that in the morning,' said Carole. 'Come on, let's all get to bed.'

Daniel darted a look from his mum back to his dad, noting that Dennis was still holding Carole's hand tightly in his. He opened his mouth to say something else then shrugged and said, 'Whatever,' and headed upstairs to bed, leaving his jacket lying across the bottom stair as he did so.

Carole looked at Dennis, and he smiled at her and flicked the switch off in the kitchen. They stood together in the darkness till Dennis whispered, 'Yes, let's go to bed.'

v

Amy

THE FIRST JOB OF THE day was fixing a leaky tap in Cambuslang. Amy must have done about ten of these a week. All that was required was replacing a washer and she often wondered why people didn't buy their own washer and fix it themselves but thank goodness they didn't or she'd be out of business.

'There's clearly a problem with the water pressure,' said the landlord after he'd got over the fact that Amy was indeed simultaneously a woman and a plumber.

With some difficulty Amy tried to focus on his eyes rather than his mouth as his first tight smile had revealed two rows of teeth, the baby teeth, brown as nuts, still there and nestling behind his big teeth so that when he smiled he looked like a shark.

'No,' she said. 'There's nothing wrong with the—'

'Look, love, if you can't sort the water pressure, just say and I'll get someone who can.'

'It's a washer that needs replacing, that's why you're getting the constant dripp—'

'It's the pressure. The boiler's ancient. I mean, I don't live here so I'm not replacing the boiler. But these people are never done complaining – "the damp patches", "the mould", you name it.'

Amy gave a deep sigh. 'Please allow me to interrupt your confidence with my expertise. All that's needed here is—'

But unlike the leaky tap, the man was in full flow. 'They're lucky I haven't upped the rent for the last three years, I'm not a shark like some.'

Amy was about to laugh then realized in time that he wasn't making a joke at his own expense and stifled it. 'Okay,' she said. 'You win. I'll sort the water pressure for you.'

The man nodded, satisfied she was following his instructions, and Amy proceeded to replace the washer and charge him for the bigger issue he was so sure he had.

Half an hour later, she left Cambuslang and headed back towards Hamilton for her second job of the day. The clouds overhead were gathering like a fist and the first drops of rain fell as Amy jumped out of the van and grabbed her bag from the back. She dashed to the shelter of the porch – no, she thought, portico was a better word for this white entrance as big as her living room, supported by broad columns and floored with a giant's chessboard.

She gave an involuntary whistle as she stepped back and admired the huge blond-stone frontage of the property. Situated at the top of Ferniegair, but some way behind the new housing estate where Amy did most of her business, she hadn't even known such a house existed. They'd all been impressed by Carole's house but this was on another scale. *Some people have all the luck*, she thought, as she waited for someone to respond to her clanging of the huge bronze bell by the side of the door.

A small and fragile man opened the door. He was gentle-looking in his soft, olive-coloured cardigan and faded corduroy trousers, and could have been anything between fifty and sixty.

His hair was almost entirely white, though still thick and long enough to cover the neck of his cardigan.

'Miss Lampton?' he said in a low, shaky voice that had Amy immediately revising her estimate of his age upwards.

'Amy. That's right. Double X Plumbers. You called about a blocked drain?'

'Ah yes. Please. Come through.'

Amy wiped her feet ineffectually on the wicker mat at the door and followed the man through the main hall into a small living room at the back. She wondered what treasures lay behind all the firmly closed oak doors they passed on the way.

'My wife's still sleeping,' he said, gesturing vaguely upstairs as they passed the huge double staircase. 'She doesn't keep well.'

'Sorry to hear that,' said Amy. 'I'll do my best not to disturb her. If you take me out to the drain.'

The man seemed not to hear her as he sat down on the soft suede sofa at the back of the room and indicated that Amy should take the matching armchair. Amy hesitated then took a seat. 'It's very cosy in here,' she said as she dropped her tool bag by the side of the chair.

The man smiled for the first time. 'This was Emily's room. She used to sit and draw here. Said the light was perfect.'

'Emily?'

'My daughter. She . . . she's no longer with us, she was run over by a drunk driver two years ago.' He pointed to a picture on the window ledge. 'She painted that one in her first year at art college. I still think it's one of her best.' He got up slowly and handed it to Amy and she heard him take a sharp intake of breath as she ran her fingers lightly over the rough surface of the picture. It was a small canvas covered in dense splodges of autumnal-coloured paint, and Amy recognized the scene as the driveway to the house, painted to show it as it would look before winter set in and made everything hopelessly white.

'It's beautiful,' she said quietly, before giving it back to him.

'She was. Very beautiful,' said the man, placing the picture back on the window ledge, adjusting its position until it was angled exactly as it had been before. 'She would have been twenty-two now, just graduated.'

'I'm sorry,' said Amy again, then, after what she hoped was a decent pause, 'Ah, the drain? Is it out the back?'

The man stirred and apologized. 'Yes, it's through the kitchen, I'll show you.'

As soon as they reached the patioed area at the back of the house, Amy could smell the distinctive, sickly scent of rotten eggs, and knew immediately the old man was right – the outside kitchen drain was clogged. She clanged down her tool bag, took out the heavy-duty industrial waste bags she'd brought with her, laid one in front of the drain to kneel on, and set to work. The man stood watching her for a few minutes, then disappeared back into the kitchen. Despite the nature of the job, she felt cleaner amidst the congealed grease and solid coffee grinds coming away with her plunger than she had done in the house, the air in which was heavy with the old man's burden and the unmistakable reek of loneliness and despair.

When she'd finished, not more than twenty minutes later, she wiped her hands down her overalls and took a deep breath. The air already smelled fresher in the garden and Amy took a few minutes to clear her head and prepare for the old man again before she knocked the back door.

'I've made you a nice cup of tea,' he said. 'I'm sorry I've

nothing better to offer you with it than these custard creams.' He pushed the little plate of biscuits closer to Amy. 'I don't think they've been in the cupboard that long.' He lifted one up to demonstrate, and Amy watched as it bent softly between his bony fingers then crumbled on to the floor.

'I'm so sorry,' said Amy. 'I can't stay. I have an appointment in half an hour.'

'Ah, of course,' he said.

She looked on in dismay as the man's face crumpled. 'Actually, I've probably got ten minutes. A cup of tea would be nice, if I could wash my hands first?'

The man gave her his sad smile and indicated the vast Belfast sink behind them. 'Then we'll go back into Emily's room,' he said, and Amy forced herself to smile back.

'And she drew that one when she was at school. Can you imagine, the talent she had at sixteen years of age?'

Amy balanced the small watercolour of a sheepdog on top of the half-dozen or so similar pictures she already had on her lap.

'It's lovely,' she said. 'Really, they all are. She was clearly very talented.'

'Very,' he said. 'Who knows what she would have gone on to achieve if she hadn't been—' He left the sentence unfinished.

Amy sat uncomfortably in the silence for a few moments, then took another sip of the lukewarm tea he'd given her, avoiding the cup's greasy rim, and trying not to gag. She placed the cup, still half-full, on the side table next to her and handed the bundle of pictures back to the man. 'I'm so sorry,' she said. 'I've really got to go now.'

'Oh. No, I'm sorry,' he said, and he bent his head so that his jowls sagged. 'I've been keeping you. We don't get many visitors. My wife, you see . . .' He looked down at the pictures in his hands.

'I understand and it's been lovely, really,' she said, standing up and shaking the biscuit crumbs off her overalls. 'I really do have to get going. But if you have any more trouble with that drain, call me and I'll be right out, okay? No extra charge.'

He shuffled behind her as she made her way back along the wide hall to the release of the front door.

She turned at the last minute and said, 'She was lucky, having a dad like you.'

She wondered whether she shouldn't have said anything because the man's already rheumy eyes threatened to overflow, and his lips parted and trembled.

'Emily would've liked you,' he said. 'She would have approved of a lady plumber.'

Amy smiled. 'I've really got to go,' she said, apologetically. She touched his shoulder and made her way back to her van, aware of his eyes upon her as she walked.

She drove slowly down the driveway, a last look in her rear-view mirror revealing a broken figure framed by the twin colonnades of his beautiful portico, waving until her van disappeared out of sight. She blew a long sigh of relief to be leaving the house and its sadness behind her, and wondered what it would have been like to have a father who loved you like that. One who praised you, and was impressed by you, and cared about—

Thud.

'Shit, what the . . .'

A small, blueish-grey object had thumped against her front

window. Amy stopped the van and ran back to see what it was. A little bird, a tiny thing, was lying face down on the ground, its wings spread out at each side. Amy watched in horror as it dragged itself along the ground by the edge of the pavement but couldn't quite lift its pathetic head off the concrete. It kept trying though, inching across the ground, its wings and underside darkening in the puddle water. Until it stopped moving.

'And that was the worst thing,' said Amy, sitting on the large floral armchair in Dr Dowling's office half an hour later. 'It didn't die right away, it just kept on trying until it couldn't keep going any longer. And then it died, soaking wet and cold on the pavement. And it reminded me of the old man who— Anyway, the whole thing, it . . . really upset me.'

Dr Dowling let the silence deepen for a moment, as was his way, perhaps hoping that she would fill it with more nuggets of personal trauma. He was sitting in his own blue leather armchair opposite Amy's, leaning forward to indicate concern or interest, as he'd been trained to do, no doubt, thought Amy. She was determined to say no more until he spoke again.

Finally, he sat back and let his eyes drift over the notes on his desk to the left. 'And is this indicative of how you've felt generally this week, or . . .'

'Things have been fine,' said Amy briskly, wondering again what she was doing here. This was her sixth or seventh appointment with the psychologist now, she'd lost count, but after each session, she'd told herself she didn't need this, what on earth was she doing spending her hard-earned cash on talking to this stranger with his cheap brown suit and fringe cut straight, like a schoolboy? What could he possibly have to say that could help her? Of course she hadn't yet mentioned her father. So far the talk had all been about Tess, their relationship, how she'd left Amy and how that had made Amy feel.

It was Tess who said Amy should see a therapist in the first place, said she had to, actually, if she was concerned at all about her sanity. She'd screeched these things as she slammed round the flat, Amy following her from room to room as she tossed her trainers and jeans and tennis racquet into her suitcase any which way, so keen was she to get out of there. She couldn't live with someone who was so angry one minute longer, she said, someone so bitter at the world, someone who *raged* against everyone and everything. And for no reason, she said, or at least no reason she was willing to share with Tess.

Dr Dowling broke into her thoughts, and surprised her by saying in his professionally soothing voice, 'I'd like to dig a little deeper today, Amy, if that's okay with you?'

Amy played him at his own game and said nothing.

'By which I mean, I'd like us to talk a little about your childhood, your family, that sort of thing?'

Ah, thought Amy. *Maybe his training counts for something after all, and he's actually going to earn his £75 an hour.*

'Let's start with your family,' he said, crossing his legs. 'Can you tell me about them? It was just you and' – he glanced back at his notes – 'Mum and Dad, is that right?'

Amy kept her eyes on the pretty paperweight on Dr Dowling's desk, a glass sphere with pink and yellow butterflies caught mid-flight in the centre of the globe. Dr Dowling, it seemed, could withstand silences of any length, but it soon grew too uncomfortable for Amy and she had to fill it.

'Only my dad now, and I haven't seen him for years. I don't have any brothers or sisters. I wish I did.' There was a pause. 'Though I did once.'

Dr Dowling leaned forward in his chair again, Amy could tell he scented blood.

'I had . . . a brother. Sean. He was six years older than me. Dad loved him.' She stared at the butterfly closest to her, noting the veins on its brightly coloured but fragile wing.

'Go on.'

'They used to go fishing together. Camping, with huge knapsacks, axes, that sort of thing.'

Amy remembered the axe well. It used to sit by the front door, the last thing to be packed into Dad's CR-V, as Sean would jump around, a boisterous twelve-year-old, desperate to get into the wild and chop down trees and eat tomato soup heated up on their little gas burner.

'Can I come?' Amy would ask from time to time, eyes down and foot rubbing back and forth on the wooden floor of the hallway.

'Don't be silly,' her dad would say. 'It's a camping trip, we'll be living rough,' like they were heading out on a Himalayan expedition rather than a few hours up the road to Glen Etive.

That sounded brilliant to Amy but she knew there was no point in making her dad angry by persisting.

Sean would smile at her apologetically and promise to bring her back the best and smoothest stone he could find from the river bed.

'And we'll have fun here, Amy,' her mum would say, suggesting shopping if she was well enough and procedures to do with colouring and shaping their nails, or videos and baking sponge cakes if she wasn't feeling strong enough to go out. None of those things sounded to Amy anything like as much fun as sleeping under the wide, blue sky, a tummy full of tomato soup and swapping ghost stories with Dad.

'It sounds like you'd have liked to spend more time with your father?' suggested Dr Dowling, in his gentle way.

Amy dismissed the suggestion. 'Nothing to do with Dad. It was the camping I fancied. Why should Sean have all the fun?'

And Sean had had all the fun, at least as far as Amy was concerned. For six years, the sole focus of his parents' adoration, lapping up the time, effort, the sheer unimaginable love new parents feel for their first-born child. Amy had come along later, a mistake − or a surprise depending on who you talked to, especially given her mum's condition. She'd suffered from fibroids right up until she died − every month requiring tea and hot water bottles in bed for three, four days at a time while Amy was supposed to look after the home and everyone in it. She'd miss school for days on end, sometimes, as she did the cooking, the hoovering, ironing the shirts, making the beds, even Sean's − though he at least had the grace to be embarrassed as ten-year-old Amy hopped over his bed to make sure there were no creases in the duvet cover. She knew none of her friends would have put up with having to miss school and play house, and was furious with herself for being so weak.

Even the normally bumpy road through puberty and adolescence hadn't disturbed her brother's equilibrium. Amy watched on, silently fuming, as Dad pinned L-plates to the car the minute Sean turned seventeen and the pair would go off for hours, their father coming home red-faced and jubilant at how well his son had handled the roundabouts or the choked dual carriageway. 'Chip off the old block, this one,' he'd say and, 'Won't be long till this one passes his test, I'll tell you that.' He'd pat his son on the head before asking the eleven-year-old Amy whether she'd thought about dinner because obviously poor Mum, with her 'women's troubles', couldn't be expected to get up from bed the way she was feeling.

'And how were *you* feeling at that point?' said Dr Dowling, looking up from his pad where he'd written what looked to Amy like a mishmash of indecipherable characters.

'I didn't care,' she lied. 'I had friends, another life outside the house by then. Dad and Sean were welcome to each other.'

Dr Dowling didn't say anything. Something about the way his eyebrows pushed together and his mouth grew thinner let Amy know he didn't believe her though.

'What?' she challenged. 'Not everyone has to have Daddy issues, you know.' She tapped her index fingers against her jeans, and wondered when the hour was going to be up.

'That's true, but it does sound to an outsider as though Sean was getting more than his fair share of attention, while you were getting less?'

Amy made a face to indicate she was fed up talking about it. 'It's all water under the bridge. Anyway, mangled at the wheel of Dad's precious CR-V and dead at nineteen is all it got him in the end, so who's the lucky one now?' Amy winced even as she spoke these words because she'd loved her brother deeply, despite the age gap and the difference in the way they'd been treated. She still found it hard to tell people he'd died, and most people didn't even know she'd had a brother. People regarded you differently if they found out you'd lost a sibling, like you yourself were a harbinger of doom.

'I can tell that it's difficult for you to talk about. Tell me, were your parents able to help you process your brother's death?'

Amy almost laughed out loud. 'We never talked about it, not ever. After the funeral, Mum shut the door behind her in Sean's old room and slept there ever after. Dad took solace from whisky and as much of it as he could handle. Which was a lot.'

Dr Dowling put down his pen. 'Okay. That was a lot for you to discuss in one session, Amy. We'll leave it there for today but I'd like you to think about something for me before you come back for our next session.'

'Homework?' said Amy, her lip curling.

'If you like,' said the unperturbable Dr Dowling. 'I'd like you to think about how your life would have been different if your relationship with your father was different. And also' – he carried on speaking as though Amy hadn't got up and started pulling on her anorak – 'if your life could be made better now if that relationship were to change.'

Amy pulled out in front of the green Fiesta and pretended she didn't see the guy at the wheel give her the finger.

'Who taught these men how to drive?' she muttered to herself, putting the van into fifth gear and speeding along the Cadzow Bridge. 'And there's bound to be nowhere to park near the library.'

In the end she had to overshoot the library and find a space in the heaving car park outside Hamilton Palace sports ground. All the school holiday clubs were running and the place was packed, parents desperate to find something to entertain their kids, given the Scottish summer weather and apparent impossibility of letting them roam in the rain the way teenage Amy had done.

She glanced over at the rugby ground where she and Tess used to train with the women's team. Amy had loved their Wednesday evenings there, the physical exercise causing the endorphins to race through her system, the laughs and the in-jokes with their teammates, but most of all, the secret smiles shared between her and Tess, and the knowledge that they'd be getting into her van and driving home together at the end of the session.

For a while after Tess left, Amy kept going to the rugby club in the hope she might see her there one evening. She thought being part of the same team and the pints they shared in the Libertine afterwards might lead to a conversation at least but, true to her promise that Amy would never see her again, Tess hadn't turned up at the club, not even once.

Amy sighed as she lifted her tool bag out of the boot, contemplated putting her overalls back on over her jeans then decided it wasn't worth the bother.

The familiar smell of the library hit her as soon as she pushed open the heavy, ornate door at the entrance. Amy didn't know how Susan could bear to work here, stuck indoors among the books all day. They'd spent so much time in the place in their last couple of years at school, it must feel like never having left.

The library was quiet as Amy walked in, and she was conscious of her Doc Martens squelching against the marble tiles and the wrench clanking against the large metal spanner in her tool bag. A whiskery old man looked up from his newspaper as she passed, staring unselfconsciously at Amy and her oversized holdall. Amy glared back and was about to offer him a photograph when Susan spotted her and called out her name.

Amy dropped the heavy bag at the counter. 'Hi, Susan, sorry

I'm late.' She looked more closely at Susan, and smiled. 'You look better than the last few times I've seen you,' she said. It was true, the wild, hunted look in Susan's eyes had gone, her lips were almost fully healed, her hands calm at her sides.

Susan glanced around her, and, seeing the front desk was empty apart from them, said, 'Yes, I am feeling better, thanks. You're right – I do worry too much and after all, they've got nothing pinning the graffiti—'

Amy put her finger to her lips and Susan mouthed, 'Sorry. They've got nothing pinning the graffiti to us.' Then in a louder voice, 'So yeah, I'm feeling better about everything, especially since I heard this morning they've finally found someone to replace me so I can start my new job next week. I'll be sad to leave here but . . . it's time.'

'Too right it is,' said Amy. 'Onwards and upwards, and not before time, you're right.'

'But first, my gift to Hamilton library – my amazing plumber friend is going to fix that permanently blocked toilet for them, right?'

Amy made a face. Blocked toilets were not her favourite part of the job and business was going so well these days that she often turned down any job offers where there was a suggestion of having to plunge her arm elbow-deep in whatever gunge or sanitary matter was lurking down these 'blocked' loos. But if she couldn't help out Susan when she asked, she wouldn't be much of a friend.

'Lead on, Macduff,' she said, picking up her bag and preparing herself for the worst.

'This way.' Susan led Amy down the steep, carpeted stairs to the toilets, appropriately located in the bowels of the building.

Their voices sounded hollow in the corridors, the walls of which were covered with off-white, pearlized tiles.

'You'd have to be bursting to brave a visit down here,' said Amy, after they'd been walking for at least five minutes.

'It's not that bad,' said Susan, defending the building automatically.

Amy pulled on her black rubber gloves, knelt at the first toilet and opened the lid. The toilet was stuffed with beige-coloured toilet roll and the top of the bowl was lined with a faint greyish brown line below the rim. The smell was overpowering.

Amy sat back on her heels, waving her hand in front of her face. 'God's sake, Susan, how long's it been like this?'

'Sorry. You know what the council are like – always coming to fix it, except they don't. Do you want a cup of coffee while you're working?'

'Yes please,' said Amy, searching her bag for the biggest plunger she could find. 'I'll need it.'

Amy worked on the toilet for the next twenty minutes, emptying the contents of the bowl into the thick blue bags she'd brought with her for the purpose, plunging the depths of the toilet to get at the blockage and continually flushing and reflushing till the water ran clear.

As she pulled off her gloves and sat back to see whether the last flush had done the trick, she heard someone say 'Knock knock' at the door behind her.

Turning, Amy saw a tall, athletic-looking girl framed in the doorway. She had a powerful, straight fringe, the same blue-black as the rest of her hair which was spiky at the crown and a little longer at the back. Her eyes were kohl-rimmed and she had a tiny tattoo of a butterfly on her neck, almost, but not quite, hidden by the collar of her sky-blue council shirt. She was carrying a chintzy cup and saucer in one hand and a small white plate in the other.

'Kiwi fruit?'

'I'm sorry?' said Amy, thinking she must have misheard.

The girl stepped forward and held out the cracked plate, which had four pieces of peeled and wet-looking kiwi sitting in the middle of it. 'Would you like some?'

'Ah, no thanks,' said Amy, scratching the back of her head. 'Thanks though,' she added, not wanting to appear ungrateful.

'Here's your coffee then. With milk, okay?'

Amy stood up and rubbed her hands down the front of her jeans. 'Perfect, thanks.'

'I'm Marion,' said the girl. 'I work with Susan.'

'Amy,' said Amy. 'I would shake your hand but . . .' She indicated the toilet apologetically.

Marion remained by the door saying nothing.

Amy felt the need as ever to bridge the silence. 'Have you worked here long? Susan never talks about her colleagues – though we do get a blow-by-blow account of whatever book she's reading this week. She reads a lot, well, I suppose you should if you're a librarian . . .' She stopped, aware she was rambling, and that this strange girl, with her silent presence, her narrowed watchful eyes under that fringe, was making her twitch with energy. She rubbed her hand over her almost bald scalp and wished she wasn't wearing jeans streaked with shit.

'Sorry about the smell,' she said. 'From the toilet, that is,' she added quickly, and was rewarded with a wide smile which changed Marion's face completely.

Amy felt a sudden heat rise up from her chest, cover her neck and flood her face.

Marion smiled again. 'I'll let you finish,' she said, turning to go.

Amy watched her stroll through the tiled corridor towards the stairs. Before she disappeared from view, she shouted after her, 'Thanks for the coffee . . . Marion.'

The girl turned and waved, and Amy caught a glimpse of another tattoo, a small blue rainbow, on the inside of her wrist.

Amy got back to the flat about six, having done two more jobs after the library and stopping off at the big Asda for the only cat food her pernickety cat would eat. Mrs Cooper was nowhere to be seen. Amy called her for a bit then gave up, knowing the cat would come and find her when she was hungry.

Grabbing a packet of spicy Doritos from the kitchen for her own dinner, Amy kicked off her Docs and tried to relax on the soft, worn leather sofa. She could hear the clock ticking in the hall, and a short high-pitched ringing from her neighbour's phone through the wall. She checked her own phone for messages but there were none. She ate some crisps and made a face as the sharp triangles sliced at the skin of her throat as she swallowed. *Even my food's out to get me today*, she thought, and threw the half-empty bag on to the table. She rested her head on the cushion again, marvelling at the silence in the flat. It was always quiet these days, not that Tess had been much of a talker. It was her presence Amy missed, she supposed, since she didn't speak much. Until that last day, when she'd spoken plenty. Like this great dam had burst inside her and she couldn't stop talking, even though Amy didn't want to listen.

And she felt guilty too, lying here half-asleep in the middle of the evening. Tess had been so sporty, so full of energy, always heading out somewhere at top speed with a tennis racquet in her hand or a bag full of swimming gear. She used to get angry at how little exercise Amy did but then Amy would grab her from behind and smother her in a huge hug until she forgot to be annoyed.

She awoke in the gloom an hour later, her cheek sticking to the leather and a crick in her neck. It was a struggle to be wrenched out of her dream about Tess, her calves strong and muscular and tanned against the white of her tennis socks. But it soon became clear what had woken her up. The flat was filled with a hideous, high-pitched whining sound, like a cat being strangled was her first thought, which she quickly batted away, remembering she was now a cat lady.

She struggled up from the couch, frowning as the screeching continued. She followed the sound – a pained, hollow screaming, but in miniature, not that of a person but an animal. She couldn't see anything in the kitchen, or the bedroom. On her way back to the living-room she spotted the trail of blood, pinpricks of red in a curving line across the hall carpet and leading into the spare room. The small howling continued and Amy covered her ears with her hands, nervous now as to what might greet her at the end of the trail.

'Mrs Cooper?' she whispered, as the trail grew thinner, ending abruptly in a puddle of viscous red, by the bed in the spare room.

Taking a breath and saying, 'Come on, Amy, you can do this,' she lifted the edge of the duvet and peered under the bed. As her eyes adjusted to the darkness and her ears tried to block out the wailing, her face fell as she saw Mrs Cooper crouched under the bed, her green eyes dull and wet, and her fur matted with blood. The poor thing tried to lift a paw to bat Amy away but lacked the strength and continued her pathetic mewling instead.

Amy sat back on her heels, not sure what to do. Would a vet come out at this time of night? Then, hot on the heels of that thought – would Tess come if she told her her cat was in trouble? She dismissed this thought as soon as she had it. She got up to call the vet emergency service – was there such a thing? – when she stopped. Mrs Cooper had dragged herself from under the bed, staining the carpet deep red all the way, her flashing eyes never leaving Amy's face.

'Mrs Cooper,' whispered Amy. 'Tess . . .'

Seconds later it was all over.

Shocked, Amy couldn't move. 'Mrs Cooper, oh, Mrs Cooper.'

She reached out her hand to pet the creature but found she couldn't touch her and ran out of the room to be sick in the bathroom sink instead.

By the time Carole got to Amy's flat, Mrs Cooper was stiff as a board. Amy had fetched the bath mat from the bathroom and laid it down on the carpet at the end of the bed, placing Mrs Cooper on top of it. The cat's eyes were open, and even in death, its stare seemed to follow you as you moved. The fur on its back was matted with blood, now crusted and dried black. Carole's stomach heaved a bit as Amy stroked the inert form on the mat.

'Thanks for helping me,' said Amy.

'Of course,' said Carole, trying not to look at the cat. 'What do you want me to do?'

'We need to bury her.'

'Right,' said Carole slowly, then as though she was talking

to one of her two younger boys, 'Is that not something the vet would do? Or—'

'Absolutely not,' said Amy. 'She's . . . she was my cat and I am going to give her the burial she deserves. There's no way she's going to be burnt to ash along with a load of other dead animals from who knows where. I can't even—'

'It's okay, Amy,' said Carole. 'We'll do whatever needs to be done. Just tell me.'

Amy looked at her gratefully and explained what they were going to do.

First, they wrapped Mrs Cooper in a plastic bag from the Co-op, her tail poking out the top. Carole couldn't help feeling it wasn't a very dignified way to go but Amy seemed happy enough and that was the main thing. They carried her between them – she was surprisingly heavy – down to the back door of the block of flats, across the road and into the lane behind the old racecourse. Amy had brought a pitted metal trowel with her and she knelt down beneath a spindly tree at the side of the lane and started digging. Tall grass covered the ground but the recent summer showers had made the earth soft and pliable and it was quite easy to dig the hole. The women took turns to break up the soil and Amy insisted that whoever wasn't digging had to stroke the cat through the plastic and say comforting things. Carole felt a bit stupid when it was her turn but, under Amy's watchful eye, she muttered stuff about cat heaven and all the treats that awaited Mrs Cooper.

When the hole was about a foot deep, Amy said that would do and Carole passed her the bag containing the cat. She laid her down gently in the makeshift grave and they both threw in handfuls of dirt from the mound beside the hole.

'There,' said Amy, wiping her hand across her cheek and smearing it with soil as she did so. There was dirt in her hair too, she looked like she'd come back from a rough training session with the Territorial Army. Carole decided she would need to take her friend in hand and make sure she didn't shave her head again. 'Okay,' she said to Amy, as gently as she could. 'I think we've finished.'

'Wait, now we need to sing a hymn,' said Amy.

'She was only a cat—'

Amy glared at her.

'Okay, okay,' agreed Carole. 'What hymns do you know?'

'I can't remember any from school. What about you?'

Carole racked her brain. 'We sang "Eagle's Wings" for my uncle Tony, it was beautiful. Do you know it?'

'No, but I don't think poor Mrs Cooper would want to be raised to heaven by a giant bird, do you?'

She had a point. 'What about "Morning Has Broken"? It's the only other holy song I know.'

'Okay, you start.'

Carole wasn't much of a singer but she knew the sooner she started the sooner it'd be over with so she began singing the first line, 'Morning has broken, like the first—' when they heard the shouts behind them.

'What's happening?' called a stocky boy of around ten or so, closely followed by his pal, both of them pushing clanky old bikes along the grass verge of the lane.

Amy swung round and shooed them away like they were scavenging pigeons. 'We're burying Mrs Cooper here. A bit of privacy please.'

The boy muttered, 'Weirdos,' and the pair jumped back on their bikes and raced off in the opposite direction.

Amy and Carole finished singing to the cat.

'That's that then.' Amy tried not think of poor Mrs Cooper under the mound of earth.

Carole patted her friend's arm. 'Shall we go back to the flat and have a nice cup of tea?'

Amy arched her eyebrow.

'Or something stronger?'

'Yeah,' said Amy, not objecting when Carole looped her arm through hers and led her away from the lane.

'I've called the girls,' said Carole as she set a pint down next to the half-finished one already sitting in front of Amy. 'Susan's to prepare Fraser's supper before she can come out' – Amy snorted – 'but Lenore's going to pick her up on the way.'

'What about you – is it all right for you to be out this late on a weeknight? Was Dennis not complaining he'd have to babysit his own kids?'

'Don't start on Dennis, Amy. Anyway, it's Daniel who's holding the fort. Dennis is—'

'Don't tell me, out working again?'

'No, actually, he's trying to find some new hobbies, stuff to do away from the office. He's out at a wine tasting tonight.'

Amy snorted again.

'What's wrong with that?' said Carole. 'Even you like wine.'

'Drinking it, not standing round with a bunch of strangers, spitting and trying to think of different ways to say "plummy".'

Carole laughed. 'You're not that upset, you can still make fun of Dennis.'

'I'm not upset at all! Honestly, I hope you didn't make a fuss and tell Susan and Lenore I'm being all pathetic.' Amy rubbed at her eyes angrily, the tears dry now but her eyes still red and sore.

'You're *not* being pathetic, Amy, no one could ever accuse you of that. Quite the opposite, in fact.' She was silent for a moment then, leaning in closer to Amy as she spoke, added softly, 'You know, you don't always have to be the strong one. Always covering up what you feel with the smart quips and the one-liners. Sometimes you're allowed to cry and say what's really bothering you and we'd help you for a change.'

Amy threw her a half-smile. 'What are you, my shrink now?'

'No, I'm your friend and I'm worried about you.'

Amy took a large gulp of Guinness. 'Nothing to worry about, I assure you. Anyway, as I remember, you were the one with problems last time we spoke. Although you seem a lot better tonight? What's changed?'

'I don't know what you're talking about.'

'Come off it,' Amy persisted. 'You're like the cat that's got the cream. You weren't like this last time I saw you.'

Carole couldn't stifle her smile. 'You're right, things are better. Dennis and me, we're—'

'Divorcing?' said Amy, almost knocking over her pint in her eagerness.

'What? No, don't be ridiculous. The opposite, in fact. Turns out there isn't anyone else, no affair, and we both . . . want things to work. Things are going to change, they already have changed, and in a way, it's all down to you and the Graffiti Girls. That's what given me confidence, belief in myself as my own person and the ability to still do things that matter. But never mind me, we're supposed to be talking about you for a change.'

'I'm fine—' Amy began, waving away her friend's concern

but Carole surprised them by banging her hand down on the table in a gesture they both recognized as belonging to Amy. 'No, you're not fine, and I don't think you've been fine for years, not since your brother died.'

Amy winced. 'Carole—'

'No, I know it's hard to talk about, but I'm your best friend and I hate to see you miserable.'

'I'm not miserable, honestly, that stuff with Sean and the way my dad treated me, that's all water under the bridge. It's just . . .'

Carole waited.

'It's more . . . that I'm raging about the way life is in general. It's not just my dad, it's all men, and the way they run the world. No, you can say they don't, Carole, but the fact is, our lives — yours, mine, Susan's, Lenore's, probably every woman we've ever known, our lives have all been fucked over by the patriarchy.'

'Oh, Amy—' began Carole.

'No, think about it. When you were at school, you wanted to study Physics, remember?'

'Well, yeah, but . . .'

'Yeah, but nothing. A girl who looked like you didn't fit into their idea of a Physics student — you liked dancing, for goodness' sake — so they steered you to the Arts subjects instead. Meanwhile Dennis, who couldn't hold a candle to you when it came to Maths and Science, he was practically forced into the science block and made to do his Advanced Physics and Chemistry. Am I right?'

'I suppose so,' said Carole, gulping down some white wine which she suddenly felt like she needed.

'And since then, you've been stuck at home bringing up the kids while Dennis has his glittering career. Why? Because he's the breadwinner and you're the homemaker, we really haven't come on any further than that.'

Carole thought for a moment. 'Okay, you're right about me – although I'm taking steps now to change that. But what about Susan? And Lenore? They've always worked.'

Amy blew out her contempt. 'Both went into professions deemed suitable for women and both have struggled since then – despite their talent, mind you – to progress up the greasy pole of success. Why? Because it's a man's world. Always was, still is.' Amy sat back, colour high and chest rising and falling with anger.

'You're right. I know you are,' Carole said quietly. 'But like I say, I'm doing things to change my own situation now, Dennis and I both are, and I think Lenore and Susan are happier with the way their lives are going since the Graffiti Girls changed things for them too.'

Amy took another mouthful of her pint and wiped her lip. 'Hmmpph,' she said. 'Maybe you're right, and we have achieved something in the context of our own lives but you know, that's small fry.'

'What do you mean?'

'I mean, what about all the other women in the world? The ones who are living in fear of their abusive partners and they go to the police only to find a culture of such misogyny that there's no way they're going to be taken seriously?'

'But that's—'

Amy carried on as though Carole hadn't spoken. 'Or what about the young girls in China that get their feet taped, or the baby girls in Sierra Leone who scream the roof down as they're mutilated, or the teenage girls in Bangladesh who work every hour God sends sewing sweatshirts till their fingers bleed, or—'

'Amy, stop! Honestly, just stop. You can't think about the injustices suffered by every single woman, you cannot be concerned about every trauma everywhere in the world. You'd go crazy!'

'But that's the point, Carole,' said Amy. 'Nobody is talking about these things, or at least not loudly enough, so they keep being allowed to happen. Okay, it's on a much smaller scale, but we're stopping that with the Graffiti Girls, don't you see? We're saying you can't pin us against a wall and assault us, and expect us to say nothing, we'll call you out. You can't pay us less for doing the same job or we'll plaster it all over your walls, we'll call you out. You can't value us only for the way we look, then write us off at forty, or we'll graffiti your premises in bright blue and red paint. We. Will. Call. You. Out.' She stopped and took a deep breath. 'Do you see?'

Slowly, Carole nodded. 'Yeah,' she said. 'Yes, I do see. Let's wait for Lenore and Susan to get here and we'll make them see too.'

An hour and a half and several rounds of drinks later, and the four women still hadn't agreed on their next move. Amy, ready as ever for action, and Carole, fired up by Amy's rage speech, were all for giving the Graffiti Girls one more outing. Lenore was on the fence and Susan was quite adamant they shouldn't risk it again.

'Honestly, the fuss has just about died down from the last time and you want to risk stirring it all up again?'

'Yes!' cried Amy. 'That's exactly what I want to do – stir things up because if we don't, who will?'

Lenore put her hand on Amy's arm to calm her down, gesturing at the two young guys at the bar looking over and listening in to their conversation. 'Look, Amy, I can understand why you want to, and you're right, we've all had a turn to say what's been bothering us and have it writ large against whatever building we choose but I don't know if you realize, the tide's turning against us.'

'What do you mean?' said Carole. 'Local women love the Graffiti Girls, women further afield too. We're acting as a loudspeaker for all the things that have been bothering them for years but haven't had the courage to say out loud.'

Lenore shook her head. 'At the beginning maybe, but folk are getting tired of seeing local property being defaced. Hamilton is *their* town, their *home*, they don't want to see bright red and green graffiti all over the council buildings, and definitely not all over their local pub.'

'Lenore's right,' said Susan.

'You would say that,' said Amy.

'You're right, I'm terrified of getting caught, but the fact is, Lenore *is* right. People come into the library every day, they talk about local issues, things that are bothering them, and one thing they don't like is their town being vandalized. I'm having to listen to people come in and complain about it almost every day and I have to keep my mouth shut and pretend it's nothing to do with me.'

'And you heard what they were saying at the Gala Day, didn't you? And you only need to look at the Hamilton Facebook page to see what else people are saying. They're not happy with the Graffiti Girls, Amy. Well, to be more accurate, they sympathize with what we're saying but they don't agree with how we're going about saying it.'

273

Amy and Carole were quiet for a bit then Carole looked up and said, 'I'm going to say one last thing. Amy came up with the idea of the Graffiti Girls—'

'Not the shite name but yes, sorry, go on . . .'

'And in the six months since we started, my life has been turned round, yours has too, Lenore, and yours, Susan. Maybe we're not exactly where we want to be yet but we're making steps in the right direction. Amy's reminded us that we're worth something, our lives matter, *we* matter – more than just the caring, sharing, doing everything for everybody else stuff we've somehow managed to get stuck with for the last twenty years – *we* matter, our ambitions, what we want from life. Amy's done that. Okay, we've all gone along with it and done our bit, with the zany slogans and the paint and the crazy outfits, but let's face it, we'd have done none of it without Amy.'

Lenore nodded, and Susan said slowly, 'I suppose . . .'

'So my opinion is, that it's Amy's turn now. And if she wants to bring attention to what's bothering her, so she can move on too, then we, as her best friends' – Carole looked pointedly at each of the women as she said this – 'should step up to the plate one last time and join her.' She picked up her glass of wine and held it high in the air. 'Now. Who's in?'

After a moment's silence, Lenore raised her hand and said, 'Okay.'

Carole smiled at her and they all transferred their gaze to Susan.

She raised her glass slowly. 'Okay. But this is the last time. I mean it!'

★

A week later, Amy left the silence of her flat around midnight. Carole and Susan were coming with Lenore so Amy made her way there on her own, Bruce Springsteen's 'Born to Run' turned up loud on the van radio as she drove. The road ahead was slick and empty, behind her only white lights and rain. She was singing along with Bruce and feeling good as she'd already made some changes. Dr Dowling was right, she'd decided. Her family issues had been a problem for her and she'd started to open up to him about how resentful it had left her. The admission alone was helping her to move on, and to her surprise, she'd found that letting go of the anger that had fuelled her since childhood was also slowly salving the blistering rage she felt towards the world at large.

The other thing she'd done was to visit the Cat Rescue Centre with Carole. 'Just to look,' she'd said but of course she'd left the place as the proud new owner of an adorable little grey and white scrap of a kitten. 'I'm calling her Gigi,' she'd said to Carole as she signed the documents at the desk to pick up her new pet in two weeks' time.

'Love it!' Carole agreed, delighted to see her friend looking more like her old self again.

It had been a scorching July day, certainly by Scotland's standards, and even though the sun was long gone and replaced by a light summer rain as Amy's dashboard clock struck midnight, it couldn't wash away summertime from the air – the smell of fresh grass and sun cream and echoes of the kids shouting in the streets, all of which was making Amy feel more positive than she'd felt since Tess left, and even before that. The graffiti campaign had brought not just her, but all of the girls, back to their old sparkling selves and if that had been all they'd achieved it would have been worth it for that. But Amy knew they'd had an impact on others in the town too. She saw it daily in the women she spoke to as she set about fixing their pipes and drains – the women who owned small businesses in the area, who now acknowledged their business skills and what they'd achieved; the stern women who called her and said they'd had enough of waiting for this or that man in their life to fix things for them, they were calling out women tradespeople, like Amy, and getting things done. As she drew up to the large white building on Campbell Street, Amy was satisfied that the Graffiti Girls had done what they'd set out to do, and that this would indeed be their last outing. That's why it was fitting they should go out with a bang.

Susan was searching in her bag for a tissue and muttering to herself in the passenger seat of Lenore's car. Lenore was tapping her clammy palm off the steering wheel, trying to keep calm. Carole sat in the back, silent, her eyes glued to the three white cars lined up in the car park in front of them, each with their unmistakable blue and yellow squares on the side, one with its blue light still sitting proudly on the roof.

'Budge up,' said Amy, rapping her knuckles on the window and getting into the car beside Carole. All three women jumped.

'God's sake, Amy, are you trying to frighten us half to death?'

Amy laughed. 'I do have that effect on people, it seems. Must be the hair.'

'You seem very relaxed, considering.' Carole gestured over to their target walls.

'It'll be fine. Are you guys all stressing because it's the police station?'

'Of course we are,' said Lenore. 'I mean, I get it – it's the symbol of oppression, dominated by men, sexist culture, I could go on . . .'

'Please don't,' said Susan, wiping her forehead. 'Is it just me, or is it really hot in here? Because I'm sweating, really sweating . . .'

'Look, everyone,' said Carole. 'We agreed the police station because of what it symbolizes with the patriarchy and the oppression of women and all the stuff Amy' – Amy gave her a hard stare – 'I mean that we are all against, so yes, this is it, this is the big one.'

'Yes and no,' said Amy. 'It's the big one because it's the finale but don't get so uptight. At the end of the day, it's the home of Hamilton's boys in blue, not Scotland Yard, and it's past midnight – they all went home hours ago for their meat and three veg and tonight's episode of *Top Gear*. We'll be absolutely fine, I promise you.'

With that, Amy got out of the car and gestured to her friends to come round to the van and help her get the paint.

'Here goes nothing,' said Susan, taking a deep breath and pulling her too-tight leggings out of her butt crack as she went.

There was a short lane at the side of the car park and the four women tiptoed through it, avoiding the main entrance to the station. The cans of spray paint were small and light, and each woman also held a miniature paint pot and soft brush for finishing touches. They crouched behind a huge rhododendron bush, which was bursting with purple flowers, and had their last pep talk from Amy.

'As usual, fast as you can is key. Quick in and out. Bit like Dennis.' She winked.

'Hey, watch it,' said Carole, shoving Amy so that she fell against Lenore and both women ended up on their backsides.

'Watch my phone, Amy,' cried Lenore, 'it's in my back pocket.' She pulled it out of her skintight leggings and, as she wiped the screen, became aware of the low buzzing that indicated she was calling someone. 'Shit,' she cried. 'I've butt-dialled Mark Lown!'

'Who?' said Carole.

'Does it matter?' said Susan. 'Can I remind you we are crouched behind a bush at the police station with cans of paint while there's an ongoing investigation into the local graffiti crisis? Who cares if some guy will think Lenore's calling him at midnight?'

'Mark— Lenore, is that the policeman?' said Amy, giving Lenore a stony look.

'Yes, but don't look at me like that, Amy, you were the one who pushed me over.'

'I think you'll find it was Carole who—'

Lenore suddenly threw her phone into the air as though it was a grenade. 'Now he's calling me back,' she cried, as her new 'Let's talk about sex, baybee' ringtone pierced the air, seemingly louder than anyone else's ringtone ever.

'Lenore? Is that you?'

The women froze.

The heavy footsteps came closer, there was a sudden rustle in the bush, and the women found themselves looking into the eyes of PC Mark Lown, with a mug in one hand and his phone lit up in the other. The top button of his shirt was undone but the rest of his uniform was intact and he looked very much like the policeman he was.

'Uh, hi, Mark, hello. Um, you remember Amy and Carole, and that's Susan over there, with her hands over her eyes.'

Susan took her hand away from her face briefly, said hi, then put her hand back over her face, as though, like a child playing hide and seek, if she couldn't see Mark, then he couldn't see her.

Mark regarded each of the women in turn, his eyes widening as he took in the outfits, the face masks, and of course, the spray cans and paintbrushes. He opened his mouth to speak but no words came out.

'How did you know I was here?' asked Lenore, standing up slowly and wiping grass and leaves from her backside.

Mark held out his phone. 'You called me, Lenore, and I called you right back. But I was standing over there' – he pointed back to the side entrance of the station – 'having my coffee break so when I called you, I heard your phone ringing from somewhere very close by. I followed the sound to this rhododendron bush and . . . well, here we are.'

'Yes, here we are,' said Amy briskly, standing up, unaware that half the bush was still sticking to the back of her thighs till Carole pulled it off. 'Thank you, Carole,' she said before turning back to Mark. 'Nice to see you, Mark, we were just . . . out for some air and now we'll be heading back to our vehicles. Come on, girls,' she said. 'Someone pull Susan to her feet.'

Mark watched in silence as the friends staggered and stumbled their way back to Lenore's little blue Skoda, Susan dropping her paint can on the way and Amy raising her eyes skywards as the can clattered back towards Mark's feet. He picked it up and handed it back to Susan, saying nothing. As Amy got into her van and Lenore started up her engine, he seemed to come out of his daze and he ran over to Lenore's side of the car. He indicated that she should roll down her window and as she did so, Susan put her hand over her eyes again. Amy watched from the driver's seat of her van which was parked directly behind Lenore's car.

'It's late now but I'm going to need to speak to all of you tomorrow.' He eyed the three women in the car, and said, 'Tell Amy – the four of you, at the library, at nine.'

'But we've got Bounce and Rhyme at—' began Susan.

'It's there or the police station, up to you,' said Mark, not taking his eyes off Lenore.

'It's fine,' she said, shaking her hair out of her eyes. 'We'll be there. At nine.'

Saying nothing more, Mark walked back to the police station, stopping only to pick up a single treacherous paintbrush that one of the women had dropped on the grass.

'I think that went as well as could be expected,' said Susan the next morning, shutting the door to the staffroom after PC Lown had left, so that neither Marion nor their new young assistant, the super-keen Olive, could walk in and disturb them.

'Bloody cheek,' said Amy, standing in front of the window and watching as PC Lown drove off in his own car.

'Aw, come on, Amy, we were as good as caught red-handed, he was well within his rights to take us in and question us for malicious damage, or whatever it is that graffitiing your local area comes under.'

'Activism,' muttered Amy but the others ignored her.

'And I think we've got Lenore to thank for that,' added Carole. 'If he hadn't fancied her so much, we'd have had no chance.'

And all the women knew it was true, even Amy. Mark Lown had come into the library in his jeans and shirt and started off by saying he was there in his unofficial capacity 'as their friend'.

'I'm going to give you a hypothetical situation, and I don't want you to interrupt me' – a significant look at Amy – 'and I most certainly don't want you to give me any information that I'd be duty bound to act upon' – Susan's turn to receive the meaningful glance – 'I am just going to set out the situation for you and how it could be resolved, okay?'

The four friends sat in silence, Carole patting Susan's arm reassuringly, as they waited to hear what he had to say.

'Let's imagine there was a small town in, South Lanarkshire, say, and this town suddenly suffered from a spate of vandalism—'

'Do you mean graffiti highlighting important issues?' Amy raised her hand as she spoke.

'I'm using my words very carefully in fact, Amy, and I mean vandalism which, you are right, in this case takes the form of graffiti. Now, if the person or, say, four persons responsible for this spate of vandalism were to promise *absolutely* never to vandalize any more property in the town, and if, sure enough, no more vandalism took place, I think that it would be conscionable for any serving police officer who was aware that the graffiti artists had stopped their campaign to say okay look, these four persons had their reasons for doing what they did but they see now they were wrong—'

'Misunderstood?' offered Amy, her hand in the air again.

'Wrong,' repeated PC Lown. 'Do we understand each other?'

Carole nodded so hard her beautiful blonde hair escaped its band, whilst Susan eyed the door nervously. Lenore remembered to pout a little in case Mark looked in her direction and Amy ran her hand over her buzz cut as though they really had any options to consider.

'And are we clear as to the consequences if even one more incident, even one' – looking at each woman in turn to emphasize his point – 'were to take place? Because even the most besotted of policemen' – Carole high-fived a suddenly grinning Lenore, then said 'sorry' and made a face as Mark raised his eyebrows – 'would have to take matters further if it happened again. And I do mean that.'

'I think we all understand, Mark. Thank you,' said Lenore, looking at her friends who muttered their thanks in turn.

After he'd left, they all sat back in relief. Amy said, 'Christ, that pompous ass, who does he think he is?'

'He's Mark Lown,' said Lenore breathlessly, 'a handsome, *besotted* policeman,' before being set upon by the others who admonished her for being such a doormat.

'Gigi,' Amy called to her cat softly, knowing she'd be hiding under the bed. They'd told her at the Rescue Centre that she'd have to be patient, the poor creature had had a troubled start in life and would need to be handled sensitively. She'd been home with Amy for two weeks now and had spent most of that time under the bed. But last night, Amy had been sitting in the living room, watching a documentary Lenore had recommended to her, when Gigi appeared at the door, back low and eyes darting round the room, checking for danger. Amy had held her breath as the animal rubbed itself against the soft leather of the sofa before springing up, and curling her little body into a tight bud on Amy's lap. They were making progress.

Amy called her again, and a few minutes later, the cat padded through to the kitchen, where Amy had laid out some food and water in two new bowls. The cat ate her lunch while Amy scrambled eggs for her own, and took it over to the kitchen table.

'Look at this, Gigi,' said Amy. 'Are you proud of me? I'm quite proud of me actually.'

Open on the table was a copy of the *Glasgow Times*, with a picture of Amy, in her dungarees and holding up a large wrench, splashed across the centre pages. Of course the other women had had plenty to say about her photograph. 'Oh, Amy, you might have had your hair done,' said Lenore. 'And given the dungarees a wash,' added Carole, but she knew they were proud of her.

No one had been more surprised than Amy when the reporter called up, asking if she'd like to be part of their feature on women in business. 'We'd love it if you would,' said the man. 'You've actually had five different recommendations from customers to be featured, that's quite the success rate.'

Since the piece had come out, she'd had so many calls for new business she was thinking she might have to take on an apprentice after the summer. And she knew exactly where she'd find one. Her new course in Plumbing Skills for Women was proving very popular, the manager at B&Q told her they even had a waiting list. She'd agreed to do an extra session on a Wednesday afternoon and was headed there after lunch.

'Okay, everyone, today we're going to talk about radiators. You might not be thinking about them in July, but trust me, you'll thank me come January. Never again will you need to wait on a man to bleed your radiator, which is just as well because they're all bleeding useless anyway, as we know.'

This got a laugh from the six women standing at their work benches, nervously eyeing the strange pieces of metal and plastic on the counter in front of them. Amy loved their attitude, the way they tackled everything she asked of them with enthusiasm and good humour, even though most of them had never handled a plumbing tool before in their lives. She wandered round the room, helping Lorraine to unlock a valve, and explaining the basics of drainage to Rhona, thinking as she did so that these were exactly the kind of women she'd been trying to reach via the graffiti campaign. She'd finally found a practical, positive way to help them and best of all, as Susan had quipped when she'd told her, it wasn't even illegal.

'That's great, Esme,' she said to the small, neat-looking woman who'd managed to bleed the radiator so that it now felt warm to the touch all the way down to the bottom. 'I'm glad you came back, we missed you last week.'

Esme flushed with pleasure. 'That's kind of you to notice I wasn't here,' she said. 'It's . . . I'm glad I came back too. Just, last week was . . . difficult.'

To Amy's dismay, the woman's already pink-rimmed eyes reddened and filled with tears.

'Thanks, everyone, that's been a great session today, I'll see you all again next week,' called Amy to the rest of the women, before turning back to Esme. 'Do you want a cup of tea, or a hanky, or . . . something?' she asked awkwardly.

'No,' she said. 'Thank you, but I'm fine, honestly. Being here today has really helped.'

Amy waited in silence, the way her therapist did, in case the woman wanted to say more.

'I've been moping since my dad died,' she said, looking at the floor. 'But it's been good for me to come out and be among other people.' She looked up at Amy. 'I mean, everyone's parents die, don't they, and in lots of ways I was lucky – I had mine right up until my fifties, but still, nothing really prepares you for it, does it? You assume they'll be around for ever and then . . . they're gone. Anyway.' She straightened up and smiled. 'Thanks so much for this, for what you're doing. Women need to be able to do this sort of thing for themselves, you're right. I'll see you next Wednesday.'

'Yes,' said Amy. 'Definitely,' and waited until Esme had gathered up her things and left before sitting down at the empty workbench, thinking about what she'd said.

Later that same evening, and on the advice of Dr Dowling who was proving to be right about most things, Amy went back to the rugby club. Although sport had always been Tess's thing, Amy had also enjoyed the feeling of being part of a team – and who wouldn't want to be in a team called the Teutonic Goddesses – but more than that, she'd missed the freedom to run and shout and forget about everything but the thrill of scoring a try. She was nervous as she entered the changing rooms but was surprised to be greeted immediately by cheers of 'Welcome back, Amy,' 'Long time no see, Captain,' and an invitation to after-game drinks at the Libertine.

'You guys take far too long to get ready,' she laughed, running her hand over her freshly clipped hair after the training session. 'I'll wait for you outside.'

The sun was burnt orange now and low in the sky, casting a warm glow over the Palace gardens. Amy put her sports bag beside her on the bench and breathed in deeply, enjoying the sweet coconut scent of the yew trees blowing in on the evening breeze. She stretched out her legs which ached pleasantly after the game, and looked around the park.

A couple of benches along, her eye was caught by an old

man, sitting with a woman about Amy's age. Amy watched as the woman carefully peeled an orange and handed it to the man a segment at a time. A young boy ran past, flapping his arms and making squawking noises like the seagull he was chasing hopelessly along the path. The old man and the woman laughed as they watched him.

Amy took out her phone and stared at the screen for a long time. Finally, like someone ripping off a plaster, she punched out a short text, pressed send and pushed her phone back into her pocket, each action performed rapid fire, without thought. She sat back. There. She'd done it, what would be would be and—

Her phone was vibrating against her hip.

An incoming call.

Amy glanced over at the old man on the other bench, then pulled the phone back out of her pocket.

She took a deep breath and swiped the screen.

'Dad? Yes, it's me, Amy . . . You saw the article? Thanks . . . It's . . . good to hear your voice too.'

VI

The Party

THE SECOND SATURDAY IN AUGUST turned out to be the hottest day of the year so far. Carole had called them all the day before in a panic, wondering why on earth she'd agreed to have a party for her birthday. She hadn't been that keen when Dennis had suggested it.

'But why? It's not even a special birthday, I'll be forty-two, Dennis. God, forty-two, I can't believe it.'

'Because we didn't have one for your fortieth, and things are different now. We're different, I want to show off my wife, the best-looking forty-two-year-old in Scotland.'

He strode across the kitchen to where she was standing and lifted her right off her feet and swung her round.

'God's sake, every time I come into a room these days, you two are at it,' said Daniel, grabbing an apple from the fruit bowl and turning on his heel.

Carole smiled. It was true, things were different now, and had been ever since the turn of the year when Amy had had them embark on their mad Graffiti Girl adventure. She'd made them all realize they were worth more than they were settling for, Carole especially. She'd enrolled on a teacher training course at City College and was looking forward to getting stuck in that September. Dennis had left banking altogether but thankfully, his financial prowess had extended to more than just helping his clients get rich; canny investment of his hefty annual bonuses meant they could afford the time to figure out what he was going to do next. In the meantime, he'd started teaching guitar at Archie and Glover's school, a fact of which both boys were very proud. He spent more time with all his kids, forever trying to get Thomas out on to the rugby field, or persuade Dan to accompany him to see one of his favourite bands. Thomas preferred clothes shopping to getting his shins dirty in a muddy field and Daniel's 'Why would I want to waste my time watching some old wankers bent over their guitars and screeching about love to an audience of has-beens?' seemed to indicate he wouldn't be joining his dad at a gig any time soon. But Archie and Glover were delighted to have him around more. He was much easier to persuade than Carole about the virtues of owning a reptile – Glover was now the proud owner of two slithery but docile corn snakes – and Archie was finally getting his chance to shine as the only son of four who actually wanted guitar lessons from his dad. Family life was better than it had been in years.

'Penny for them,' said Dennis, watching his wife's secret smile and reaching for her in that obsessed way he'd done when they'd first met, like he couldn't get enough of her.

'No time for compliments,' Carole said, batting away his hand. 'If we're going to have a party, let's do it right and make sure everything's organized.'

But as her birthday grew closer, she realized that although Dennis was the new and improved version in many ways, that didn't extend to taking on the role of party organizer and it soon dawned on her that it is very hard to enjoy the run-up to your own party. Quite apart from worrying about what her four sons might get up to, she also had the burden of ensuring that her eighty guests were fed, and more importantly watered, and had someone to talk to, music to listen to, and entertainment to be entertained by. As she looked down her to-do list and noticed how few items she'd ticked off, she remembered why she'd never been that keen on parties.

She should have known her friends wouldn't let her down. Amy had turned up in her dungarees and Doc Martens, ready to jump up ladders and put banners all along the walls of the hall. Susan sat in a corner with a huge mug of tea, blowing up countless pearlized pink, white and silver balloons. Lenore, meanwhile, pranced into the hall in a red and white stripey apron with the words 'English teachers do it better' emblazoned across her chest. 'What?' she'd said to a grimacing Amy. 'They do.' And proceeded to dance around in the adjoining kitchen in her apron, conjuring up mini pizzas, quiches and a mountain of fluffy cupcakes with 'Fab 42' in pink letters on the white icing.

'What a spread, Lenore, thank you!' said Carole.

Lenore gave a deep bow, delighted her friend was pleased. 'You're welcome,' she said. 'It's amazing how much better food is when you allow yourself sugar and butter, isn't it?'

With everything prepared, Carole began to relax. Back home, she had her bath and doused herself in the Chanel No 5 Dennis had given to her that morning, before suggesting, while clicking their bedroom door shut, that they begin the real celebrations before the younger boys came bounding in looking for Cheerios and toast.

Smiling at the memory, Carole brushed her hair and gave herself a last check over in the mirror. She was satisfied with what she saw but in any case, the more she looked into training for a new career, the less her looks mattered to her. She couldn't believe she'd spent so much time defining herself by the smoothness of her skin, the symmetry of her perfect cheekbones, the slimness of her waist. All of those things meant nothing if you weren't also happy with the way you were living your life, and Carole was ready to start living hers better.

'Ready to go—' began Dennis, coming out of their en suite. 'Wow, you look stunning.'

Carole was still able to blush at compliments from Dennis all these years later, and she did so, her dimpled cheeks glowing. Dennis brushed the back of his fingertips lightly against her soft upper arms till the fine blonde hairs stood on end. His eyes played games with hers as he pulled gently on the little silver butterfly at her ear.

'You gave me these on my twenty-first – do you remember?' she whispered, resting her palms against his chest.

'Of course I do.' He pulled her closer, kissing her full on the mouth. The kiss grew deeper and his hands moved to her waist until Glover's shout of 'Muuuuuum, are there any frozen mice left to feed Homer and Marge before we go?' made them draw apart and start laughing.

'Later,' said Dennis, taking Carole's hand in his and leading her downstairs.

Carole stood in the doorway to Greyfriars Hall, satisfied with what she saw. The place looked magical in the evening sunlight. The main doors were thrown open so that guests had to enter through the huge stone archway which Amy had adorned with swirling garlands of pink and white roses.

'Like a bloody wedding,' she'd muttered as Carole had handed her the flowers and told her what she'd wanted.

'Exactly,' said Carole, dreamily, ignoring Amy's tone completely.

Amy had done a great job though, the effect was like the sweet entrance to a hidden garden. Once into the main hall, the effect continued as the low vaulted ceilings were hung with wisteria, trailing low enough to touch and smell. There were about a dozen tables set around the wooden dance floor, each covered in a pristine white cloth, and trailing their own pink and white carnations around the silver cutlery and various items of glassware. Beside each place setting was a small white nameplate with each guest's name painstakingly written out in calligraphy by Lenore's third years.

Bloody hell, thought Amy, as she arrived ten minutes later and looked round the hall. *Not bad for a hastily arranged party for a woman in her forties.*

'Like it?' said Carole, coming over from the bar as soon as she saw Amy. Amy turned and took a sharp intake of breath. Carole was wearing a white one-sleeved toga dress, cinched in at the waist with a thin strand of gold braid. Her hair was gleaming, half of it held up in a long golden ribbon, half of it streaming down her back. Her skin glowed and she carried herself with the air of one truly contented with the world.

Carole faltered. 'Too much?' she said, picking up the skirt of the dress awkwardly.

Amy tried to speak but no words came out. She licked her lips and tried again. 'Carole. No, you look . . . you look amazing.'

Carole smiled up at her. 'Really? Thank you. You too,' she added, indicating Amy's navy blue jumpsuit and huge silver hoops in her ears.

'Ha,' said Amy. 'I think we all know that's rubbish. But hey, I did put on my lipstick.'

'Who's wearing lipstick?' said Lenore, sashaying in through the front door and coming over to join them. She too had made an effort, and the effects of her recent healthy eating regime were obvious in her radiant, lightly tanned skin, but more importantly in the way she held herself, knowing that she wasn't thin, but knowing too that this was her body and she was proud of it, showing it off in her fifties-style polka-dot party dress, all dips and curves and bright colours meant to enhance her figure rather than hide it.

'You are,' said Amy briskly. 'And a bit too much of it, if you ask me, but no one ever asks me so that's fine.'

The women were still laughing as Susan walked in, closely followed by Fraser and his girlfriend, their arms linked. Susan did a double-take as she saw Carole and indicated her own long-sleeved jersey dress that she'd bought in the sale from George at Asda because it was 30 per cent off. 'I should probably have made more of an effort,' she said, looking round their group.

'No one could match Carole so best not to even try.'

Carole waved away their remarks impatiently. 'If there's one thing I've learned in the last few months in my incarnation as a Graffiti Girl, it's that there's more to us than the way we look, so let's stop comparing ourselves to each other and finding fault and celebrate who we are. Right?'

'I'll drink to that,' said Amy. 'Come on, girls, let's get this party started. Who's coming to the bar?'

As the clock struck ten, Amy stood at the main door, facing out to the trees bordering the Clyde. She hadn't been to Greyfriars Hall for years, had forgotten how beautiful it was down here – the calm and the peace, with the waves shimmering in the moonlight. It was an unexpected choice for the party – though maybe not since Carole and Dennis had had their engagement party here, more years ago than Amy cared to count. She remembered that night well – Carole had looked spectacular in her hip-baring cargo pants and tight-fitting, almost-there white tank top, like she was auditioning for a part in an All Saints video. Amy had been unable to look away, while Dennis's parents had looked on askance as Carole and their precious son had writhed on the dance floor, leaving no one in any doubt as to the basis of their mutual attraction. Dennis had insisted on reuniting with that tragic band of his and playing one of their own even more tragic compositions. He'd strutted his stuff and made a complete arse of himself while all their friends looked on, not sure if they'd rather be going out with Dennis or living the dream life with Carole. Eight months later and Carole was screaming 'Give me pain relief, all the drugs, *all* the drugs' in Wishaw maternity, and no longer the envy of all her pals.

Looking back into the hall though, and seeing Carole and Dennis intertwined on the dance floor, his hand on the small of her back and her eyes closed as she swayed against him, Dennis whispering God knows what into her ear, and not enough space to put a cigarette paper between them, even Amy had to admit that maybe they'd done something right. She wasn't sure what had happened, how they'd managed to flick the switch from sure-fire divorce to Hamilton's most loved-up couple, but she knew without a doubt that some such change had taken place.

She turned away from the couple kissing and swaying on the dance floor like a pair of teenagers. Her feelings for Carole would always be complicated but she knew she'd never stop loving her and wishing the best for her. She picked up a smooth, grey pebble and tossed it as far as she could but it didn't quite reach the river. She bent down to try again when she heard a voice behind her.

'Come on, Amy, are you going to stand out here all night or are you going to come in and dance with me, show these pretenders what real dancing is?' Lenore was behind Amy, lifting up her flouncy skirt and shimmying like a fifteen-year-old at the school disco.

'Not me, thanks,' said Amy, deftly stepping out of Lenore's way. 'I'm not a dancer, you should know that by now.'

'Oh come on, you're never any fun at these things. After all the drama you've got me involved in these last few months, the least you could do is have a dance with me. Drink a few more pints and you'll soon be up there.'

'Looks like you've already drunk enough for both of us,' said Amy, but laughing, happy to see Lenore back to her old vivacious self, Tommy's departure and that business with Dave Bates well behind her. She thought again that people could say what they liked but her plan to broadcast their complaints throughout the town via graffiti was having a positive effect on all of them, whether they admitted it or not.

A tall figure joined them from the shadows.

'What about me?' came a voice behind them. 'Will I do as a dance partner?'

It was Mark Lown, looking less like a policeman tonight in his off-duty navy chinos and red polo shirt.

'Mark. What are you doing here?' Lenore hoped he hadn't been watching her dance about on her own. 'You're not here to arrest us, are you?' she said suddenly, her hand at her chest, grabbing the treacherous GG necklace that was swinging between her breasts as she danced.

He laughed. 'No, whatever can you mean?' he said, raising an eyebrow and putting one finger to his mouth. 'It turns out my son Finn's at school with one of Carole's boys. We got talking at the last parents' night and she invited me along. I was . . . hoping you'd be here.' He looked down and kicked some dirt along the ground.

'Off you go then,' said Amy, with a smile, as Lenore seemed rooted to the spot. 'Go and get some dancing done.'

'Are you okay out here on your own?' Lenore suddenly wondered why Amy wasn't joining in the party.

'Of course. I'm just taking the air, I'll see you in there in a bit.'

Mark held out his hand to Lenore and said, 'Shall we?'

Amy watched as they headed back to the dance floor, holding hands, Mark throwing his head back and laughing at whatever Lenore had just said.

'I'll have a white wine please. Large,' said Susan when she finally got to the bar which was three lines deep in Carole's family members, all of them dressed up to the nines and seemingly every last one as glamorous as she was. Susan took her wine and wandered back to the side of the dance floor, wishing she hadn't come. Then she spotted Fraser and Fiona spinning each other round to a Pretenders song, Fiona's long red hair fanning out behind her as she danced, Fraser smiling at her, his eyes shining. Susan couldn't remember the last time she'd seen him look so happy or carefree. He was right, she reflected, he did need downtime from his studies, and the last few weeks getting to know Fiona had made her realize she wasn't so bad after all.

'They make a nice couple, don't they?'

Susan turned to see a small, vaguely familiar-looking man standing next to her. He had a slightly chubby but pleasant face which, like hers, was covered in freckles. His muted ginger hair was receding, revealing freckles even on the top of his head. He smiled at her, a lovely smile, broad and unguarded.

She smiled back. 'Have we . . . I'm sorry, have we met?'

'No, not yet, but looking at how well my daughter and your son are getting on, I think it was only a matter of time, don't you?'

'Oh, you're Fiona's dad? That makes sense because you look so like her.'

The man laughed. 'She's the new and improved version, wouldn't you say? I think it's safe to assume I won't be appearing on the cover of a magazine any time soon.' He held out his hand. 'Geoff. Geoff Young. Lovely to meet you finally, Fiona's told me a lot about you.'

'I'm Susan. Pleased to meet you too. You have a lovely daughter.' As she said it, Susan realized it was true. Having spent time with Fiona at last, she now understood what her son saw in his beautiful young girlfriend, who wasn't at all the vapid, vain creature Susan had anticipated. Over coffee one morning, Fiona had told her that she only wanted to work as a model to help fund her way through uni, but long term she planned to be a vet. Put that way, strutting your stuff in fancy clothes and having someone pay you to take your photograph and fund your education didn't seem like a bad plan. Not at all.

'It's been a real pleasure getting to know her these last few weeks,' she said, realizing that she meant it.

'That's kind of you to say so. I'm grateful to you for making her so welcome.' He focused on the drink in his hand and added, 'Though it can be quite lonely when she's at your house all the time.' He scratched his cheek and looked back at Susan. 'Sorry. I know people don't admit to loneliness.' He kept his eyes on hers. 'I don't know why, it's not a personal failing, is it?'

'No,' said Susan, warming to Geoff. 'It's not at all. It's pretty common in fact. If people just admitted it.'

A broad smile spread across Geoff's face. 'And Fiona was telling me you're a librarian. That must be so rewarding.'

'I was a librarian for years. I'm a communications officer now, still in the book business though. Are you . . . do you like books?'

'I do, very much. Which makes my profession quite difficult at times.'

'Oh?' Susan loved the way his eyes crinkled at the sides when he smiled, and he smiled a lot.

'I run a second-hand bookshop in town. Near Candleriggs, if you're ever passing . . .'

'I'd love to come and browse round the books. There's nothing I'd like better, in fact.' Susan's freckled skin glowed and she was glad she'd remembered to smear some Vaseline on her lips before she'd come out.

'Excellent. In the meantime, can I top up that white wine for you? And when I get back, I'm going to try and guess your favourite book, and I bet you I'll get it right. Give me two minutes.'

Susan watched as Geoff made his way back to the bar, turning and giving her a wave as he reached the counter.

Amy remained outside, the evening chill setting in now, despite the still-violet sky. She looked out on to the water and watched the greeny-blue waves lap over and over each other.

'I like wild swimming.'

'You nearly made me jump out my skin,' cried Amy, spinning round at the sound of a low voice, and a soft touch on her shoulder.

Standing behind her, and looking at the waves, was a woman Amy half-recognized but whose name she couldn't place.

'Marion,' she said. 'From the library.'

Amy considered her more closely. She'd eschewed the sky-blue council uniform for the evening and was wearing a pair of black jeans, with purple glittery Doc Martens poking out from the bottom. The little blue and red butterfly tattoo on her neck was on full show, as was the white flesh of her shoulders as she wore a strapless black mesh bodice, tight enough to make any doctors present nervous about her ribcage. She wore even more black kohl round her eyes than before and had added a dab of purple lipstick on her bottom lip only.

'You look . . . different,' said Amy, taking her gaze from Marion's smooth shoulders and locking eyes with her.

'No kiwi fruit.'

Amy laughed. 'That's true.'

'I was looking for you. I came out to talk to you.'

Amy raised her eyebrows. 'Well, you found me. Here I am.'

'Yes,' said Marion, staring at the water. She hesitated then said, 'I thought we might have a bit in common.'

Amy rubbed her palm across her stubbly head. 'I shouldn't think so. You've probably got more in common with Susan, I imagine?'

'Oh no,' said Marion. 'Susan and I have nothing in common. At all.'

'Except books, presumably?'

'True, we both read books.' She looked up at Amy suddenly. 'Do you?'

Amy paused, distracted by Marion's shoulders, and the way she was looking at her so intently under that fringe and through the soft kohl. 'Yeah, of course,' she said eventually. 'Of course I read books. Who doesn't read books? I mean—'

'You don't, do you?'

'Well, no . . .' agreed Amy, laughing.

'But I still think we'd have a lot in common.'

They both stared at the water for a bit then Marion said, 'Do you need another pint? I could get us both one and come back and sit with you? If you like?' She pressed her lips together so that some of the purple lipstick transferred to her top lip. One hand swung by her side while the other gripped her opposite arm, the black nails striking against her pale flesh.

'Erm, yes,' said Amy. 'That would be . . . lovely. Thanks. Shall I sit over there?' She indicated the wrought-iron bench at the front of the chapel house, overlooking the Clyde.

Marion took her hand from her arm and gave her a slow smile, before sloping back into the hall to get the drinks. She turned at the door and said, 'Don't go anywhere' before disappearing inside.

★

It was almost midnight. The DJ was still taking requests, the dance floor was filled with friends and family crashing around and bumping hips and elbows, and the bar was still half a dozen people deep.

Carole was pleased with the way the evening had gone. She looked up at Dennis, who was sitting beside her at the once beautifully set table, now strewn with crushed white roses and paper plates smeared in chilli sauce and covered in crumbs. His arm was tight around her shoulders and she snuggled further into his chest. 'This has been the perfect evening, hasn't it?'

'Almost,' said Dennis, looking across the hall, where Thomas and Jaxx were dancing opposite each other and doing the Macarena with all the aplomb of professional flamenco dancers. They'd been together on the dance floor all night, Thomas in a white shiny jacket with a pink love heart on the back, and Jaxx, with a long silver shark's fin dangling from his left ear lobe, in black leather trousers with a wide red sash.

'Versace,' he'd said to Dennis proudly at the start of the night.

'More like Liberace,' Dennis had whispered to Daniel, who didn't get the reference and shrugged, more at ease with his brother's choices than his father. 'I like the fact they don't care what other people think. Takes courage to go against the crowd,' he'd said, leaving his father feeling sheepish as he headed to the bar to find his friends.

'What do they look like?' he said, watching Jaxx put his arms round Thomas's waist and swing him high in the air.

'So what, Dennis?' said Carole. 'Come on, look at him. He's dancing, laughing. Look how happy he is!'

'I suppose so,' Dennis agreed reluctantly. 'And Dan's right. You need to be pretty brave to plough your own furrow in life.' Carole raised her eyebrows in surprise, but she nodded, and they both watched as the music changed and Thomas squatted impressively low to the floor like a Cossack, his arms folded tightly across his skinny chest.

'Go, Thomas,' called Dennis, standing up and giving his son a thumbs up and a wave. Thomas lifted his arm in salute and kicked alternate legs straight out in front of him, Russian-style.

'Mind you,' said Dennis, sitting back down, 'I'd still rather see him doing what Dan's doing.' They both looked over to see Daniel lunge towards the brunette he'd been chatting up all night and proceed to snog her with all the passion of a teenager on Diamond White, whilst winking at his friend Mordecai who was standing behind them.

'I'm not so sure about that,' said Carole, 'but yeah, he's happy too. And look at Archie and Glover – Glover's never been off his iPad all night, busy researching reptile habitats, he says, but Archie's been the apple of his grandma's eye, chatting to her and all the old dears about his guitar and all the tunes he can play and loving being the centre of attention. They're just different, Dennis, four equally beautiful but entirely different human beings. We have to accept that.'

'You're right, I know that.' Dennis turned to Carole and, smoothing her hair away from her face, kissed her forehead tenderly. 'We've done okay for a couple of teenagers no one expected to last five minutes, haven't we?'

Carole smiled and Dennis took a deep intake of breath as he thought again how beautiful she was, and how lucky he was to have her. He interlaced his fingers with hers and she waited for him to lean in and kiss her properly.

Suddenly the atmosphere changed as the last frenetic burst of the weird Russian rap was replaced by the thumping bass of the Prodigy's 'Firestarter', long one of Dennis's favourite tracks. He drew back immediately and held his hand out to Carole. 'Now we're talking. Come on, Mrs Dungreavie, let's do what Mr Flint says and set that dance floor alight.'

'Oh no, Dennis,' laughed Carole. 'I can't, honestly, this is the first time I've sat down all night. Find someone younger and more energetic than me.'

'No need for a partner for this one,' said Dennis, and headed off to set the dance floor on fire on his own.

Carole laughed as she watched the crowd going up and down as one body, and she had a sudden flashback to a girls' night out in the Toledo Junction in Paisley when she and Lenore had danced their socks off to that song, among others, while Susan and Amy had stayed at the side of the dance floor egging them on. She realized she hadn't seen any of the girls for a couple of hours. Scanning the dance floor, the desecrated buffet table, and the bar, she couldn't spot them and wondered if they'd all gone home already. She wouldn't have blamed them. After all, whatever Lenore said, they were none of them getting any younger, and they'd all been drinking and dancing for hours. She'd speak to them tomorrow, she thought, hoping they'd all had a good time.

She headed to the exit and stood at the door for a few moments, breathing in the cooling night air as the party went on extravagantly behind her.

She shivered a little and turned to go back in when she heard voices outside. That was definitely Amy's voice setting forth some opinion or other, followed by Susan's lower-pitched laughter and Lenore's good-natured 'For goodness' sake, Amy.'

'There you all are,' she called to her friends, who were perched together on the bench overlooking the River Clyde. Susan was wrapped up in the anorak she wore to work, Lenore was still braving the cold to make sure everyone saw her in her strapless polka-dotted dress, while Amy was busy pouring them all more wine into a line of plastic tumblers she'd persuaded the guy behind the bar to give her.

Amy noticed her first. 'And there's the birthday girl herself. Come and join us,' she cried, gesturing to Lenore to budge up on the bench and make space at the end for Carole to sit down.

'So this is where the party's at,' said Carole, accepting the cup of red wine Lenore handed to her and taking a large mouthful, then wiping her mouth with the back of her hand.

'Not at all. All the action's in there and it's been a fantastic night.'

'Really?' said Carole, hoping her friends had enjoyed it as much as she had.

'Really,' said Susan. 'We've all had a ball, don't worry.'

'What are you all doing out here then?'

'We were just . . . reflecting,' said Amy.

'Yeah,' agreed Susan. 'Talking about how far the Graffiti Girls have come these past few months.'

'We really have, haven't we?' said Carole, swirling what was left of her red wine round the bottom of the plastic cup and taking another sip.

The women sat and contemplated the river in front of them in silence for a few moments, enjoying the calming effect of the waves lapping against the shingle, the quicksilver flash of tiny shrimp and the sway of slimy reeds in the water, the full moon throwing shadows on the trees. The muted sounds behind them of dance music, laughter and chaos seemed far away.

Amy turned and looked at each of the three women she'd known since school. They were best friends, for ever friends, who'd stick together no matter what life threw at them. But as she gazed at the faces she knew so well, she knew they'd always be okay. And if they weren't, well, they had each other to lean on until they were.

As the clock struck midnight, she stood up and raised her plastic tumbler full of wine.

'What are we drinking to?' said Carole, as she, Lenore and Susan stood up to join Amy.

'To us, of course.' Amy smiled. 'And Graffiti Girls everywhere.'

Acknowledgements

Huge thanks to the wise, funny, and prodigiously talented Clare Gordon – everything you could wish for in an editor; to copyeditor Liz Hatherell and proofreader Charlotte Atyeo; and to all the team at HQ, especially Isabel Williams, Dawn Burnett, Kate Oakley, Halema Begum, Angie Dobbs, Sarah Renwick, Tom Han, Georgina Green and Fliss Porter.

I am very grateful to all the wonderful women from Primadonna and Curtis Brown who set me on the path to publication, and who have continued to help and support me ever since, especially Lisa Milton and Cath Summerhayes.

Thank-you to my first reader, Claire Mannion, who read an early draft despite being so very ill. How I loved getting Claire's messages with feedback, always full of encouragement, love, and a million exclamation marks and emojis. I hope I have done her proud.

Big thanks to my sons, Luca and Sebastian, for giving me a window into the weird and wonderful world of teenage boys – love you!

Finally, since *Graffiti Girls* is all about good friends, I'd like to raise a glass to mine, especially Susan Henderson, Alison Gray, and Farah Ahamed – Graffiti Girls one and all.

ONE PLACE. MANY STORIES

Bold, innovative and
empowering publishing.

FOLLOW US ON:

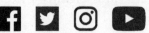

@HQStories